to kill a nice man like the Judge?

The burglar alarm was ringing, deafening Bea as she stooped over the body of the Judge. Stunned, she could only imagine his heart had failed until she saw the blood on her hand where she touched the still warm corpse.

Who would want to kill this distinguished man? What was the killer searching for in the old Connecticut mansion? And what would happen to Bea, who was heiress to the dead man's estate—and to his legacy of evil?

Suddenly Bea could trust no one, not even the man she was to marry, as she realized the hand of death was poised, ready to strike again . . .

WARNER BOOKS EDITION

Copyright © 1973 by Mignon G. Eberhart
All rights reserved.

This Warner Books Edition is published by arrangement with
Random House, Inc.,
201 East 50th Street,
New York, N.Y. 10022

Warner Books, Inc.,
666 Fifth Avenue,
New York, N.Y. 10103

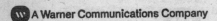 A Warner Communications Company

Printed in the United States of America

First Warner Books Printing: December, 1983

10 9 8 7 6 5 4 3 2 1

One

The judge lay in the shadow, but the eerie red light from the burglar alarm flashed from its box under the eaves of the house at swift intervals and momentarily lighted lawns, shrubbery and the inert figure.

Bea bent over him. "Uncle Judge—Uncle Judge."

One arm clad in a white shirt threshed a little; the judge moaned. Then he said clearly, "Doctor . . . Will . . . Seth . . ." and died.

The flashes of light from the house sent out tremors of rosy reflections which touched the tall pines, the glossy laurels, the stone wall beyond the shrubbery. The alarm kept squawking raucously.

But he can't be dead, Bea thought, and knew that he was. His hand had relaxed and dropped. She tried to remember whatever she had vaguely heard about resuscitation: move his arms, move his chest so his heart will keep beating, breathe air into his lungs. It was no use. Without being aware of her own action, she had found his wrist and hunted for a pulse, but there was not even the slightest flicker in that suddenly flaccid arm.

The burglar alarm kept on: *wow-wow-wow*. The whole countryside must hear it. Surely the doctor would hear it; the Thorne house lay across and only a couple of hundred feet down the road. Rufe Thorne, too, would hear the alarm and come.

Instead there was the nearby sound of a car racing behind the stone wall, and then it shot into the Salcott drive. It had a red light too, whirling and flashing on top of it: police car. The alarm connected with the Valley Ridge police station, and somebody there must have radioed a patrol car. Before Bea could more than stumble to her feet, two men were getting out; she could see their black silhouettes against the car lights. She ran, calling to them, "Here! He's here—"

They heard her, turned and came plunging toward her. She seemed to be shouting, yet her voice sounded thin and faraway in her own ears. "The judge! He's dead! Down there—"

Each man had an enormous flashlight. The lights turned upon her, dazzling her, showing every fold of the blue dressing gown she had yanked on when the burglar alarm went off.

She cried to them to hurry. She could be mistaken; the judge, so full of energy and determination, could not have died so quickly.

One of the men said, "All right, Miss Bartry. Take it easy—"

They jogged on, their flashlights dancing everywhere, down toward the wall and the crowding thickets of the laurels and pines—and the judge.

She had to tell Clara. She saw then that the study door at the end of the terrace was open as she had left it. Clara stood there, her little figure clear against the light behind her. "Bea," she called. "Bea! Is it the judge?"

Bea made her way toward the terrace and Clara. The alarm was now very near, shrieking to all the world that the judge was dead.

Clara didn't need to be told. "That man Meeth! He was let out yesterday. He said he'd kill the judge when he was released. He killed him."

"I don't know. Come back into the house, Aunt Clara."

"He killed him! I knew he would. He swore he'd kill him—"

"Aunt Clara—" She drew her back into the study. "Dear, I think he fainted or . . . or something." Her attempt at a lie sounded unconvincing.

Clara knew. "No. No, he's dead. He was murdered."

"I'll call the doctor, he said to call the doctor. He said to call Seth—"

"Neither Seth nor the doctor can help now. How did he kill him? I didn't hear a gunshot."

"I don't know. He might have had a stroke and lost consciousness. You know the doctor warned us—"

Clara pointed at Bea's dressing gown. "He didn't have a stroke. That's blood."

Bea looked down. There were vividly red, wet blotches along the front of her dressing gown and on one sleeve. She remembered that she had tried to lift the judge. Suddenly the unusually warm spring night seemed cold. She felt it in her bones. "I'll call the doctor. The judge said to—"

6

"He talked to you? Didn't he say what happened?"

Bea reached for the telephone on the judge's big desk. She dialed the doctor, a number she had always known well, especially since Rufe came back from Vietnam.

Clara stood like a statue in her prim dressing gown, belted at her plump little waist; her gray hair was neatly netted, her pretty round face stony. As Bea waited for the ring of the telephone she saw the judge's jacket lying on the desk. It was old and shabby but the judge loved it; it was almost a part of him. The burglar alarm was still going. Somebody ought to turn it off; it will run down the battery, Bea thought. The judge couldn't have been murdered. Yet that man Meeth *had* been released from prison; he *had* sworn to kill the judge. A feminine voice said thinly in her ear, "Dr. Thorne's answering service—"

"I want the doctor. I must have the doctor—"

Footsteps came running across the terrace and Rufe Thorne plunged into the study. "Bea—Aunt Clara—Bea—"

"I'm calling your father," Bea said.

He came to her, took the telephone and put it down. "He's coming. He heard the alarm. He's down there with the police. Can't you turn off that thing?"

Bea said something, but Rufe ran out of the study and up the stairs to the panel controlling the alarm in the linen closet.

A sudden silence fell upon the night. Bea took a long breath. But then she heard clearly the metallic sound of voices coming from the drive, calling the police station. Soon there would be more police. Rufe came back into the study. "They're calling Obrian—" Obrian was the Valley Ridge chief of police.

Dr. Thorne came slowly in from the terrace. Accustomed to night calls, he had got into a dark turtleneck sweater; he carried his small medicine bag as if it were a part of him. "I'm sorry, Clara."

Clara gave him a stony look. "I know that man—that Meeth killed him, didn't he?"

Dr. Thorne's face was set too; he looked older and very tired. He was the family physician and their friend. "I don't know."

"But it was murder," Clara said. "I know it was murder. We heard the alarm and Bea found him."

7

Dr. Thorne came to Clara and put his hand on her wrist. "Yes. He was murdered. He was shot—"

"I knew it! That man Meeth—"

"Now, Clara—" The doctor took her arm, his silvery head towering above her. She went with him as if she didn't know what else to do.

Rufe came to Bea and put his arm around her. It couldn't be very late, for he was still dressed. "I'm sorry about the judge." He looked at her dressing gown. "Bea!"

"Yes. I leaned over him. I tried . . . I couldn't believe . . . but then he died. He just died."

"Bea!" He held her close to him, his face down upon her own. "Dear, don't tremble like that."

She clung to him, thankful for the warmth of his arms and the solid rock of his body. "Oh, Rufe, he died. And he didn't forgive me. He only said something about your father. Get the doctor I think he meant. Oh, Rufe, I wish he had forgiven me. We quarreled tonight—after dinner."

"About me." It was a statement.

"Yes. He said . . . well, you know the judge. Lately he's been so difficult."

"A kind word for it. But then the poor old guy couldn't help it. My father explained it to me."

"Your father told me too, and Aunt Clara. He said we mustn't let him be upset or excited. He said—Oh, Rufe, I feel as if I had killed him myself. That quarrel!"

Rufe's arms held her tight. "You couldn't have killed him."

"I lost my temper and said that as soon as you had your appointment we were going to be married and that he couldn't stop us. He turned so red—"

"Yes, he was like that with me."

Bea's head jerked up. "With you! You weren't here!"

"Yes, I was. I knew he'd get himself worked up when you told him we were going to be married, so I came across the road after dinner and tried to talk to him. It was no use."

"I didn't know you were here!"

"You and Aunt Clara were upstairs. I could hear her television going. I came here to the study door and saw his light. He was still moody."

Bea waited a moment. "I suppose he said the same things to you that he said to me."

"I imagine stronger."

"He told me that he wouldn't let me marry you. I reminded him that I'm of age. And I—Oh, Rufe!"

"There, there, Bea. Things will be all right."

"Rufe, if it's murder . . ."

"If this man Meeth did it, it shouldn't be hard to run him down."

"What else did Uncle Judge say?"

"He said that I had only passed the examinations, and that the Foreign Service is a long and demanding career. He said you'd been accustomed to every luxury, that he had given you every care and an expensive education. He said that he'd been like a father to you—"

"He always was. Until lately."

"He couldn't help his recent condition. But then—"

"I know. He said it to me too. He said—" Bea swallowed hard. "He said that I probably expected all Aunt Clara's money and his too—what there was—to come to me eventually. He said that it was a great help to a young Foreign Service officer to have a wife with money, or even expectations of money."

"He said all that to me and more. I reminded him that he had helped me all along the line—character reference, study of international law, everything. He was really worked up. He said that he wouldn't have helped me if he'd known that my intention was to marry you and eventually get his money and Clara's. He said—" Rufe checked himself for a moment and then went on. "Well, never mind all that. I lost my temper too, so I thought I'd better leave. He was so furious, I was afraid he'd blow up then and there. Bea, how did you know he was out there?"

"I didn't know. I was half asleep. The burglar alarm went off. Aunt Clara and I both ran into the hall. I knew she had set it, thinking that the judge had come upstairs. She's done that a time or two and it made him very angry. It's still new to us—the alarm, I mean. Aunt Clara had it installed when she learned that Meeth was to be paroled. We were supposed to phone the police if it was a false alarm. It's connected with the station. The men who installed the alarm said that all the doors and windows downstairs, and both front and back stairs too, were—he called it bugged."

"Go on."

"Then the judge didn't come upstairs. I ran down. The

lights were still on in the study and the terrace door was open. I thought he'd gone out for a stroll around the place; he did that sometimes. I thought the door must have blown open, or something. I expected him to have heard the alarm and come back to the house, and when he didn't I was afraid he'd fainted or had a stroke or—I didn't know what. So I ran down to the hedge along the stone wall. All the time the alarm kept going. I ran along the laurels, and then I stumbled over his feet, I think, and fell and . . . he said something about the doctor and . . . and died. I felt his pulse and he was dead. Like that."

"He must have had only a moment of consciousness."

"Not more than that. He just said 'Doctor . . . Will . . . Seth . . .' He must have meant for me to call Seth too. I only thought of your father. Rufe, who is Will?"

"I don't know. We'd better call Seth."

"We don't need a lawyer!"

Rufe's face changed slightly; it seemed guarded. "Well, he'll know what to do. The police will question everybody."

"But surely it was that man he sent to prison. Who else could have killed him?"

"I'll call Seth."

"Is he in town?"

"I saw him on the street yesterday. Do you know his number?"

She couldn't think of it. When Rufe let her go, she felt she couldn't stand without his supporting arms. He hunted through the telephone book, and then, as he dialed, said, "But I don't know any Will!"

"Oh, of course! He didn't mean Will Somebody. I know what he was thinking of. He told me that if I married you, he and Aunt Clara would change their wills. He accused you of being a fortune hunter. He must have meant that Seth was to draw up new wills. He didn't realize that he was dying."

Rufe spoke into the phone. "Seth? Rufe Thorne. Something awful has happened. The judge was murdered."

Bea could hear the rumble of Seth's powerful voice. Rufe replied, "Shot. A few minutes ago. Seth, can you come? The police are here. A patrol car came and by now they've sent for help, and Aunt Clara and Bea are alone except for me and my father." Seth's voice came again; no words were clear, but Rufe replied, "I think Aunt Clara is all right. My father took her upstairs. He's seeing to her." There was another pause, a short one, and then Rufe said, "Tony was in the patrol car."

Tony? Bea thought, and remembered: of course, Tony Calinas. He and Rufe had known each other since they were boys; they had been inducted into the service at the same time. Rufe had written: "We were in the same outfit at first. I really miss him now."

Rufe replied to something Seth said. "I don't know, I'll ask . . . All right." He put down the telephone. "He'll be here right away. He's only a mile away. He said not to talk to anybody, police or anybody."

"What did you say you would ask?"

"If either you or Aunt Clara had heard a gunshot."

"No, only the alarm. Aunt Clara was watching a Western on her bedroom television. She's a little deaf, so she turns it very loud. It was full of gunshots; I could hear them from my room. She must have turned it off only a little before we heard the alarm."

Rufe went to the door and looked out. Over his shoulder she could see headlights and hear the racing roar as still another car came hurtling into the drive.

"Obrian must be here by now. I'll go down and see what they're doing." Rufe gave a swift glance to the smears on her dressing gown. Again his face seemed to alter a little. "Bea, go upstairs and take that off. Put on a dress."

She started numbly for the living room and the hall but he caught her by the shoulder and turned her back. "Bea, the police will have to question you and Aunt Clara. Don't talk to them till Seth gets here. Take as long as you can about dressing. It will give you time to pull yourself together." He leaned over, kissed her swiftly and then ran out the terrace door.

She went slowly through the living room, as if she were drugged, and pulled herself up the stairs which she had come down so short a time ago to find the judge, to placate his wrath at Clara for setting the alarm too early—so short a time, yet so long a time.

Bea couldn't remember when the judge had not been an important figure in her life. It was true, he had told her—accused her in a way—that he had stood between her and the world; he had taken her in when her own parents had died; her only claim was that she was the daughter of his nephew.

He hadn't been particularly fond of her mother, but he and Aunt Clara had made her their child. Nothing was too good for her.

At the top of the stairs she met Dr. Thorne coming from Clara's room. "She's all right," he said quickly. "I gave her as strong a sedative as I dared. Her heart is really better than she thinks, you know, but still, she's not young." He gave her a faint smile. "She's a bit of a hypochondriac, as we all know, but I won't let the police talk to her tonight. How about you?" His eyes and Rufe's eyes had the same piercing concentration. "I think I'd better give you something to make things easier for you, just for a while. Come on. You'd better lie down until the police—" He broke off and, as Rufe had done, stared down at the smears of red on her dressing gown. "How did you get those?"

"I leaned over him. I thought I could do something—"

"Take it off." He spoke as tersely as Rufe.

From off in the distance there rose an ululating wail. Dr. Thorne's head lifted.

"Is that—" she began.

He nodded. "The ambulance. Don't worry, child. Here—" He went into her room with her, gently took off her dressing gown, disappeared into the bathroom and returned. "I hung the thing over the shower rail. They'll find the stains, of course, but don't worry. Perfectly clear how you got them. Don't look like that, child."

"Doctor, was there anything I could have done for the judge?"

He considered it. "No. He must have been unconscious—"

"He spoke to me. Just a few words."

"He couldn't have lived, Bea. Here, get back into bed."

Her bed was tumbled as she had left it. The doctor opened his medicine bag, got a capsule from a small bottle and gave it to her. "Take that. It won't put you to sleep but it'll calm you down a little." Again he lifted his head sharply and listened. "H'mm, they got here in a hurry."

"You mean the Valley Ridge police—Obrian and—"

"Oh, they were on their way when I came. I expect they've called in the state police."

"State . . ."

"We don't have many murders in Valley Ridge. Fact is, I

12

can't remember one. The state police have facilities we don't. Besides, the judge was an important man. Now take it easy, Bea." He went out. The door closed behind him. Though he and Rufe, father and son, naturally resembled each other, Dr. Thorne was thin where Rufe was strong and sturdy, and now the doctor's frosty hair retained only a tinge of red, while Rufe's was still a stubborn auburn.

For a long time she sat on the bed. She was aware of a tumult and activity around the house—cars dashing into the drive, doors opening and closing, voices—but the capsule the doctor had given her began to dull the sounds for her. After a long time she began slowly to dress. She'd wait until they sent for her. The state police!

A voice from below her window shouted, "We looked in the barn right away. Nobody there!"

Another voice shouted back, "Search the house."

Two

They searched the house, room by room, swiftly. Two troopers in state uniform knocked politely at Bea's door, then went through the room, the closet, the bathroom, even the wastebasket, like two terriers clad in smart gray uniforms. When they thanked her and departed, one of them was carrying her blue dressing gown with its sickening red patches.

She knew that the nearest state police barracks was in Welbury, not far from Valley Ridge. Dr. Thorne had said the state police had "facilities"—he must mean for the detection of criminals. She thought vaguely of fingerprints and guns. *Guns!* The judge had had one in the drawer of his big desk. But he would never have killed himself. She sat on the bed again, huddled against the pillows. She wouldn't budge; she wouldn't speak to anybody until Seth came. Suppose . . . suppose the police found out that not only had she quarreled with the judge, but that Rufe had actually been in the house not long before the judge was killed and that he too had quarreled violently with him about their marriage. Yet the judge

13

had had nothing against Rufe; he had done everything possible to help him during his training to enter the Foreign Service.

Rufe was a part of her being. There had been few things in her life that Bea loved. One was Clara's library; another, her dog Shadders. But the most important, for as long as she could remember, was Rufe. She loved Clara and the judge and was grateful to both. But Rufe she loved with all her deepest instincts. She had adored him when she was a gawky girl in her early teens and Rufe, older, would come home for vacations and skate with her or take her for a ride in a sled with Shadders bounding happily beside them. She had adored Rufe even when he was in love with Lorraine, Clara's niece, and couldn't stay away from the house because she was there. She had prayed when he went to Vietnam; she had hated Lorraine for so swiftly casting him off in favor of marriage to Cecco. She had agonized over the letters he wrote, which Lorraine either glanced at or sometimes didn't bother to open.

Bea had written to him herself so that he'd get letters from home. She had written when old Shadders died; she had written when, as everyone had long expected, Miss Dotty, the doctor's office nurse, gliding silently along a country road on her bicycle without reflectors, had at last crashed into a car. For a long time after that Miss Dotty was rather subdued and very careful about her bicycle riding at night. Rufe had answered all of Bea's letters and had never asked about Lorraine.

When he came home from Vietnam he seemed much more mature, so much older that Bea was at first shy and felt herself awkward again and childish. But he came to the house to talk to the judge and Clara, and then, gradually, he began to come frankly to see Bea. They would go to a movie, or just for a drive. He told her of his desire to go into the Foreign Service and why. Even in the beginning, she knew that he was dedicating himself to something which he believed might help the cause of peace in the world.

She remembered the first time he had kissed her; it was in the late fall, with a cold hunter's moon, and they were standing on the steps of the terrace. Rufe had been home for a few days and she had cherished every minute of their time together. They had gone to a movie, and she was about to go into the house when Rufe had pulled her coat collar closer around her throat and then, unexpectedly, almost as if he didn't mean to yet couldn't help himself, leaned over and kissed her. Then he had kissed her again, and they were in each other's arms. The world changed for her. The hunter's moon was white and the world was magic.

But he hadn't mentioned marriage until he was home again for a few days at Christmas time, and then it was in the most casual way in the world. They were skating on the little pond, and he had said in the middle of a conversation—"so when I get an appointment we can be married."

Married. Again the world became a magic place and life was full of meaning. They had skated on for a while. Then, when he helped her off with her skates, he said, "I didn't make a very romantic proposal, did I?"

She had laughed and said truthfully that he needn't be romantic.

No, there was nothing dramatic, no sweeping, earth-shattering romance, but she had always felt theirs to be an inevitable love, something they could count on all their lives.

She had struggled with German and French, as had Rufe; she had a little advantage on him in French because she had learned the rudiments in school. Rufe had the advantage in his aptitude for learning any strange language; he picked up grammar and accent more easily than she did. He had worked hard; the requirements for the Foreign Service were exacting. He had gone to law school but had interrupted his education when he went to Vietnam; when he came home he decided to train for the Foreign Service. Seth had not discouraged him; he only said that it was a hard course, and he too had helped him. Seth was a lawyer but he also had a specialized knowledge of international problems, for long ago he had turned from his law practice to politics and now was a senator.

Surely nobody could say that Rufe had anything to do with the judge's murder. Meeth had killed him.

The capsule the doctor had given her had blurred the edges of her mind. It struck her in a distant and half-dreamy way that the past was always amidst the present. Another judge—younger, vigorous, indulgent—seemed to walk through the present; yet in fact the judge had changed recently. He knew it too; he had resigned from the bench before the required age of seventy, saying impatiently that he preferred to resign before his ability for careful reasoning and judgment was impaired and the Bar Association was obliged to ask for his resignation. He had been right to resign, and Bea knew that Clara accepted it. At times he was perfectly lucid and natural, but in a second he could change into an unreasonable and querulous old man, touchy to the point of irrationality. The doctor had told Bea and Clara that there was no firm dividing line to define his mental state; they must simply be patient and not permit him to fall into a rage.

The last had been impossible; no one knew what might send the judge into a burst of flaring, violent temper. She had done so that night, sitting at the dinner table with him after Clara had taken herself upstairs to her Western. And when he had flared up, Bea had been fiery and defiant, too. What was done was done; she couldn't have stopped herself. However distant, she was of the judge's blood, and she was young and had strength and passion. Out of gratitude and a real affection she had trained herself to be calm and obedient, but there were some things the judge could not demand of her. She would have liked his approval of her marriage, but she could do without it. She could do without anything, she had thought in sudden blazing anger, except for Rufe. Yet surely the judge had guessed how things stood between her and Rufe? She wondered if that was one reason why he had been so intent and helpful about Rufe's training. He must have known that Rufe would receive only a minor appointment. The judge could have reasoned slyly that Rufe would be sent far away from Bea, and that for a long time he wouldn't be able to afford to support Bea in—the judge was right when he called it luxury. But now her own love for the judge and her own reason tried to deny that suspicion.

Until her quarrel with the judge, it had been a great day. Rufe had come that morning to tell her the news that he had passed his final oral examinations. They had walked away from the house, past the old red barn which now served as a garage, and along the path to the pond, through the spring woods. A few swamp maples were flaming red; there was a golden haze around the willows. "I'm still shaky in French," Rufe had said. "German was all right. Duties requirements, those were all right, and so were tactics and strategy in the event of war."

16

"War?"

"Required instruction. 'War is a projection of policy when other means fail.' "

It was obviously a quotation. "Who said that?"

"One of our greats, Robert Murphy. What a Foreign Service officer hopes and tries to do is prevent failure."

After a moment she said, "Where are they going to send you?"

"Where are they going to send us, you mean. Oh, Bea!" Rufe had laughed exultantly. "We'll hear soon, I expect." He sobered. "It's what I've wanted to do ever since I was sent to Vietnam. If this world is to be saved, it's by communication. We've got to learn to talk to one another, to understand one another. It *can* be done by Foreign Service officers, by diplomacy. We've got to understand one another—nations, I mean —as people."

"I know." She had heard him talk like this many times. It was as if his experience in Vietnam had opened his vision; he was dedicating his life to the hope of being even a small thread in a mesh that could help bind the world of nations together in friendship and common cause.

The Foreign Service was strict in its demands, but surely the fact that Rufe's intended wife's great-uncle—so remote an association—had been murdered could not possibly endanger his career.

Suddenly she realized that a long time had passed since she'd come upstairs. She wondered what the police were doing. She started as someone knocked at the door and then opened it. "Seth!"

Seth was tall and lean, like Dr. Thorne; he had a long face with sharply aquiline features, a Yankee face, although it always seemed to Bea that in a portrait his neck should be surrounded by a ruff, like a Spanish grandee. But no Spanish grandee would wear such old and baggy tweeds. "Dear Bea, I'm so sorry."

"Seth, I quarreled with him tonight! Seth, can this possibly hurt Rufe's career?"

"No!" He said it too vehemently, in his strong orator's voice, the voice that had helped him in his own career. Apparently he heard himself, for he added quietly, "Don't think of such a thing! How could it hurt Rufe? He had nothing to do with this."

17

"Was it Meeth?"

"They're trying to find him. Now, Bea, listen to me. The police have a warrant. They've searched the whole place—the judge's study, everywhere. They want you to tell them how you happened to find him, but tell me first."

She gave a careful, brief recital, and as he listened his angular face cleared. "All right. They'll make a record of everything you say, you know. I just wanted to be sure there was nothing that you—oh, that you might later wish you hadn't said. Stick to the facts and you'll be all right. Obrian is down there, and you're not afraid of him, are you?"

Obrian, the chief of the Valley Ridge police, had known Bea since her childhood; indeed, he had once caught her sailing full tilt down Main Street on roller skates. She couldn't remember how she had got there undetected, for the Salcott place (Clara's property, which in spite of her marriage to Judge Bartry was still called the Salcott place) lay over two miles from the quiet little village of Valley Ridge. Unluckily, Mrs. Benson had emerged from Bellow's Fancy Fruit Store just as Bea shot past. But she didn't shoot past; she butted full speed into Mrs. Benson. Even more unluckily, Mrs. Benson was wearing an immaculate white linen dress and fell into a tray of blueberries and red raspberries. Mr. Bellow had burst from the store; Obrian, already chief of police, had heard the commotion from his office and had taken Bea home after administering a sound whack to the seat of her blue shorts. Nobody was supposed to rollerskate down Main Street. The judge had been most apologetic to Mrs. Benson and had scolded Bea, but there had been a twinkle in his eye. Mrs. Benson was not one of his favorites.

Seth said, "Now then, wash your face; you'll feel better."

She did feel better after splashing her face with cold water. "Comb your hair," Seth directed when she emerged from the bathroom, and obediently she did that too, unable to repress the thought that Seth thus carefully advised clients before their appearance in a courtroom.

Seth stood behind her and watched in the mirror as she brushed her hair. "You're a beautiful child," he said unexpectedly.

"Me!"

"Look at yourself. Dark-blue eyes—but they can flash with anger. Hair like silk, sort of brown and gold. When you were

18

a kid you had great golden curls. Your face was rounder then; now it shows character."

"Seth!" But she eyed herself in the mirror, momentarily distracted.

"Black eyelashes, black eyebrows, good strong nose and— Oh, don't look so surprised, Bea, you must have seen yourself. Rufe is a lucky fellow. A beautiful wife, and one with character. Soft on the outside," Seth said. "Concrete inside. Well, perhaps that's not very flattering. Marble on the inside."

"You're trying to stiffen my backbone."

"I don't think it needs stiffening. All right now, come with me—"

"Oh, Seth—" She rose.

"You'll have to talk to them. Just be yourself and— Control yourself, Bea, don't let them work on your emotions."

"No." She rose. "Seth, the doctor said they had called the state police."

"Oh, yes. They've been conducting the search."

"Two of them were here in my room."

"They haven't found any intruder——Meeth or anybody. The territory is hard to search. There are all the woods belonging to Clara's property, and those of the Ellison place on one side and the Carters' on the other. The Carter place hasn't been occupied since old Mrs. Carter died. The Ellisons are away and there's only a caretaker there. It's easy for somebody to hide. They've tried to find and identify tire tracks along the public road, but I don't think they found anything. The medical examiner came, he's gone now. He says he'll have a full report in the morning, but there's no doubt that the judge was shot. He says the bullet entered by the shoulder just above the heart, but too close. He called it the anterior chest wall." Seth's voice took on a sharp note. "He says . . . Well, you'll have to know. The medical examiner insists that whoever shot him tried and probably succeeded in removing the bullet from below his shoulder blade. I don't know how he can be so sure, but that's what he says. You'd better sit down!" He pulled Bea toward a chair barely in time. "Put your head down. I thought I'd better tell you here."

A dizzy swinging sensation descended on her like a curtain. "Did the judge know that? Was he conscious? How long could he have lived?"

He shook his head. "I doubt if he was conscious at the time

19

the bullet was extracted—if it was extracted. I really don't think he suffered, Bea."

"He was conscious for a moment, just long enough to tell me to send for you and the doctor—"

"That's all he said?"

"That's all, Seth. There's simply nothing I know that could help the police. Nothing!"

"Well, then," Seth said, "take it easy. They won't know whether the murderer really succeeded in getting the bullet out until the medical examiner has made X-rays. He may be all wrong about the bullet being extracted. As a matter of fact, it seems to me they're being a little too fast about calling it murder. The judge was shot, yes, but knowing him and knowing that he was aware of his own physical condition, he just might have shot himself."

"But the bullet—"

"Could have gone straight through his body and is somewhere in the ground. If the medical examiner should be right, of course somebody must have shot him and believed the bullet could be traced. But suicide seems to me more likely."

"Not the judge."

"They found a gun near him. It may prove to be his."

"I didn't see a gun."

"You weren't in a state to see anything. Come, Bea—"

"He wouldn't have killed himself! Not the judge!"

"They'll try to trace the gun they found. We'd better go down. There's a lieutenant of the state police. The medical examiner let them take the judge away after he'd seen him; there was an ambulance. There are two detectives, men in plain clothes. Don't let anybody frighten you. Tell them what you told me, but don't say any more than that."

There was a significance in his words that she had to search out. "What do you mean, Seth?"

"Murder is a capital crime. The police never give up on a murder case."

"You mean more than that."

"I mean that one never knows just how entangling the evidence in a murder case can be. It's a good rule to say no more than you have to say and stick to it. Now don't look at me like that, Bea. You and Clara—good heavens, nobody will suspect either of you! But just do as I say. Talk to them as you talked to me, but not another word."

Rufe knocked and opened the door. "Bea, they want you to tell them how you found him."

She took a long breath and went down the stairs, following Seth, Rufe holding her hand firmly. In the study there was a group of men, some state policemen, some in the blue uniform of the village police, and, as Seth had warned, two men in plain clothes stood beside the desk. All of them turned as she came in, and Seth introduced them. The lieutenant's name was Abbott; she didn't hear the other introductions.

Chief Obrian surged heavily out of an armchair. "I'm sorry about this, Bea," he said. He was trying to put her at ease. "Now, these officers want you to tell how you happened to find the judge."

Lieutenant Abbott stepped forward, and politely, as if he had memorized an exact formula—as indeed, she thought vaguely, he must have—gave her a formal warning to the effect that as a witness she must be willing to make a statement. Another policeman took out a stenographer's pad and a pencil. She told her story, aware of the alert eyes and ears around her and of the swiftly moving pencil of the man taking notes.

When she finished, Seth said in a low voice, "It will be typed up and then you'll be asked to sign it. All right?"

Bea nodded as they began to question her. She knew that her answers were being added to the notes.

"Now this burglar alarm," one of the men in plain clothes said, "I've seen many of them. It goes off when a door or window that has been bugged is opened. You say this door"—he jerked his head toward the terrace door—"was open when you came down. How much time elapsed while you and Mrs. Bartry talked up there in the hall before you decided to look for the judge?"

"I don't know; only a few minutes. The alarm makes such a noise. I got into a dressing gown and slippers, and when I came downstairs the judge wasn't here—"

"We understand that. But the medical examiner says that whoever killed him had to have time to dig out that bullet. Now, if the judge had gone outside after Mrs. Bartry set the alarm, it would have sounded then."

The second man in plain clothes cleared his throat. The other nodded. "Yes, I'm coming to that. There's a caretaker on the Ellison place next door. Name is Griffin. He heard and

21

saw the police cars and came forward with some information." —

Willie Griffin, Bea thought; she knew him. Any information he had to give was probably accurate. It also proved to be difficult to understand.

"He says," the first detective went on, "that he heard not just one shot but two shots. Heard them distinctly. After that, he is sure that it was maybe ten, fifteen minutes after the two shots that he heard your alarm go. Any answer to that, Miss Bartry?"

Bea shook her head. "Two shots?"

"So he says. We found only one gun. It had been fired once as far as we can make out at this time. You're sure you heard no shots at all?"

"No, no, I told you—"

"If this man Griffin is correct, then the judge must have gone outside before the alarm was set. So it looks as if whoever shot him had time first to dig out the bullet and then come back in the house, setting off the alarm. The judge—or the murderer—apparently closed that door when the judge went out. After that the alarm was set. When the murderer came back to the house and opened the door, the alarm started. At least that's the way it looks now."

All of them seemed to conclude that it was murder; nobody even mentioned suicide. But then Bea herself wouldn't have accepted suicide.

The detective asked thoughtfully, "Why would anyone come back into the house? It was a terrific risk. What could anybody want? Money?"

"We never keep much cash in the house."

"Jewelry? Did anybody have time to do any rummaging around for jewelry after you and your aunt heard the alarm?"

"No."

"Well, whoever killed him wanted something from the house pretty badly."

22

Three

"But there isn't anything." Bea said.

There was a long and thoughtful silence. It struck her that there was a faint, grimy dust over almost everything in the study, particularly on the judge's desk; it must have been to get fingerprints. Rufe took her hand and pulled her down into a chair. Finally the lieutenant said, "There's another consideration. If that bullet was removed, whoever dug for it must have had some kind of surgical experience. He'd have to know where to dig and how, in the dark—"

Dr. Thorne was sitting in a chair in the corner; Bea hadn't seen him till he spoke. "I have certainly had medical, even some surgical experience, but I assure you I didn't shoot the judge."

Rufe said suddenly, "That bullet would have had to come from a thirty-two, wouldn't it?"

All the men looked at him sharply.

Rufe said, "Well, it stands to reason. A forty-five would have been too destructive. A thirty-eight would probably have gone through the body. A thirty-two is my guess. My father's gun is a thirty-two. You can look at it yourself. He always keeps a gun in his car—"

"Why?" the lieutenant said, surprised.

Dr. Thorne answered, "Because I'm a doctor. I make night calls. The country is different now—you never know. Well, I have a permit, and you can examine the gun. I don't think it's ever been fired, thank God."

"He hasn't even cleaned it," Rufe said. "Believe me—"

"You pointed out the fact that the gun that killed the judge was likely a thirty-two," one of the detectives said slowly. "Now, if the judge had worn that coat of his"—he nodded at the heavy, shabby tweed jacket which now lay neatly folded over a chair—"the bullet probably wouldn't have gone so far through to enable anybody to try to extract it from his back. You've had army experience, I understand?"

Rufe replied shortly, "Of course."

"I expect you have a gun."

"I had one. I turned it in with the rest of my gear when I got out of the service."

"What did you do in the army? I mean your special job."

Rufe's face became the reserved mask which was partly natural and partly cultivated since he had been training for the Foreign Service. He replied agreeably, "I was a medical corpsman for a while."

The lieutenant's face sharpened. "How did that happen? I understood from Obrian that you had studied law."

"I did. But my father's office is in our home, and from time to time since I was a kid I'd hang around and give him a bit of help now and then. Anyway, I knew something of first aid, so they made me a corpsman. Of course, they gave me some training."

"You'd know how to dig out a bullet," one of the detectives said almost to himself.

Rufe remained agreeable. "I've dug out plenty of bullets. Made plenty of splints and all that, too. But I had help—lights for one thing, and assistance."

There was another long silence. Everyone was wondering how anybody could successfully extract a bullet in the dark shadows of the laurels. Finally one detective, small, thin, gray, put another question to Rufe. "You were a corpsman all the time you were in Vietnam?"

"No. I was transferred to another outfit. They called it intelligence. I was new at it and green. Mainly I only had to interview prisoners or villagers, try to get at the truth of things."

"But did you understand their language?"

Rufe looked rather grim. "No. You understood—oh, other things. Gestures, attitudes—I can't explain it. I picked up a few words."

Seth said, "He was good at it. His commanding officer gave him a fine recommendation for Foreign Service training."

The detective looked soberly at Seth and then back to Rufe. The lieutenant fingered his own polished holster from which protruded a businesslike revolver. "But you know something about guns."

"Quite a number of young men know something about guns," Dr. Thorne said wearily.

Seth said, "Can Miss Bartry leave now? She's had a fright-ful shock. She'll talk to you any time. But tonight . . ."

Obrian's face seemed relieved at the idea of a respite. He heaved himself out of his chair. "I do advise that, Lieutenant."

Rufe said, "When did you get the alarm at the police sta-tion, Mr. Obrian?"

He turned a fat face toward Rufe. "I'm not sure. Tony!"

Tony Calinas stepped forward. "Yes, sir."

"When did that alarm come on?"

Tony replied promptly, "I was in the patrol car, and we got the alarm from the police station at ten forty-five almost to the second. I made a record of it."

"There'll be a record at the station too. What's on your mind, Rufe?"

"Whoever came into the house and set off the alarm must have got out fast."

"The alarm scared him away," Obrian said. "At least that's what it is supposed to do."

The lieutenant said, "We've got to find out when Mrs. Bar-try set the alarm—"

Dr. Thorne interrupted him. "You cannot question Mrs. Bartry tonight. If you insist on it, I cannot be responsible for the consequences. You can get her statement tomorrow."

There was another pause; then one of the men in plain clothes spoke. "The point is, what did the murderer want?" He eyed the three steel filing cabinets that stood behind the judge's big desk.

Obrian looked from the files to Bea. "You acted as your uncle's secretary. Do you know of any record or anything that somebody might have wanted?"

"No. Only the usual letters and accounts. And he was working on his memoirs."

The little gray detective turned to her, his ears seeming to prick up. "Memoirs?"

Obrian's plump face tightened. "His autobiography?"

"They're in the files. He'd talk into the dictating machine and then I'd transcribe the tapes." She thought of all the pages, most of them flat and dull, which she had laboriously typed out to the accompaniment of the judge's rather harsh voice on a tape. "You can look at them—they're in the files.

But I'd remember anything that—that anybody might want. There must have been some other reason for the murderer to come into the house. We didn't hear or see anybody." Her voice rose unsteadily.

"It's all right, Bea," Seth said.

The lieutenant tapped his fingers lightly on his revolver holster as if he were playing some tune which only he could hear, and addressed nobody in particular. "Now, the time the alarm came in at the police station was, say, a minute before the alarm reached the patrol car. So whoever came into the house had to be here before ten forty-five but after Mrs. Bartry set the alarm. So"—he addressed the ceiling—"if this fellow Meeth should happen to have an alibi for that time . . ."

He paused, and after a moment Obrian said heavily, "Then we'll have to look elsewhere."

"That's our job," the lieutenant said shortly. Having got that off his well-tailored chest, he seemed to feel better and stopped playing tunes on his holster.

The detective with the gray suit, gray hair and grayish face said, "The judge had a gun, Miss Bartry?"

She nodded.

He said, "Could you identify it?"

"No. But he had it registered."

"You've seen it?"

"Yes. He showed it to me."

"When was that?"

"About a couple of weeks ago."

"Any special reason for showing it to you?"

"Yes. He'd had it for some time, but he never wanted my aunt to know about it. She's nervous about guns and she was upset because Meeth was about to be released from prison. That's why we had the burglar alarm installed."

"Why did the judge show you his gun?" said the detective.

"He told me how to load it and where he kept it."

"But why? Was he afraid of something—or somebody?"

"He said that I ought to know he had it, that was all."

"Was it loaded when he showed it to you?"

"Yes. He said there was no use keeping a gun around unless it was loaded."

"Was he afraid of Meeth?"

"No! He said once that if he were afraid of everybody he sentenced, he'd never have an easy moment."

"Where did he keep the gun?"

"In a desk drawer."

"Which one?"

The detective's voice was quiet, yet there was tension in the room when Bea went to the desk and pulled open the third drawer from the top. The police seemed to crowd around her, but it was Rufe who said quietly, "It's not there. Maybe he changed the place. Look in the other drawers."

The gun was nowhere in the desk.

"How about the files?" the lieutenant said.

One of the detectives shrugged and pulled open the top drawer of the nearest filing cabinet; it slid out easily and heavily, disclosing labeled, packed papers. He gave a look of dismay at the others, then quite openly glanced at his watch.

Abbott seemed to sigh. "We can't go through all those tonight. What about the rest of the drawers?"

Bea said, "They're almost full, too." ·

Obrian said thoughtfully, "I guess as people get older they save more and more. No sense to it, but they do."

Bea pushed her hair up from her temples wearily. "There are tax records, bank statements, my aunt's brokers' statements, letters—quite a number of them, both copies of letters he sent and the replies. There are the records of insurance premiums paid, and he kept paid bills for five years. His notes for the memoirs are in the lower file drawer on this side—"

Obrian said, "Now, these memoirs—"

Bea understood him and said firmly, "There was nothing in the judge's memoirs that could hurt anybody. It gave him something to_do." She remembered how often she and Clara would hear the judge's voice, not as resonant and commanding as it once was but still with a certain authority, rumbling along at all hours; they would exchange a kind of conspiratorial glance which said "It keeps him occupied."

Obrian's great hand closed the packed drawer of the filing cabinet. "The point is, the judge couldn't have shot himself and then tried to dig out that bullet."

The little gray detective said in a tired voice that they could check tomorrow on whether the gun they had found belonged to the judge.

The other detective heartily agreed with him. "We can't do any more just now. Have to find this man Meeth, take a look through the judge's desk and files. That'll take time."

The lieutenant said, "We haven't taken Miss Bartry's fingerprints."

The second detective grunted. "She's not going to run away. But I'd suggest leaving a man here in the house who'll keep an eye on"—his gaze went to the filing cabinets—"things," he finished, his underlip protruding.

"I can't spare a man. God knows what's going on right now at the barracks. But—" The lieutenant made up his mind and turned to Obrian. "Have you got a man you can leave here tonight?"

Tony stepped forward smartly. "I can stay, sir."

Obrian frowned. "That'd be overtime for you. Sure you don't want me to get someone else?"

"No, sir, it's all right."

The lieutenant seemed unhappy but yielded to the pressure of time and to the obvious desire of the two detectives to depart. "All right." He gave Tony a severe stare. "Just don't go to sleep. Keep your eyes open. Now then, men—"

They were leaving. The young policeman with the stenographer's tablet put it carefully in his pocket. Bea saw that the small gray detective was carrying her dressing gown over one arm.

There was the measured tread of feet along the terrace, then the roar of cars starting up in the drive. Nobody spoke until the thud of the engines had diminished down the drive. Then Dr. Thorne took up his medicine bag. "I've got to get home to check my answering service. Bea, if your aunt wakes and gets restless I left two capsules on her bedside table. Give her one. Coming, Rufe?"

"I think I'll stay here tonight, Pa—that is, if Bea wants me."

"Yes—" Bea began, but his father interrupted, "Of course. Well—" He put a hand on her shoulder in a gesture which was meant to be comforting. "The judge couldn't have recovered, Bea. He was getting worse all the time—everybody knew it. He'd get something on his mind and brood over it and build it up and . . . It must have been very difficult for you and Clara. He was a proud man. Wouldn't surprise me at all if he used his own gun to—"

Rufe shook his head. "He couldn't have dug out the bullet, Pa."

"But suppose the medical examiner is wrong. He's new

28

here; I don't know much about him. Suppose the judge killed himself. I'm not sure I could tell whether the bullet was extracted or whether its velocity had torn the flesh.''

"You could tell," Rufe said.

Seth said thoughtfully, "When I used to go hunting, I'd sometimes dig out a bullet, but I'm not sure I would have known afterward whether it was dug out with a knife or whether it just came out. It was a messy business, anyway."

"Don't—" Bea said in a small voice.

"Try to sleep, Bea," the doctor said and went out the terrace door.

Seth said, "I'll be going too. Unless you want me to stay."

Bea saw his own weariness; his aquiline face seemed to fall into sagging lines, so that his tight iron-gray curls looked even crisper than usual.

"No, Seth, thanks."

"I'll come by tomorrow. There's his will, you know. He had me draw up wills for himself and Clara when I was home last fall. They fixed it so everything Clara and the judge had is to come to you eventually—"

"To *me!*" Bea stared at Seth. "But I—That's not fair!"

"It's the way he wanted it. I'll explain it tomorrow—"

He broke off, for at that moment the terrace door flung open and Lorraine swept into the room along with green chiffon, sables and perfume. Afterward it seemed to Bea an almost shocking example of Lorraine's gift for timing that she should arrive at the precise moment when Seth was talking about the judge's will. But in her astonishment she said only, "You can't be here! You're in Italy!"

"In Italy? What do you think? Darling Seth! I hear you're still a senator. It must be almost your third term. You don't look a day older! Just as handsome as ever. More so!" She swept over to Seth and kissed him warmly. Then she swirled around to Rufe and embraced him warmly too. Altogether too warmly, Bea thought.

Lorraine had been her rival for years—no, Bea had to amend that, for the fact was that though Rufe had once been in love with Lorraine, it was a long time ago.

Lorraine perched on the corner of the desk, her slender white hand on Rufe's shoulder. "And they tell me," she went on, "that you're going into the Foreign Service, Rufe. You'll be a great man. It's wonderful."

29

"I didn't know you were here," Bea said lamely.

Lorraine gave a high-pitched, shrill laugh, like a bird's song —but a glittering, flashing, predatory bird. "I've been here two days. I'm staying at the Bensons'."

"The Bensons'! Why on earth?"

"Oh." Lorraine laughed lightly again. "I knew the judge wouldn't welcome me here. I thought I'd take a few days to see how the land lay—that is, if there was a chance of softening him up. He told me never to darken his door again." She giggled. "He really said that, just like a stern father in some old melodrama. All because I wanted to marry Cecco. That is"—she caught herself and seemed to snuggle her lithe body toward Rufe—"I *thought* I wanted to marry Cecco. I wouldn't have done it if the judge hadn't opposed the marriage. I couldn't let him bully me. But it happens that the judge was right. I've left Cecco. Will you help me get a divorce, Seth?"

Seth said soberly, "Don't you know what happened tonight?"

"Oh, of course. That's why I came. I was at a dance at the club with Ben Benson. Somebody heard the news and told us, so I got Ben to bring me here and . . . here I am." Her eyes danced toward Bea. "My clothes are at the Bensons'. We'll have to get them tomorrow. I'll stay here now, of course. Aunt Clara will want me. Aunt Clara always loved me. It was the judge who got upset about my marriage. Too bad he'll never know how right he was." Lorraine laughed again and tossed back her head so that the black locks of thick hair framing her narrow, heart-shaped face displayed her high cheekbones, her bold white forehead, slanted black eyebrows and red lips to advantage. The gesture was so graceful that it seemed practiced; nevertheless it was attractive.

Rufe's face showed neither pleasure nor surprise as Lorraine leaned against his arm.

Seth said, "Are you sure Clara will want you here, Lorraine?"

"Oh, yes!" Lorraine said confidently. "I'm her niece, her only blood relative."

Seth said, "I'll be going. Try to rest, Bea."

"Seth, wait," Bea said quickly. "What will happen now?"

"An investigation. An inquest—"

"When?"

30

"Possibly not for some time, and unless they have very strong evidence, the inquest may be adjourned or there may be a verdict of murder by a person or persons unknown. After that," Seth sighed, "well, if they can secure strong evidence against some person, there'll be a warrant sworn out, that person will be taken into custody and then the evidence will be presented to the grand jury."

"And after that?"

"If the grand jury brings in a true bill—that is, indicts someone—there may be bail set, later a trial . . . Oh, don't think about all that now, Bea. Besides, I still don't see how the police can jump so fast to the conclusion that it's murder. I suppose that Meeth's threats set them off. That, and this medical examiner saying the bullet had been dug out. Still, this talk about murder isn't really conclusive. Of course, they have to consider it and investigate—that's their duty. But I'm not sure—" He shook his head.

He was certainly not as handsome as Lorraine had proclaimed but he did have a distinguished air in spite of the baggy clothes he wore, which Bea always suspected were assumed to fit his political image, that of a New England lawyer from a small town. Yet it was like Seth to refuse to put on airs.

Tony had removed himself unobtrusively to the corner by the door. His dark face was lowering and angry. Why? Then Bea remembered that he had been with Rufe in Vietnam; he must know of the many letters Rufe had written to Lorraine, and of Lorraine's failure to reply to them. Out of sight, out of mind must have been one reason for Lorraine's swift rejection of Rufe, but another was because she had met Cecco. Tony gave Lorraine a baleful glance, which she noted instantly. Sliding off the desk, she went over to Seth and lifted her charming face again. "I never knew a senator could be so handsome," she said softly. "But then, you always were handsome, Seth—"

Seth gave a short laugh. "I'm working up to fifty, Lorraine. No blandishments, if you please. Better ask Clara what she wants you to do." His glance took in Bea and Rufe. "I'll see you," he said, and left.

"Ciao," Lorraine called after him, and then turned back to Forty-five or whatever isn't too old. Did he ever marry?"

Rufe. "Goodness! I always thought of Seth as being ancient.

31

"No."

"H'mm." Lorraine was thoughtful. "Living in Washington, knowing all those famous people. Why, he really needs a wife, a hostess."

Tony abruptly and unexpectedly changed the subject. "Now don't worry, we'll see to things, Miss Bartry."

"You're not married either, Bea?" There was a teasing quality in Lorraine's voice. "And so many men around! Why, I thought you'd have been married long ago."

Tony moved restlessly, watching Rufe from the corners of his dark eyes.

Lorraine gave that graceful little toss of her head again. "Well, it was smart of you to make yourself useful to the judge and Aunt Clara. She's so rich!"

"Lorraine, it's been a dreadful—" Bea's voice broke a little.

Rufe made a move toward her, but somehow Lorraine was between them, stooping to pick up the sable scarf she had dropped at his feet.

Bea went on, "I think that Aunt Clara would want you to stay here. I can give you a nightdress. Is Ben waiting for you?"

"Oh, no, I told him to go home before his mother got upset and began to phone all over the place." There was an edge to Lorraine's voice. "If ever anybody was tied to his mother's apron strings, it's Ben Benson. Of course, I'm very sorry about the judge, but Ben did tell me that he had been ill, so possibly he just decided to kill himself," she said airily. "I don't see how they can possibly be sure that somebody shot him."

"They can be," Rufe said shortly. "Take it easy, Bea. I'll stay down here with Tony." He came to her, lifted her face and kissed her.

Over his shoulder Bea saw Lorraine looking knowing and a little amused. "Come on, Lorraine," she said, breaking away from Rufe. "We'll have to be quiet. The doctor gave Aunt Clara something to make her sleep."

But Lorraine had not finished. "Tony!" she cried with delight. "Why, of course! I knew that I ought to remember you. You used to work at the filling station on Oak Street."

Tony nodded.

Lorraine swept on, apparently overcome by rapturous admiration. "And now you're a policeman!"

"Yes," Tony said. "And I was told to stay here tonight."

Something in his voice and lowering face put Lorraine off her stride. "Oh, well. That's very good of you. And you, Rufe. We'll feel so safe. I'm coming, Bea."

Tony's adamantine face was a small triumph; Bea could have kissed him. She led the way, Lorraine's sables brushing against her arm, up the stairs, lightly, in the hope of not rousing Clara. It seemed remarkable that nothing in the house had changed. The lower hall was wide and gracious; the big mirror above the table reflected the two young women, flashes of green chiffon and black hair, flashes of herself, pale and tired-looking, in her brown sweater and skirt. Nobody, not Seth or even Rufe, could think her beautiful now. She had always felt gawky and pedestrian in Lorraine's presence, but now she felt it acutely when they entered her room. She took out a nightgown for Lorraine, who laughed, but checked it when Bea put her finger to her lips. "It's the nightgown," Lorraine whispered. "Nobody wears nightgowns!"

"Well, don't wear it if you don't want to. Nobody cares!" Bea snapped.

Lorraine eyed her. "What's all this between you and Rufe?"

Suddenly Bea's fighting blood surged up. She said forcefully, "We're engaged. We're going to be married as soon as Rufe gets his appointment."

"Oh, *are* you?" Lorraine smiled. "You've taken my room, and apparently you've tried to take my place with Aunt Clara as well as with Rufe. I'll go to that big guest room."

She seemed almost to dance out of the room. If anybody regretted the judge's death, it wasn't Lorraine. Exultance was in her every move and word.

Bea pulled her sweater over her head and paused to look at herself again in the mirror. There were shadows under her eyes; her face was pale and seemed oddly determined. Seth had called her beautiful either to distract or encourage her, but now she told herself to accept his compliments and proceed as if they were true. Lorraine was no ordinary rival.

Sometimes Rufe had said something flattering, and even the judge sometimes had given her a swift, hard look, usually over the dinner-table candlelight, and said that she was *en beauté* that night. It was one of his fancies to use French or Latin phrases. Apparently it hadn't occurred to him that if

33

there was a special sparkle in her face, it was because of Rufe.

But the judge was perceptive. He couldn't have been as surprised as he pretended to be when she told him that she and Rufe were going to be married as soon as he got an assignment. He had been pleased when she'd told him the good news that Rufe had passed his last tests, but he had taken that as a credit to himself and whatever assistance he had given Rufe. Yet she could not reasonably ignore the fact that the judge simply preferred to keep her at home because she was useful. Clara had plenty of money; even now she could have contrived to employ a chauffeur, a secretary for the judge and a housekeeper; instead there was only Velda Mathers from the village who came in by the day. Somehow she kept the big house in order with Bea's help. Sometimes Clara deplored this, but not often, for the judge's wishes came first in her life.

Bea was sure she couldn't sleep. She was tired to the bone, but not sleepy-tired. Lorraine had said something about divorcing Cecco. Obviously it wasn't because of his lack of money. She remembered the rings flashing on Lorraine's white hands, the sable scarf she had dropped on the floor as if it were a rug, the adroitly designed green chiffon dress. Perhaps Lorraine had simply tired of him.

Certainly she had taken a swift interest in Seth, a longtime senator who, Lorraine had said, must need a wife and hostess for all those important people in Washington. But she had also instantly flirted with Rufe. Did she feel sure of getting him back again?

But naturally Lorraine would feel sure of getting anything she wanted.

Eight years older than Bea, Lorraine was the daughter of Clara's only sister, who had divorced her husband and remarried. Then her father had remarried too. Bea had never heard the entire story, but she did know that Lorraine had been welcome in neither household and that Clara had lovingly offered her a home. She must have been about twelve or thirteen when Bea herself was introduced into the household, but even then Lorraine possessed a certain sophistication. She hadn't paid much attention to Bea; she wasn't interested in small children. Later on, though, she had permitted Bea to watch while she prepared to go out with some boy. She would fix her hair in this arrangement or that; put on lipstick and then wipe it off to try another color, leaving her lips bare but inviting; would let Bea watch her try on her dresses and perfume.

Bea didn't know when it was that she began to recognize Lorraine's facility for lying, but was always astonished at the way she could coolly lie to Clara or the judge.

Bea was also very much aware of the progress of her cousin's interest in Rufe. Lorraine would laugh in a satisfied way and tell her how Rufe adored her, how he felt that she was the only woman for him!

Bea didn't know how much she had believed as a child, but certainly Rufe's behavior had confirmed at least some of Lorraine's smug statements. He was always underfoot, the judge had said once testily, but Clara had intervened. They had known Rufe all his life, and they couldn't find a better husband for Lorraine.

Lorraine had looked rather sulky at that and said she didn't need to have anybody find a husband for her; she could do it herself. This bothered Clara, whose faint eyebrows drew together over her troubled pale-blue eyes. Clara had taken a motherly interest—almost too great an interest—in Rufe since his own mother had died many years before. Rufe had complained once, but laughingly, saying that Aunt Clara would still have him in long woolen underwear if she could. But he loved her and called her Aunt, a courtesy title.

Yes, both Clara and the judge would have accepted him as Lorraine's husband. But then Rufe had gone to Vietnam, Cecco had arrived on the scene and Lorraine had fallen for him—or perhaps vice versa. In any event, the judge had opposed their marriage so violently that in the end they had eloped and gone to live in Italy.

Gradually as Bea grew older she had become like a daughter to both Clara and the judge. She knew that they loved her, knew that they had grown to depend on her, and so she had made it her task to take on more and more responsibility.

Long ago Rufe had taught her to skate on the pond down by the woods; he had romped and run with old Shadders, the dog the judge had given her, a stiff-legged Airedale whose manners were also rather stiff at first acquaintance. But he had loved Rufe, and Bea had loved Rufe too, counting the days to his vacations even though she knew that he would be coming to the house because Lorraine was there.

But then, years later, Rufe had come home from Vietnam and went into the arduous training for Foreign Service, and he and Bea were now engaged to be married. She held that fact close; Rufe wouldn't be taken in again by Lorraine.

Or would he?

Now the shadow of the judge's death fell over her again. How could she think of anything else! She debated briefly whether to reset the burglar alarm; all she had to do was go to the linen closet where the tiny panel was set into the wall. There were two small lights in the panel and a smaller push button; if the bugged doors and windows were properly closed, a white light showed; if not, there was no light at all. When the white light showed, one push of the button would switch it off and turn on the red light, showing that the alarm was set.

She decided against setting the alarm. Tony or Rufe would be strolling around the house and might open one of the doors. She was thankful for their presence; she would go to sleep safely. But her mind was like a pinwheel whirling around and around, shooting off sparks: the judge's death, the gun, a police inquiry. Hadn't Seth said something about the judge's will, something that affected her?

The spark of consciousness floated off and vanished into darkness. She went to sleep as if she had taken some of Clara's medicine, drugged into insensibility. Yet she dreamed; she was telling Lorraine again that she and Rufe were going to be married, and Lorraine was looking at her with brilliant green eyes and saying again, not quite restraining laughter, "Oh, *are* you?"

A sound aroused her; she sat up, wondering what burden had fallen on her and at once remembered. It was a dull day; gray light came through the curtains. Somewhere there were voices. Lorraine was saying, piercingly and sweetly, "Darling Aunt Clara! Of course I came at once to be with you," and a man's voice murmured in a low tone.

Four

So the day began. After a quick shower Bea dressed in her usual casual fashion, but she brushed her hair into a shining mass, even though she knew it couldn't rival the dramatic effect of Lorraine's hanging black frame of hair. As she walked down the hall she saw that Clara's door was open; Lorraine was there, still in her green chiffon, perched at the foot of Clara's bed. Seth was there too, lanky and sober, sitting on a straight chair. "—no, his will doesn't have to be probated at once, Clara," he was saying as Bea paused in the doorway. "I'll stay home as long as I can. But the sooner you get all the business details over with, the better."

Clara had a breakfast tray across her lap. Her hair was neat; her face a little pale but firm; she wore a fluffy, coquettish bed jacket and eyed Lorraine with a troubled gaze. Lorraine waited, as still as a cat about to pounce upon a mouse.

Then Clara's worried gaze caught Bea, standing in the doorway; she smiled. "Come in, dear. This concerns you, too. Tell her, Seth."

Seth politely offered Bea his chair. She shook her head and went to the other side of Clara's bed, taking the same position as Lorraine, but in her yellow sweater and blue tweed skirt Bea looked, she was sure, anything but glamorous.

Seth wriggled his angular body back into the small chair. "I started to tell Bea last night but I don't think she paid any attention. It's the judge's and Clara's wills."

Clara touched a lacy napkin to her lips. "Explain it to Bea, Seth."

"Yes. Well, in a way it's unusual, yet the judge wanted it this way and Clara agreed."

Clara gave a little nod. Lorraine sat statue-still and seemed to be holding her breath. Seth locked his hands together and looked at them as if he were consulting a brief. "I drew up both documents. The judge asked me to do it; he and Clara have separate wills of course, but they amount to the same thing."

37

Lorraine did move then. She put out one white hand on which diamonds flashed. "But you're still a senator!"

"I've always kept up an office here. Joe Lathrop sees to things, real-estate transfers, title searches, that kind of thing. But once in a while an old friend asks me to do something as the judge did. I wasn't sure it was a wise move on the judge's part but it wasn't my business to advise. Anybody can do anything he wants to in a will. And Clara agreed——"

Clara said, "Of course I agreed."

"Naturally," Seth said rather dryly. "You always agreed with the judge. The point is this, the wills are so written——" He turned to Bea. "If the judge predeceased Clara—as tragically he now has—then her property as well as his own were to be made into a trust for Clara's lifetime. After that the whole of the property, Clara's portion as well as the judge's, was to come to you, Bea."

"That's what you meant," Bea began in astonishment. Yet she had taken in enough the night before to say that it wasn't fair. She said it again. "But that's not fair to Lorraine."

Lorraine made no sign that she even heard Bea. Seth said, "As you know, Clara has a great deal of property and money. She was content with the judge's arrangement—weren't you, Clara?"

Clara eyed her empty coffee cup and nodded.

"The fact was, I suppose, that the judge didn't quite depend upon Clara's judgment about business." Clara's eyes went up to Seth's face and a slight smile touched his lips. "I can't say that I agree with the judge. This kind of arrangement—that is, Clara's care of her own property, to hinge on the judge's predeceasing her—is unusual but it's perfectly legal. Nothing I could do to stop it as long as Clara agreed. But Clara always wanted to please him. Now, as we all know, the judge had not been himself recently; he was very uncertain in his mind. He would get—notions," Seth said gravely. "And nothing in the world could change his decisions. So I drew up the wills. He and Clara signed them. Joe Lathrop and the office girl he occasionally employs both witnessed them. The original documents are in my office safe. I expect the judge put copies in his safe-deposit box. Unless they are in the files in his study——" He looked inquiringly at Bea.

She shook her head. "No, I'd have seen them. That is— well, I'm not sure. If I had just gone about the usual filing

38

routine I might have missed them, I mean the judge might have slipped them into the files under some other heading, something I would not have been likely to notice. But I'd remember it if I had seen them."

"It doesn't matter. The point is the judge's will must be probated and I want Clara to tell me whether she wants the original arrangement, the trust fund, to stand or whether she wants to make another will. You don't have to make up your mind now, Clara."

Clara crumpled her lace napkin and dropped it on the tray. "I'll think about it."

Bea felt Lorraine's sudden movement and heard what sounded like a sigh of relief.

Seth rose. "Now if there's anything I can do, Clara——"

Clara's little hands fluttered. "The obituary, Seth. It's got to be right."

"I'll see to it."

Lorraine pushed back her hair. "I saw the morning *Times*. It was delivered just as Tony and Rufe were leaving. I was downstairs and—dear Aunt Clara, the account of the judge's death is in it. Short. Somebody must have phoned it in late last night."

Seth said comfortingly, "It was news. There are always reporters interested in anything that goes on at the Welbury barracks. They must have got the facts from somebody. I saw the account, too. It is brief and—no sense looking at it, Clara."

Clara looked up in a composed way. "But he was a well-known man. I expect there'll be a great deal in the papers. But first— Let me see, this is Saturday. You can phone in his obituary in time for tomorrow's papers. You write it, Seth. You know about the judge."

"You'll have to help me. My memory may not be as accurate or as complete as yours."

"Of course. What about a photograph?"

"Oh, I expect there'll be a photograph in the morgue."

Clara's eyes opened wide. Seth added hurriedly, "I mean the file the newspapers keep on well-known people. I'll go downstairs now and work on it. The police will want you to make a formal statement, Clara. I'll stay with you. Probably once they know you are here, Lorraine, they'll want a statement from you. Oh, yes. There may be reporters around, too.

I'd only advise you to remember——well, since the police think it is murder, the least said the better just now."

His lanky figure in its baggy and unpressed tweed slacks and jacket went out. Lorraine said softly, as if to herself, "He really does need a wife to see to him. His clothes! Aunt Clara, I'm so thankful that I happened to be here just now when you need me. That is, darling, if you do need me, I want to stay."

Clara's little hands went out lovingly toward Lorraine. "I want you to stay. Where else would you go? I'm so thankful that you have left that dreadful person, Cecco. Bea, will you take Lorraine to the Bensons' and get her clothes now?" She moved to get rid of the tray, and Lorraine sprang up, took it from her and put it on a table. "Now, you girls run along. I'll be dressed by the time you get back."

Lorraine's green chiffon swished softly as they went down the stairs. The keys for the car were on the hall table. Bea took them and opened the coat closet. "It's foggy. Here——" She handed her own raincoat to Lorraine, who took it without thanks; Bea put one of Clara's coats around herself. At the front door both girls stopped abruptly, for there were three cars in the drive, and the instant the door opened men tumbled out. "It's the reporters!" Lorraine cried, and stopped to pose, her head up.

"Oh, come on. We've got to get past them to the garage." Bea hurried on, but could not evade the two reporters who bounded up at her elbow and asked if she was Miss Beatrice Bartry.

She said something, anything, and hurried to open the two halves of a door of the ancient red barn which had been turned into a very outdated garage. The doors were fastened together with only a bolt, which one reporter obligingly pushed upward for her. "Miss Bartry——"

"Not now. Please." Bea slid into the judge's gleaming Mercedes, which he ususally had permitted only Bea to touch and only when he wished her to drive for him. Household errands were accomplished in a tiny, rather shabby and unreliable car that stood humbly beside the Mercedes. She heard Lorraine's high voice, sweet and sorrowful as she told somebody that it had been a tragic shock, yes, and she was Mrs. Bartry's niece.

Bea started the engine, its roar shutting out whatever else was said. Lorraine appeared then and leaped into the seat beside her. Bea thought that a reporter had to spring out of the

40

way hurriedly as she backed out of the garage. She went as fast as she dared past the cars parked in the drive, aware of poised cameras as they went.

Salcott Road (named for the ancestor of Clara who long ago had had the perspicacity to buy two hundred acres near Valley Ridge, then really a village) wove its way around curves and over bumps. Clara had kept the entire piece of Salcott property intact in spite of many offers to buy with the intention of cutting it up into two-acre tracts and building houses. The judge had agreed with her, although he had looked rather serious when he figured just how much money that two-hundred-acre tract would now represent.

They turned on Stony Road, passing Seth's ancient little house, which his father had used as a summer place until he retired and spent the rest of his life there. Seth Hobson had continued to use it as his only home even though he spent so much time away from Valley Ridge. They went on to the Bensons', where Mrs. Benson greeted them coldly. She was a tall, stately woman who, Bea suspected, had never forgiven the blueberry, red-raspberry incident of Bea's childhood. Her long face lighted a little, not much, when Lorraine explained that Aunt Clara wanted her to stay with her and she wished to get her clothes.

"You ought to have gone there in the first place," Mrs. Benson said. "I can't imagine why you didn't. But of course, when Ben explained that you wanted to stay with us for a few days, you were very welcome," she added, lying in her very white false teeth. "You know the guest room. Now, Bea, what is all this I hear? Is it true that that awful man Meeth shot the judge?"

It was true that the judge had been shot, Bea told her.

Mrs. Benson's gaze sharpened. "Aren't they sure it was Meeth?"

"I don't know."

"I see. I suppose the police don't take you or Clara into their confidence." She thought for a moment. "Someone told me once that the judge had been writing his memoirs."

"Yes."

"Had he finished them?"

"No."

"You seem to know—— But of course, I remember, you did all his secretarial work for him."

41

"Yes." Bea wished Lorraine would hurry.

Mrs. Benson thought for another long moment. Then she said, "Was there anything in his memoirs that would—oh, give you an idea about a—a—" She stuck there.

Bea said wearily, "A motive for killing him?"

"Well, I—yes, I suppose that thought crossed my mind."

Bea did not reply, for Lorraine came running down the stairs. She had changed out of her green chiffon and into black slacks that fit as if molded to her handsome legs, and a dark-green turtleneck sweater which brought out the emerald gleam in her eyes. Mrs. Benson said goodbye, something intent and baffled in her light-gray eyes. She pointedly did not ask Lorraine to drop by sometime.

Lorraine giggled as they got back in the car. "She thinks I'm after her Ben!" she said with scorn.

When they returned to the Salcott place the reporters were gone. "I expect Seth got rid of them," Bea said as she stopped the car. "I'll park here in front of the house."

"I'm hungry." Lorraine lugged a large suitcase up the steps. "There's a servant of sorts, isn't there? At least a female in yellow-and-green plaid brought Aunt Clara's breakfast. Why not a uniform?"

"She wouldn't think of wearing a uniform. And don't let her hear you call her a servant."

"What do you call her?"

"Velda. Velda Mathers."

Lorraine tugged at the suitcase, and Bea let her tug; however, she relented sufficiently to hold open the big front door so Lorraine could deposit the suitcase in the hall. Lorraine shook back her hair. "I've got to have breakfast."

For once Bea agreed with her. Velda, summoned to the dining room, did not. "Don't you know it's nearly eleven—" Her gooseberry-green eyes focused on Lorraine. "Why—why, it's the niece! Mrs. Bartry's niece! Now I know who you are —you're the one that married that Italian fellow. People said he was a count or something and—"

"Coffee," said Lorraine tersely. "Orange juice and an egg, three minutes."

Velda flared in instinctive rebellion. "I got breakfast for Mrs. Bartry and somebody had fixed coffee and things in my kitchen early this morning before I got here." Tony, Bea thought, and Rufe.

42

Velda said, "Not that I was on time. Mr. Obrian came to my house early this morning and I had a long talk with him." Her manner was sinister with heavy implication.

Obrian? Bea thought. What could he and Velda have had a long talk about? The obvious answer was that he wanted information about the judge or about anything whatever in the Bartry household. Bea thought uneasily of her quarrel with the judge the previous night. Only the night before, and now the judge had been killed!

Velda, eying Bea, suddenly relented. "Oh, all right. I'll fix you something. But stay out of my kitchen."

This was contrary to the rule; usually Bea had breakfast at the kitchen table while she and Velda planned meals and shopping for the day. Clara peaceably, Bea prudently, even the judge, on occasion, accepted Velda's demands. The judge had been inclined to be impatient with her assumed authority, but both Clara and Bea knew how nearly impossible it was to get anything remotely resembling a servant.

Bea got place mats and silver from the enormous buffet, wondering what Velda had told Obrian. Lorraine sat down at the table. "Why, when I was young we had two gardeners, I remember. A cook—and a good one—and I think two housemaids floated around—"

"That was some time ago. Things had begun to change before you eloped with Cecco."

"Really, I don't remember."

"Well, I do." Bea plunked silver down before Lorraine. "I was lucky to get hold of Velda. Don't hurt her feelings. She says she's very sensitive—"

"Sensitive!" Lorraine's eyes flashed. "I promise you, now I'm home to stay we'll have some decent servants—"

Unfortunately Velda, bearing coffee, came in through the pantry in time to hear. "Decent! I'll have you know I'm a decent woman. All Valley Ridge knows me. I think I'd better leave now, Miss Bea. I didn't undertake to cook for anybody who says I'm not decent. I'll leave this morning."

Lorraine gave a genteel snort. Velda's angry gaze zeroed in on Bea. It had been the judge who thundered at Velda, ordering her to say Miss Bea; at first, with fine democracy, Velda had addressed her merely as Bea.

"Please don't think of such a thing, Velda. You know how much we need you. Especially now. It's so terrible. The judge

43

—" Bea shuddered as she thought of the horror of the night before and heard the renewed sense of shock in her voice.

Velda softened. "Well, all right. Seeing how Mrs. Bartry needs me right now." She flounced off into the pantry.

Lorraine said, but this time in a whisper, "She wouldn't leave for anything. Just think how she can report everything to the village!"

Velda could gossip. Bea knew that. But surely there was nothing to gossip about that all the village did not, probably, know by now.

The pantry door swung open again. Velda's pale face and pale hair and pale but avid eyes appeared. "I'm really sorry, Miss Bea. But Obrian said I had to tell the truth. He's the law."

"Tell the truth—"

"About your quarrel with the judge last night." Velda did look embarrassed. "I was here in the pantry, doing the silver. Could I help it if I heard every word you and the judge said? Both of you shouting like that. That is, the judge shouting. But you were holding your own, all right. I never heard you talk like that. You must have been good and mad. I heard the judge say you'd have to marry Rufe over his dead body. Oh—" Velda turned an even pastier color. "I didn't think of *that*."

Lorraine's black head jerked up. "He said *that*?"

Velda nodded, cast Bea a worried but sharp look and vanished again.

Lorraine turned to Bea. "I didn't hear about this."

Bea poured coffee into Lorraine's cup and her own. "The judge didn't want me to marry. He had nothing against Rufe. You haven't been here, Lorraine. You don't know how the judge had changed. He was different."

"He didn't want me to marry Cecco either! But I went right ahead just the same. I must say I wish I hadn't. Why did the judge object to your marrying Rufe?"

"Because he didn't want me to." She couldn't say it was mainly because he wanted his own smooth way of life to continue. "He said that we should wait. He knew that Rufe's salary wouldn't be large enough at the beginning."

Lorraine seemed deep in thought as she sipped coffee. Velda brought in toast and orange juice and whisked out again. Lorraine said finally, "Over his dead body! Dear me! I wonder what the police will make of that."

"Nothing can be made of it." Bea hoped that she was right. "The judge was angry. He had moods like that. Explosive——"

"Over his dead body." Lorraine bit into toast with a snap of very small, very sharp white teeth and chewed meditatively.

A car came up the drive. Another car followed it. Doors were banged. Lorraine turned to look toward the hall. The front door was closed and there was the sound of feet marching along the terrace. "They're going to the garden room. It must be the police."

Bea's heart went down in spite of herself and in spite of the fact that she had of course known the police would return.

It seemed odd, now, for Lorraine to call the judge's study the garden room. It had been the garden room when Lorraine eloped with Cecco. After the judge retired he had chosen it for his study; he said, truly, that the library was dark and dismal. So he had had his filing cabinets, a typewriter for Bea, his big desk and chair, his dictating machine placed where he wanted them. The office furniture looked out of place among the wickers and rattans of the big room with its long windows looking out on the lawn and, further, the garden. But the judge liked it, so the change suited Clara.

As Bea was finishing her breakfast, Seth appeared in the dining-room door. "It's the police," he said unnecessarily. "They want your fingerprints, Bea, and yours too, Lorraine. It seems that Tony reported your arrival last night, so they want to question you, too. Oh, yes, and they want Velda's fingerprints."

Velda was close to the pantry door and she popped it open; her face was pale and apprehensive. "My fingerprints! I'll let them have no such thing. Senator, can't you tell them to mind their own business?"

"This is their business, Velda." Seth's voice was soothing but definite too. "They took fingerprints from every surface in the judge's study last night."

Bea remembered the film of faintly grimy dust. Seth said to her, "You and Clara were upstairs. But they took Rufe's prints, the doctor's, mine. Now they want yours, Bea, Clara's, Velda's. Yours, too, Lorraine, now they know you were in Valley Ridge last night. It's only to eliminate."

"Eliminate?" Velda was suspicious.

"I mean if your fingerprints turn up on, say, his desk, they'll be able to segregate your prints from any others that are there. You'll have been dusting, a perfect reason for your fingerprints. Understand?"

Velda understood perfectly. "Why, certainly, Senator. I'll come right away."

"No need for that." Seth turned as two men in uniform came from the hall. "All right, here are the two young ladies and Velda Mathers. I'd suggest the pantry . . ."

It was a rather gruesome little ceremony, but Velda seemed to be pleasantly interested in seeing her own fingerprints, black little marks. Afterward one of the policemen obliged with a fluid to remove the ink from their fingers. This didn't satisfy Velda, who instantly scrubbed her hands thoroughly at the pantry sink and then handed the soap to Lorraine and Bea.

"If you've finished breakfast," Seth said, "the police want to talk to you, Lorraine, and you too, Bea."

About my quarrel with the judge, Bea thought, and then thought of the gun they had found beside the judge. "Seth, did they find my fingerprints on the gun?"

"I don't know."

But they *had* found fingerprints on the gun. She could see that in the faces of the two young policemen who were neatly storing away all those tiny black and identifying curves. "They found mine," Bea said. "I touched it. The judge put it in my hands when he showed it to me and told me how to load it and——"

"You already told the police about that," Seth said as he swung open the pantry door.

Lorraine went ahead. The two young policemen followed them into the study, where the lieutenant and two men in plain clothes waited, where Clara sat and looked calmly at Obrian, who knew that Bea had quarreled with the judge and that the judge had said "Over my dead body."

Clara was composed. "They've asked me to tell them everything I know," she said. "What time I set the alarm, everything. They were very polite. They asked me if I was willing to make a statement and of course I said yes. Somebody took it down. But there wasn't much I could tell anybody about last night." She folded her hands quietly, with an air of having finished with the police.

Lorraine went to stand beside Clara. Bea went to a chair, to hold its back and brace herself for what she knew was coming. It came at once. Obrian said, "First I have to tell you that there is no question of its being suicide. The medical examiner is absolutely certain it was murder. So we have to proceed on that basis, no doubt about it." He turned to Bea and went on with a shade of apology in his attitude. "I guess you know I talked to Velda Mathers. Now she thinks you had a quarrel with the judge last night. She says you sounded very angry. That right?"

"Yes," Bea said helplessly.

Five

But they couldn't believe that she had murdered the judge. It wasn't possible. She looked up gratefully as Seth's lanky figure moved to stand beside her. "Did they find any fingerprints on the gun?" he asked directly.

The lieutenant's head jerked up; he was about to speak when Obrian said, "Yes."

"Whose fingerprints?"

"Now, Seth, you needn't act like a lawyer—"

"I am a lawyer," Seth said. "If you found Bea's fingerprints on the gun, she has already explained how they got there. The judge showed her the gun, gave it to her to tell her how to load. Naturally there could be her fingerprints—"

Obrian eyed the ceiling uneasily. "The gun has been fired recently. Last night, they think."

The lieutenant shot a glance at the two detectives, neither of whom moved.

Obrian spoke again. "There were her fingerprints, yes. There were some smudges too—" He gave the lieutenant a warning look as if he dared him or either of his men to interrupt.

"There were smudges all over it. You can't tell, fingerprints or even gloves or— But the point is," he went on hurriedly, as

47

if the lieutenant or one of the detectives might try to stop him, "they did the autopsy. Whoever killed him got the bullet out all right. Remember Griffin heard two shots. The judge's gun has been fired only once."

"So," Seth said, "you can't be sure whether the judge was shot with his own gun, or another gun was used and taken away by the murderer."

Obrian shook his head. "Whoever it was took a chance, digging out that bullet, working so fast. The medical examiner said it wouldn't be difficult to get out the bullet; it could have popped right out under a knife. But he's sure that the exit wound was made by a knife. The murderer might have had a flashlight, but he took a big chance. Maybe he used the judge's gun and then left it there, but it doesn't seem likely."

"He *could* have just forgotten it," the lieutenant said.

One of the detectives, the one in the gray suit again, said gently that was how murderers were caught; often they simply forgot something. "If they were really intelligent, they wouldn't murder," he added dryly.

"Never mind all that. We'll find whatever gun was used to kill him," the lieutenant said shortly.

Obrian sagged down into the judge's big chair and looked at Clara. "Mrs. Bartry, we haven't told you. We—rather the state police—got Meeth. He was here last night. Admits it. But says he didn't hurt the judge, didn't even talk to him."

"Meeth!" Clara's calm deserted her.

Once more the little man in gray took over. "Picked him up in a rooming house where he'd lived before the judge sent him to prison. Admits he borrowed a car from a friend and drove here last night. Parked out in the road. But he says he didn't intend to hurt the judge; he'd got all over that idea. He did want to give him a piece of his mind, though. And it's a fact that people did think the judge was a little harsh—didn't direct the jury, couldn't of course, but just as good as told them to give Meeth a stiff sentence."

Lorraine said, "Who's Meeth?"

Clara replied quickly, "He's a man who murdered his wife. The judge was convinced he was guilty—first degree. Made it quite plain to everyone. That was before he retired. The jury sentenced Meeth to a long prison term. But then recently Meeth was paroled. The prison doctor and a psychiatrist said his wife's murder was not premeditated, and the parole board

48

voted to let him out on probation. I knew he'd come straight here. He was beside himself when he was sentenced. He swore he'd kill the judge. *You* may believe that he came here with no intent to kill the judge, but I say he did!"

Lorraine slid down to the arm of Clara's chair. "But I never heard a word of all this."

"Naturally not. You were in Italy with that dreadful—I mean with your husband. I don't know how Meeth got hold of the judge's gun," Clara said firmly. "But clearly he did. And then . . . then he got out the bullet and then . . . well, forgot the gun. What have you done with Meeth?"

"But there were two shots—" Obrian began.

The lieutenant interrupted. "We're holding him now as a material witness. He had quite a story to tell." He glanced at the detective in gray, and for the first time Bea heard his name. "Smith, maybe we'd better get young Thorne to hear Meeth's story."

Smith said, "Yes, I agree. Where is he?"

"He stayed here all last night." Bea heard the unsteadiness in her voice. "He went home early this morning—"

Why did they want Rufe to hear Meeth's story? What *was* his story? She had not seen him the previous night; she had never seen him. She had heard little of Meeth's case in fact, until recently when the judge had learned and strongly disapproved of the decision of the parole board.

The lieutenant turned snappily toward the terrace door and as snappily another policeman in uniform came into view on the terrace. "Get that young fellow Thorne, lives across the road—"

"Yes, sir."

Clara put her small hands tightly together. "I don't know what Meeth said, but Rufe had nothing at all to do with the murder of the judge."

Detective Smith opened the drawer of one of the filing cabinets, gave it a rather despairing look and turned to Bea. "Did he use this dictating machine much?"

"Oh, yes. Letters and his memoirs and things."

"Where are the tapes?"

"In that cupboard, in the corner behind the door." She nodded.

Smith walked over to the cupboard, opened the door and gave the boxes a long look. "All those?"

49

"Yes," she said, but hastened to add, "The tapes now mainly have my own French practice on them. After the judge had used them I used the same tapes; they erase as you go, and I put on the new——"

"I know." Smith nodded shortly and then looked puzzled. "What's this about French?"

"I practiced and then listened to myself. I was trying to learn to speak it more fluently."

Obrian said, "She and Rufe Thorne are going to be married as soon as Rufe gets his appointment. I expect she wanted to learn languages. Rufe has been training for the Foreign Service." He paused, brushed his chin nervously and added, "As you know."

The lieutenant nodded at a policeman who had a pencil and pad of paper ready, and addressed Lorraine. "We'd like a statement from you if you are willing to give it."

"Certainly," Lorraine said promptly.

"I understand you arrived in Valley Ridge two days ago, Mrs. di—di Pall——"

"Pallici," Lorraine said. "Yes. I stayed at the Bensons'. Last night I was at the club dance with Ben Benson."

"How did you learn of the judge's murder?"

"Ben—Mr. Benson and I had left the club. It was a warm evening, so we drove around a little. Then we dropped back at the club for a nightcap. By that time someone had heard of the murder or seen the police cars or something. Anyway, they were talking about it, the people who were still there. I was very shocked. I didn't quite know what to do. My aunt didn't know that I was in Valley Ridge——"

Detective Smith interrupted smoothly. "Why didn't your aunt know of your presence?"

"Because I didn't tell her," Lorraine replied as smoothly, but added with candor. "The fact is, I wasn't sure that the judge would welcome me. I thought I'd stay at Mrs. Benson's a day or two and find out just how the land lay, so to speak. That is, if the judge had forgiven me——"

"For what?" the detective said smoothly again.

"For marrying my husband. I thought I'd see my aunt alone and— But I hadn't yet."

"So when you heard of the murder, what did you do? I understand that you arrived very late, after we had gone."

"I suppose Tony reported it. However, you'd have soon

heard of my arrival. Well, I was very shocked and, as I say, I didn't know what to do, so Ben drove me around again for a while, a long time, I think, and then we decided that my aunt would want me here. So I came."

The lieutenant glanced at the detective, who returned his look; they might as well have said audibly: We'll talk to Ben Benson and see if he agrees with your story.

Clara reached up and took one of Lorraine's hands in her own, lovingly.

After a short silence the detective said, "May we see your passport?"

"Certainly," Lorraine replied again with great promptness, flashed out of the room and up the stairs. In a moment she returned and handed over her passport to the detective, who said he would return it to her soon, and put it carefully in his pocket.

There was another brief silence while the two men, as if overwhelmed by the long task awaiting them, opened and studied the contents of one file drawer after another. There was nothing there, Bea knew, that would serve the slightest purpose in their search for evidence. Smith moved away, eying her as if she were responsible for that mass of papers. "Are all those boxes of tapes jammed full of French lessons?"

"I think so, yes."

The detectives exchanged sadly resigned looks. The lieutenant at the terrace door seemed to stiffen in a military way. "Here he comes."

Rufe came in; he was dressed casually, but he had taken time to plaster down his rebellious hair. He had also taken time, Bea thought, half amused even then, to assume a very dignified and quiet expression. A Foreign Service officer must never seem troubled and nervous, Rufe had told her, laughing. Now there was a serious need for self-control. He said a general kind of good morning, which included Clara and everyone in the room, shot a swift glance at Bea, who nodded as if to say she was all right, and then said pleasantly, "All right, Lieutenant. Your men tell me you want to question me."

The lieutenant gave Smith an admonitory jerk of his chin. Obrian sank further back in his chair and looked at his sturdy shoes. The policeman taking notes adjusted his pencil and paper. Smith sighed. "It's this way, Mr. Thorne. Did you know of the judge's will? And of Mrs. Bartry's will?"

"Yes," Rufe said coolly.

"Who told you?" Smith seemed to have taken over the proceedings.

Seth stirred, putting one long leg over the other. It was like a warning gesture, but Rufe ignored it. His chin stuck out in the way that Bea knew was indicative of controlled anger. "The judge told me."

Clara guessed what was coming. "Oh, no! No, Rufe!"

Rufe smiled at her reassuringly, but said to Smith, "Apparently you know that I came here to see him last night after dinner."

Seth unfolded his legs and rose. "Now, Rufe——"

Rufe gave another casual smile, this time at Seth. "They'll find out. They already have found out, apparently. Yes, I came here last night. I thought I could talk to the judge. I guessed that he wouldn't want Bea—Miss Bartry—to marry and leave him. He was always a good friend of mine but he was also interested in his own comfort. Miss Bartry was like a servant here——"

"Rufe," Clara said quickly, "the judge was very grateful for all of Bea's help, so was I. But"—she shook her head reprovingly—"Bea has never been like a servant. You should know that."

Rufe was apologetic. "No, of course not! I didn't mean to say that. But I knew that the judge wouldn't approve of our marriage. I thought if I could talk to him— But I couldn't, he wasn't——" Rufe paused and added wryly, "Talkable."

The lieutenant frowned. "Talkable?"

"He was already seething. Miss Bartry had told him we intended to marry as soon as my appointment comes. He was already like a firecracker ready to go up. And the minute he saw me he exploded."

There was another silence, but a short one. Smith asked, "What did he say?"

"What didn't he say! Among other things, he accused me of wanting a rich wife. Or one who would some day be rich. He said a rich wife is a great help to a poor young Foreign Service guy. About then he turned so purple that I was afraid he was going to have a stroke. He hadn't been well, you know, lately. He'd get moods like that and——"

Smith broke in. "He told you about his will?"

Rufe nodded in an unperturbed manner. "The judge's will and Mrs. Bartry's will. He said that if he predeceased his wife, she would probably alter her will so there wouldn't be a trust frund at all but everything both of them had would go to Bea. At least he told me that I must be counting on that. And then he said——"

"Rufe!" Seth Hobson went to him and took his arm.

Rufe shook off Seth's hand good-naturedly. "Keep your cool, Seth. The judge said the shock of his death would undoubtedly kill his wife——"

Clara said firmly, "It didn't."

Bea wished that Rufe would not keep his own cool with such infuriating——and dangerous——candor. He went on calmly, "So I left. There was no use in trying to talk to him."

The lieutenant glared at the two men in uniform who had gone to get Rufe and who now stood behind him, near the door, as if to prevent his escape. "So you had to tell him what we wanted him for!"

Rufe intervened. "Certainly not! Neither of them said a word except to tell me that I was wanted for questioning. It wasn't hard for me to guess why. I suppose someone saw me and it's possible that same someone heard our conversation. The door here was wide open. It was a warm night. Someone could have stood outside on the terrace. Who was it?" Rufe asked in a conversational way.

Both detectives looked at him very sharply. Clara said, "They've found that man Meeth. He was here last night."

That did surprise Rufe. "Meeth! But I didn't see him!"

Smith took over again. "He parked his car down in the road. He came up here and saw the lights in this room and saw the judge. He saw you and heard you. Said the door was open. He heard every word."

"Oh, Rufe!" Clara pulled her hand from Lorraine to put both out beseechingly toward Seth. "Seth, stop him."

"I tried to stop him. But it's true, Rufe. They got that story out of Meeth, and a fishy story I'd have said. But——" Seth turned toward the detectives and the police lieutenant. "That's all Rufe is going to say. I doubt if you find it strong evidence for a warrant. And I doubt if the grand jury would call it evidence for arraignment."

"But Thorne has confirmed it," Smith said gently. The lieu-

53

tenant took his gun from its gleaming leather holster and looked at it reflectively.

Rufe said, "Was it the judge's gun you found?"

Obrian answered. "Yes. He had had it registered."

"What about the bullet?" Rufe asked. "Did the medical examiner find that?"

Obrian shook his head. "No. It was gone, all right. Cut out sort of botchily with a knife. That's what the medical examiner says."

He remembered Clara's presence and gave her an apologetic glance, but Clara was unmoved. Seth said, "Who is this medical examiner? He must be new here. How can he be so sure?"

"Oh, he's sure," Obrian told him. "He's new here, yes. But he's had considerable experience. He was a naval surgeon all during World War Two. Says he can tell the difference between— Well, if you don't mind, Mrs. Bartry—"

"Go on," Clara said firmly.

"He said between a hurried botchy kind of job done with a knife and a normal exit wound a bullet would make. I believe him, Seth. A jury will believe him. However, there's no bullet, so there's no way to prove it did or did not come from the judge's gun."

For the first time a trace of steel seemed to underlie Rufe's almost casual manner. "So either it came from the judge's gun or it came from some other gun. You have your work cut out for you, Lieutenant."

Obrian stirred in a worried way. "Now, Rufe—"

The lieutenant eyed his revolver almost affectionately, certainly wistfully, it occurred to Bea. Seth apparently shared her feeling, for he said, "Obrian, surely you're not going to accuse Rufe on such flimsy evidence as this! That man Meeth would say anything to clear himself after all the threats he made against the judge's life."

Obrian rose ponderously, debated for a moment and said, "I don't know what the state police will say. I for one would like to have some good hard evidence."

"Right." Seth nodded. "Of course you want firm evidence! In my opinion you haven't got it."

"Now, Seth," Obrian began, "don't try any of your orator's tricks on us—"

"I wouldn't think of such a thing!"

But Bea knew that was exactly what Seth was going to do; his voice was his talent both in law and politics. As he spoke she could almost feel the adamant attitude of the two detectives and Lieutenant Abbott weaken. "Now, this boy isn't going to run away. I'll answer for that. But the point is you wouldn't want to ruin his career by charging him with murder —on the say-so of a man who *is* a convicted murderer. An arrest now—when this boy has just passed his Foreign Service examinations, a boy who had a fine record in Vietnam, a young man respected in this community! Why, his father has the respect and love of everybody in this town. You wouldn't want to make a mistake like that, one you'd regret always."

"They tell me," Smith said softly, "that you could have been one of the best defense lawyers in these parts, Senator, before you went into politics."

Seth said frankly, "I still could be, I think."

The lieutenant's mouth opened and shut. Obrian, liking Rufe, liking Bea, said, "Something in what he says, Lieutenant."

The lieutenant thought hard. "But there's a motive."

"Motive?" Seth appeared to consider it. "Well, call it that. Far-fetched, though, isn't it? Nothing to keep Miss Bartry and Rufe here from going off and getting married any time they wanted to. Now my guess is that Miss Bartry talked to the judge about her marriage because she was fond of the judge, she wanted his approval. Same reason Rufe tried to talk to him. Everybody in town, though, knows that the judge hasn't been—"

Obrian interrupted. "He's been off the beam. Begging your pardon, Mrs. Bartry. People respected him and made allowances, but that's the fact. No telling what's in those memoirs of his—facts or nonsense."

"But I told you," Bea said, "there is simply nothing that could hurt anybody."

"All the same," Obrian said, "let the judge get some notion in his head and *whoof*—fireworks! Like you said, Rufe. I agree with you, Seth. Better take some time than make a howler of a mistake, Lieutenant."

The lieutenant's jaws worked rather in the exasperated manner of a hound who sees his rabbit dashing into a briar patch, but he nodded. "All right. But don't try to leave, Thorne. Smith, Whipple—"

Whipple, then, was the name of the other detective, Bea thought.

Smith took off his coat, obviously preparatory to tackling the files. Clara rose. "Rufe, nobody believes for an instant that you killed the judge."

Smith's eyebrows rose. Whipple sighed and stared at the filing cabinets. The lieutenant touched his gun, wistfully again. Clara went on in a cool and motherly manner, "You go on home, Rufe, and get a shave. Dear me, your chin— And I expect Miss Dotty will want to give you some more breakfast."

Miss Dotty was not only Dr. Thorne's office nurse; in fact she was everything—nurse, housekeeper, and, some said laughingly, keeper, for Dr. Thorne was getting older and more forgetful. Miss Dotty was a firm and formidable woman.

Clara said, "Now, if that is all, Lieutenant, I wish to talk to the senator about—about the judge's obituary." Her firm voice did falter then.

A rather troubled and sheepish look came over Obrian's face. The lieutenant didn't look sheepish but he did bow in a polite fashion and slid his revolver, regretfully, Bea was sure, back in its holster. He and Obrian left together.

Rufe lingered for a moment. "Anything I can do, Aunt Clara?"

"Not now, Rufe. I think the judge would want you to be one of the pallbearers. I do want everything about the services for him to be just as he would want them. When can we hold the services, Seth?"

"I'd say about Tuesday. I'll talk to the police about it."

Rufe gave Bea a look of, she thought, reassurance, waved his hand with admirable nonchalance and went away too.

Lorraine gazed after him, sighed and said, "Dear me, he certainly is attractive."

Seth eyed the two detectives, who were starting to work on the masses of papers in the files. "Do try to get things back in the right order."

Whipple gave him a reproachful glance. "This is part of our business."

Clara said, "Come into the library, Seth. Bea dear, there are people who ought to be told about the judge's death—not read it in the papers first. I'll give you a list."

The day turned suddenly from a police inquiry about murder into a conventional routine of which Velda showed she knew every nuance of etiquette. When callers began to come, it was Velda who brought out sherry and small cookies and emitted an occasional lugubrious sniff which obviously she felt was appropriate.

Between visitors and frequent telephone calls Seth and Clara wrote the judge's obituary, and Seth telephoned it to Joe Lathrop in his office, who in turn was to telephone it to the *Times*. "And the Bridgeport papers," Clara told Seth. "And Hartford. After all, the judge was well known."

Bea spent most of the day in the dismal library working on the little personal notes Clara wished her to write; some of the messages went at Clara's wish by telegraph. "And be sure," Clara said, "to try to find out who is coming to the services."

Seth talked again to Obrian, who conferred with the state police, who apparently said that the services could now be arranged at any time. Bea telephoned the Reverend Cantwell to arrange for the church services and to set a time, which was two o'clock Tuesday afternoon. She hurriedly began to add that to her notes and telegrams. Seth sat in the judge's study while the two detectives minutely yet rather speedily too, as if well accustomed to their work, went through all the judge's files. Seth did some of the telephoning for Bea, as Clara's friends came in a decorous stream to make their calls of condolence.

All this was in the Valley Ridge tradition, and it was a heart-warming tradition, Bea thought, as she interrupted her task time and again to speak to each caller briefly and listen to their expressions of sympathy.

Rufe did not return, as Bea half expected him to do. Seth and the detectives were still in the study when she gathered up all the little notes, put on a coat and took the car quickly past the other cars in the drive and then on to the village post office in time to catch the last mail. Even so, of course, it being Saturday, none of the notes would reach their destination before Monday, but in any event that gesture of amenity had been made.

It seemed strange that the main street, the red-brick post office were just the same. She did think that people on the street eyed her rather closely, but she shrugged that off as imagination. By the time she reached home again, the living room was empty, the detectives and Seth had gone and there was the rather brooding silence in the house which follows a storm. She trudged upstairs, feeling tired and dirty, took a long hot shower and changed her clothes.

She was fastening her dress when Lorraine came in. "The reporters have all gone. Seth wouldn't let me talk to any of them. Where is Rufe?"

"At home I suppose. He was up all night."

"Are we going to be alone tonight?"

"I hadn't thought of it."

"I can't say I like the idea. Of course, Rufe wouldn't hurt *me*. Or you."

"*Rufe!*"

"He did know about that will of the judge's and the one Clara made. And the police seem to feel it does provide a motive. Aunt Clara has complained about her heart ever since I knew her. A shock like the judge's murder——"

Bea restrained a desire to reach out and pull Lorraine's hair viciously, but borrowing a leaf from Clara's book, she said quietly, "But she didn't die. She's taking all this very well."

Lorraine's green eyes glinted reflectively. "She acts almost as if it's a relief, really. Living with the judge all these years, especially since he's been out of his head, can't have been much fun."

"He wasn't out of his head. He was only . . . he only had moods . . . and Aunt Clara adored him."

"I expect she did. In her way. You know, it never struck me until today that Aunt Clara has a very strong character. Of course, she'd have to be pretty firm, trying to cope with the judge. But still, I wouldn't have expected her to react as she has. Calm as all get-out. Not a tear."

"She's not the weeping kind."

"Nobody around this house appears to be the weeping kind." Lorraine lifted slim black eyebrows. "I haven't seen you dissolving in grief."

"There's been too much to do. And too much——"

"Yes. Police. They're not through yet either. I heard the judge say one time that a murder case is never closed until they nail the murderer. Isn't that right?"

"I think so."

"It really would be too bad if they arrested Rufe. Even if

later he was proved not guilty, he'd never get a job in the Foreign Service. They go through everybody's records. Why, if he'd even so much as been fined for speeding, it would count against him. I think." Lorraine added frankly, "I don't really know much about it."

Someone knocked on the door and then opened it. Velda stood there. She was no longer lugubrious and long-faced; her gooseberry eyes were shining at Lorraine. "There's somebody to see you. He says he's your husband."

Lorraine shot up, straight and tall. "Cecco! Oh, no, no!"

But it was Cecco. He came up behind Velda, moved her to one side and smiled at Lorraine. "Glad to see me, darling? I heard of the murder. I felt my place was at your side."

"But you can't *be* here!" Lorraine cried, much as Bea had cried on seeing Lorraine. "You're in Italy!"

"You left me there, darling. But now I'm here. And this is little Bea, quite grown up. Dear Bea—"

He took Bea's hand, bowed and kissed it. She had a fantastic impulse to count her fingers; somehow one did count her fingers after Cecco di Pallici kissed them. Cecco himself was the very picture of an old-time Italian nobleman, tall, slender, his dark features aquiline, dark eyes dancing, his white teeth shining.

Lorraine said, "You can't stay here. I'm getting a divorce."

Cecco smiled, showing all those white teeth. "I think I'll be the one to get the divorce, darling. Unless of course you wish to change your mind."

Six

There was a slight rustle in the doorway where Velda stood riveted, watching the scene. Bea could do nothing about that, or the fact that Cecco so openly implied his knowledge of something which, Bea thought wildly, could show Lorraine in a very poor light. She really shouldn't mind Lorraine's being shown in a bad light, Bea told herself firmly, yet she could not help feeling a tug of the family tie, a desire to protect the other girl. Although not related by blood, she and Lorraine had

59

grown up as cousins in the same household, and she couldn't deny that bond.

Lorraine, however, seemed to need no defense; she said coldly, "Why did you come here?"

"I told you. When I heard of the murder I rushed to be at your side—"

"You couldn't have come here from Italy. You were in New York!"

"Well—"

Lorraine's eyes flashed fire. "Or right here in Valley Ridge!"

Again Cecco bowed suavely.

There was something about him—his high cheekbones, high thin nose and forehead—which for a fleeting second reminded Bea of Seth's New England face. But Seth would never be done up in a natty, broad-shouldered pin-stripe suit and glistening oxfords with very thin soles; Seth wouldn't have been caught dead in a fantastically colored tie of geometrical design and a turquoise pin in it.

"The taxi is waiting," Cecco said. "He wants money!" He shrugged in an entirely Latin gesture.

Again Lorraine's eyes blazed. "Do you mean to say—"

"I managed to have a little money you couldn't touch."

"I suppose you got another mortgage on that decrepit rock pile you call a *palazzo?*"

"Now, now, darling!" Cecco shrugged, a ripple right down his spine. He spread out his hands and a rather dubious-looking diamond flashed on one finger. "There was only enough money for my plane fare. And I had enough left over from that to come to Valley Ridge by train. But not enough to pay for my hotel bill and not anything at all for the taxi driver, who may be getting a little restless."

"Hotel?"

"I think they call it the Valley Inn. Small place but pleasant."

"So you arrived last night. You went to the Valley Inn."

"Where could I go? I didn't think you—or at least the judge—God rest his soul," said Cecco and this time bowed presumably to the judge's soul, "would give me a welcome here. Or Ben Benson—"

"Here! Wait—" Lorraine ran out of the room.

Cecco glanced at Bea; there was a merry twinkle in his dark eyes.

60

"I suppose you always get what you want," Bea said tartly. "She's probably gone to get some money to pay off the taxi. Our American cabbies are a little emotional about not getting paid."

Cecco nodded graciously. "But I knew Lorraine would pay him. Couldn't have talk around town, you know. Cecco di Pallici without enough money to pay a taxi! Ah—"

Lorraine flashed in again, a handsome black handbag under her arm. From it—the jewels on her fingers glittering (not dubious jewels, those, Bea thought)—she extracted some bills. "Pay for your taxi and go back to Valley Inn and pay your bill there, and then take the train to New York. After that I don't care what you do, but stay away from me."

The bills flicked out of sight and into Cecco's pocket so swiftly that Bea scarcely saw the motion.

Cecco looked at Lorraine and said, a tone of mock-sadness in his voice, "No, darling. I wouldn't think of leaving you just now. The tragedy of the judge's death—murder— Oh, no, my place is here with you. I'm sure your aunt will agree."

Velda, still in the doorway, made a sound not unlike a robin choking on a particularly active worm.

Bea looked at her. "Velda?"

"He's right, Miss Bea. Mrs. Bartry will want him to stay until . . . well, until . . ."

Velda could be trying at times but she had her very good points too, and one of them was a sure sense of Valley Ridge propriety.

Bea nodded. "Aunt Clara will want him to stay here, Lorraine. Until . . . well . . . for a while. You see, everybody in town would know that he was here and didn't stay and—"

Cecco's eyes gleamed merrily. "You see, Lorraine darling. Your aunt would not like any talk."

Lorraine seemed to debate with herself for a moment, then said, "All right. If Aunt Clara says you can stay. Have you got any baggage with you?"

"One small bag in the taxi. A couple of others at the inn."

"We'll get those later. Now pay the taxi man and bring your bag up here—"

Clara said from beside Velda, "There's a taxi waiting outside but I didn't see anybody— Oh!"

"Madam—" Cecco again performed his lithe and graceful bow. He took Clara's astonished hand and kissed it. And, Bea

61

thought with a quiver of laughter, Clara too looked at her hand thoughtfully when he released it, exactly as if she also had an instinctive impulse to count her fingers. There was simply something about Cecco which induced suspicion.

"You," said Clara inadequately.

Velda spoke from the doorway. "He was at Valley Inn last night, Mrs. Bartry. I was sure that you'd want him to stay here—at least just now. I mean you wouldn't want people to talk—"

Clara had got her breath back. "You are quite right, Velda."

Suddenly, irrelevantly, Bea thought: But Velda could be very wrong too; it was she who had blurted to Obrian about Bea's fiery quarrel with the judge. At this moment Velda caught her eyes and apparently read her thoughts, for a pinkish flush crept up into her face.

Cecco, secure now in his position, smiled graciously all around, then went swiftly out and down the stairs. Lorraine watched him go, fury stamped on her face. Then she, too, left. "He can't stay in my room," she said over her shoulder, and disappeared.

Velda turned to Bea and said earnestly, "Miss Bea, I did tell Obrian about your quarrel with the judge. I shouldn't have, I know. I didn't mean to get you into trouble. He got it out of me before I—well, I was shocked, you see. I hadn't known a thing about the murder. Obrian arrived before I'd so much as had a cup of coffee, and before I knew it—well, I'm sorry. But it really didn't do you any harm, did it?"

"I don't know. That is— Oh, it's all right, Velda. I see how it happened."

Clara, who had been standing quietly, seemed pleased that Bea had accepted Velda's explanation. Now she turned almost eagerly to change the subject. "Put Mr. di Pal—mal—Oh, put his things in that other guest room, Velda. Show him where it is."

Velda nodded. "They used to say that he's a count. Doesn't look like it to me."

"You may be right," Clara sighed.

Velda made for the stairs to meet Cecco and steer him to his room.

Clara, still sighing, said, "I can never get his name straight. But then, I've had so few letters from Lorraine. In answering

62

them I always had to look in my address book to get the name straight. No, I suppose he isn't a count. I wonder how anybody got that impression—unless from Cecco himself. In fact"—Clara frowned—"I can't even remember who brought him here to Valley Ridge. I do remember that there was a sort of impression that he had money and a fine *palazzo*—is that what they call it?—in Italy. But Velda is right about these things. She's lived in Valley Ridge all her life. As I have. There's enough for people to talk about; let's not add to it. Seth's gone. The men in the study have gone, too."

"They couldn't have found anything of interest in the judge's papers. If there were anything, I'd know," Bea said.

"It was Meeth." Clara spoke with simple obstinacy. "I don't care what anybody says. He waited around till after Rufe had gone and then he got into the study and the judge got out his gun. Meeth took it from him and he made the judge go down to the road—outside the house so we wouldn't hear him—and then he . . . then he shot him."

"When did you set the alarm, Aunt Clara?"

"It was during the commercial. The ten-thirty one. I told the police about it. I thought the judge was upstairs, so I came out and touched that little button, then I went back and listened to the program for a few minutes. I had turned off the program just before the alarm went. The police say the report of the alarm came in at close to a quarter to eleven. That would be about right. Oh, Bea, if I hadn't had that program going I might have heard the gunshots. But there were so many gunshots . . . I mean in the program . . . and I'm a little deaf. The judge always said I turned my programs on so loud he could hardly hear himself think, let alone sleep."

"You couldn't have stopped anything, Aunt Clara. And it does seem reasonable," Bea said slowly, "that Meeth did exactly that. Somebody had to get hold of the judge's gun, so the judge himself must have taken it out of the desk drawer. And somebody could have forced him to go out toward the road, away from the house."

"That's the way the police will see it," Clara said firmly. "They just need a little time to do all the things they're supposed to do. Police routine, the judge used to call it. I see you've freshened up for dinner, dear. That's right. We really must go on as we always do. That's another thing the judge used to say. Conventions are made for emergencies. But I do

63

wish that dreadful man Cecco hadn't followed Lorraine here."

At that moment Cecco came bounding lightly up the steps; he was carrying his own bag. Velda followed him, gave a firm wave of her hand toward a guest room beyond the one Lorraine was using, and said, "I've got to see about dinner, Mrs. Bartry." She rustled back down the stairs.

Cecco gave them both a flashing smile as he went to his room. Clara sighed again, then said she, too, would change for dinner. Bea watched her go, her pretty head held high, into her own room, and then went downstairs to help Velda, who accepted her aid with a grunt. "Not a very nice dinner. Can't help it. I've had a busy day. You better mix some strong cocktails, Miss Bea. Your aunt is bearing up very well, but I can tell, she needs a drink. If you can't keep your spirits up," said Velda rather surprisingly, "put some down."

Bea made martinis as the judge had taught her, and as Velda advised, a large and strong quantity.

"Where's that Rufe?" Velda asked, watching as Bea stirred the contents of the tall pitcher.

Velda might permit herself to be browbeaten by the judge to the extent of saying Miss Bea—or Miss Lorraine—but never would she have referred to Rufe as Mr. Rufe, not the doctor's boy whom she had known more or less all his life.

"I don't know. I expect he had to sleep some. He and Tony were here all last night."

"Oh, I know that. Rapping away all night, I suppose."

Sometimes Velda was startlingly *au courant* in her way of picking up the latest slang.

"I suppose they were. They must have had a great deal to talk about."

"Got into my refrigerator. All that pie is gone. We'll just have to have ice cream out of the freezer tonight. You don't think your aunt will mind not having soup."

"She'll not notice." Bea tasted her martini mix, blinked and shoved more ice in it.

When she carried it and glasses on a tray to the living room, Lorraine and Clara were already there. Lorraine took over the chore of pouring the drinks. Cecco came gracefully into the room in time to take the first glass from her hand and present it, with another spine-wriggling bow, to Clara.

Clara eyed it rather doubtfully, as if he might have

64

dropped in a touch of cyanide, Bea thought with a hysterical little quiver of mirth, but took it. At this point Rufe arrived, this time an orderly, brushed and indeed almost dressed-up Rufe. Clara's face brightened. "Oh, Rufe! I hope you've come to dinner. We've had such a day——"

"I know. I saw all the cars. Thank you, Lorraine, I can do with that." He took the pitcher, saw that Bea had a glass in her hand and poured one for himself. A good thing I made enough, Bea thought. Rufe pulled up a footstool near Bea, balancing the martini glass neatly, and sat down. "I've got to go to Washington on Monday. Somebody phoned me today. Is that all right, Aunt Clara?"

"Of course, Rufe. But you must be back for the services Tuesday."

"I'll get back Monday night or at the latest Tuesday morning. Miss Dotty told me the time. I've phoned Obrian to ask if it's all right for me to go to Washington for the day. I explained it to him. He said sure, go ahead, and then my father got on the phone to find out what the police are doing."

"Is there any special news yet?" Clara asked quickly.

Rufe shook his head. "Nothing new."

"Oh, I think I'll just have another martini, Lorraine."

But Cecco, who had been sitting thoughtfully in a corner, rose swiftly to take her glass. Rufe apparently had not seen him, for he jerked around on the footstool. "Why—why, I didn't know anyone else was here! That is——"

Lorraine didn't quite bite off the words, but almost. "My soon-to-be former husband. He arrived in Valley Ridge last night. Stayed at the Valley Inn."

"How do you do," Cecco said happily. "So you are my defeated rival. Ah, yes. You had gone to Vietnam, wasn't it, when I came to Valley Ridge?"

"It was Vietnam." Rufe stood; the two men shook hands. "Well, well." Rufe eyed his victorious rival. "You weren't expected here, were you?"

"A happy surprise to my dear wife." Cecco's white teeth gleamed.

Lorraine uttered something which perhaps fortunately was not entirely audible.

Velda came to the door and said, "Dinner!" as if she were firing a cannon.

Rufe collected the martini pitcher, still not quite empty. "May I bring this to the table, Aunt Clara?"

Velda gave him a swift glance. "Might as well stay here and finish up those good martinis. I wasn't expecting you, Rufe. I'll have to put on another place. That is, if you're here for dinner."

Clara replied serenely, "Oh, yes, Velda. You know he's always welcome."

"It's not much of a dinner," Velda said. "But it's better than what Miss Dotty would give you." Velda did not like Miss Dotty, who, Velda said, put on airs.

Cecco deftly took the pitcher from Rufe, and assuming the air of the man of the house, the host, poured more drinks. Lorraine's eyes glittered viciously at him; her jewels glittered too, a bracelet, rings, a stunningly huge diamond clip. Bea wondered briefly how Cecco had got the money to pay for all those jewels. Lorraine had not changed into a dress; she still wore her skintight black slacks and dark-green sweater, but apparently considered the display of jewels sufficient for a home dinner—and indeed, Bea thought tartly, the jewels would have been sufficient decorations for a ball.

Clara told Rufe of the callers that afternoon. Cecco brought Bea another martini, which she took, and then wished she hadn't, for she began to feel distinctly dizzy. Luckily Velda appeared again and they went in to dinner.

It wasn't a very good dinner. Perhaps Velda had had an ulterior purpose in speaking so encouragingly of martinis, hoping for their euphoric effect. Clara obviously was affected by her unusual double dose of drinks, for as she speared a mushroom she said, "It's a good thing we keep a store of canned mushrooms and things," and then added unexpectedly, "Soup."

Velda had been hovering at the pantry door. She stuck her head in. "Soup, Mrs. Bartry?"

Clara shook her head. "No, no. I was thinking of something else. How do you manage?" She said to Lorraine, "I mean doesn't your hair sort of get in the way when you have soup?"

Lorraine looked up with a gasp, shoved both heavy curtains of black hair back, anchored them behind her ears and said sweetly, "That's how I do it, darling Aunt Clara."

But Clara was still doubtful. "Your uncle wouldn't have liked your hair, dear. It doesn't look tidy."

Rufe choked. Velda disappeared into the pantry and brought out the coffee tray, which she carried into the living room. Cecco's black eyes danced but he said nothing. By the time they had finished Velda's hastily concocted dessert of ice cream and pound cake—at which Lorraine looked with marked distaste—and returned to the living room, Lorraine had recovered her poise. She seated herself, the daughter of the house, behind the coffee table and began to pour. "I'll cut off my hair, darling Aunt Clara," she said sweetly. "If you don't like it, certainly I'll have it cut."

Clara was troubled. "Dear Lorraine, it's *your* hair. And beautiful too." She seemed to brood for a moment, then put down her cup and added apologetically, "But you might just do it up for the services, Lorraine. Everybody in town will be there."

Cecco's eyes met Bea's; she turned away from him, but he said, smiling, "Little Bea has grown up so properly. No longer braces on her teeth, an excellent coiffure and, may I say, a figure—"

"I'll have more coffee, please," Clara said sharply.

Rufe said, "Come walk with me, Bea, unless of course you'd like me to stay here tonight. If you do—"

Cecco again took on the position of the man of the house. "Not at all, my dear fellow. Not at all. I am here."

Perhaps it was the unaccustomed martinis that still affected her, or perhaps it was the firm calm which Bea was beginning to observe was a part of Clara's nature that during the judge's lifetime she had somehow contrived to conceal. Whatever the source of her poise, Clara told Rufe he need not stay. "Thank you, though. It's like you. But if anything should happen, we'll call you. And we'll set the alarm." There wasn't even a quiver in her voice as she mentioned the alarm, the alarm that had announced the murder of the judge. Yes, Bea thought, Clara had a courage and strength which in deference to the judge, Clara must have tactfully concealed during their life together. She would never have opposed the judge about anything. Even about their wills.

Bea went with Rufe. When they were outside, on the terrace, he suddenly laughed. "So that's Cecco! You wrote to me about that time, when he came here. Who introduced him?"

"I think it was Ben Benson. I don't remember. Just all at once Cecco and Lorraine eloped. The judge didn't want her to marry him. But not for the same reasons he didn't want me to marry you."

"To think that once I was desperately jealous of him!"

"Lorraine says she's going to get a divorce."

"A good idea," Rufe said in an absent way. "Funny though. Cecco seems to speak English very fluently, no trace of an accent."

"I believe he went to an English school."

"Doesn't have that kind of accent either. I'd be inclined to think—" He paused. They strolled on down the drive. Finally Rufe said, "Are you sure that was his first visit to America? I mean when he came here to Valley Ridge and got acquainted with Lorraine?"

"Why, I—I don't know. I just assumed it was."

Rufe walked on in thoughtful silence for a moment; then he said, "You were in your teens when Lorraine met and married him."

"Yes, of course."

There was another thoughtful silence on Rufe's part. Finally he said, "How did he get to know Ben?"

"I don't know that either."

"Miss Dotty said that the news of the judge's murder was on the radio today. Every local news broadcast. I suppose that's how Cecco knew of it. That, or someone at the inn told him."

"Rufe!" Bea stopped abruptly to look up at him. "Could he have killed the judge?"

"I didn't say that."

"No, but—could he?"

"I doubt it. He doesn't strike me as a very violent man. Besides, if Lorraine is leaving him, how could he possibly expect to gain anything by the judge's death?"

Bea thought for a moment, then said slowly, "Suppose he believed that Clara's heart is really so bad that the shock of the judge's death might kill her too. Suppose he thought that Lorraine, Aunt Clara's only blood relation, would inherit from Aunt Clara. Suppose he relied on his charm—I suppose you'd call it that—to get Lorraine back again."

"That's quite a bit of supposition." Rufe took her hand and held it tightly. "Let's forget Cecco. I really don't think he murdered the judge. And I think it's safe to let him stay in the house. Only remember, Bea, it was murder."

68

"Aunt Clara is sure that Meeth shot the judge. She says he must have waited until you left and then came in the house, the judge got out his gun and Meeth got it away from him—the judge was rather feeble in a way, you know. She says Meeth made him go outdoors and down by the wall and—"

"I know. Apparently the police think that's a possibility too, otherwise they wouldn't hold Meeth as a material witness. I didn't see his car parked in the road when I left. But I wasn't paying much attention to anything then. I do remember, though, a car came along, going in the direction of Valley Ridge just as I was crossing the road. Lights came full on me. So I was seen all right. But the car went on. It could have been Meeth's car and he's not saying anything about it. It would put him on the spot as I was leaving. He says he had gone before I left. It's possible that he shot the judge. That coat of the judge's bothers me though."

"Coat? Oh, the old tweed one that was on his desk?"

"Yes. Nobody can avoid the fact that a thirty-two—if that was used and I think it must have been—wouldn't have had the force to go right through that thick tweed and the—the judge, and then reach a spot in his back from which it could be readily extracted. So how did the judge happen to remove his coat?"

They turned and started up toward the house again. Gravel crunched beneath their feet. "It was a warm night. It turned suddenly cold later. But it had been too warm for this time of the year," Bea said at last. "He may simply have taken it off because of that."

"He was wearing it when I talked to him. I'm certain of that. The judge was a kind of—oh, formal man in his way."

"But the coat was there, over his desk."

"But, Bea, who could have induced the judge to remove his coat?"

"Maybe the murderer got the judge's gun, knew he'd have to get the coat away from the judge and just—just did it."

"By force? Holding the gun at him? No. The judge was no fool. Remember Griffin says he heard two shots. I don't think the bullet that killed the judge came from the judge's gun. I don't think the police believe that either. It's the same question. Why dig out that bullet, taking such a chance, and then leave the judge's gun? The police checked on my father's gun.

69

I was right. It hadn't been fired, hadn't even been cleaned lately. They searched through his surgical instruments, too."

"His surgical— Oh, for the knife that was used to extract that bullet. Do you mean to say that Miss Dotty allowed them in your father's office?"

Rufe chuckled. "Yes. I was surprised she didn't take a knife to the lieutenant."

"Rufe, I've been wondering. The judge must have made other enemies besides Meeth. He had a long career on the bench. First as judge of the juvenile court, then the superior court."

"You typed his memoirs. You ought to know."

"There really wasn't a thing that could indicate any danger to him except Meeth's threats."

"Something may develop. There's not been much time for the police and the detectives."

They had almost reached the steps to the terrace. Bea put her hand on Rufe's arm. "Rufe, this trip to Washington. Why? What do they want?"

"I don't know. I was just told to come."

"Is it about"— Bea swallowed hard—"the judge's—the murder—"

"Why should it be?"

"They must know about it. They seem to know everything about you."

"Well, then," Rufe said cheerfully, "they'll know I didn't murder the judge."

"I do wish you hadn't admitted coming here and talking to the judge. You could have let them think that Meeth was lying."

Rufe laughed shortly. "Darling, how could I tell a lie!" He sobered. "No, I wasn't so hell-bent on telling the truth as it seems. I remembered those car lights. I'm sure that sooner or later somebody will come forward and tell the police he saw me crossing the street. I thought I'd better get my story in first."

"But nobody has told the police that he saw you."

"No. And that is rather odd in a way. However—"

"Rufe," Lorraine called from the terrace. Bea turned. She couldn't see Lorraine's face; the light from the open door was behind her. But she could see her lovely figure outlined against the light. Lorraine came down the steps, and ignoring

70

Bea, put out her hands in a pleading gesture to Rufe. "Oh, Rufe! If only you hadn't gone to Vietnam just when you did. We were so much in love with one another. I was a fool to marry Cecco. I don't know how it happened!"

"Because you wanted to marry him, of course," Rufe said pleasantly. Bea could now see Lorraine's face, for she had moved closer to Rufe. She was lovely in that half-light—or in any light, Bea admitted in honest appraisal.

Rufe said, "Goodnight, Lorraine." Then he turned and bent over Bea and kissed her, but rather lightly. He went off quickly down the drive. Lorraine looked after him and then at Bea. "How easy it will be to get him back! That is, if I want him."

Seven

"You needn't be so sure of that!" Bea spoke with assurance, but she could not help but feel that it could be easy for Lorraine to get any man—if, as she said, she wanted him.

No, Bea told herself. Not Rufe!

Aunt Clara had already gone upstairs. Cecco was still there, smoking one of the judge's cigars. He went with Bea as she made a little tour of the house, shutting doors and windows. Velda had gone long ago, leaving a sparkling clean kitchen and the back door unlocked. Bea locked it.

Both Cecco and Lorraine watched over Bea's shoulder as she set the tiny button on the burglar alarm. Cecco said thoughtfully, "Oh, I see how it works. That white light shows that the doors and windows that are bugged have been closed. Then you punch that little button and the red light comes on, instead of the white. After that—"

"After that," Lorraine said sharply, "don't even go down the stairs, Cecco. Front stairs or back stairs. Isn't that right, Bea?"

"Oh, yes. It would set off the alarm."

"Loud?" Cecco's eyes were intent.

"Loud enough to wake the——" Bea caught herself.

Lorraine finished for her. "To wake the dead. Except it didn't."

"He wasn't dead then. He died— Oh, please don't talk about it."

After she had got into her own room and closed the door, Bea went to the window. In the summer the heavy foliage of the woods shut off lights even from nearby houses; now in the early spring, she could see a faintly yellowish area reflected in the haze above the village streetlamps. She could imagine—almost hear—how the whole village must be buzzing. Murder in Valley Ridge just did not happen, yet—knowing the town and its people, Bea guessed that those men who had guns had taken them out and loaded them. And those who had no guns had probably spent the day driving to Stamford or Bridgeport or even to New York in order to buy them. And she was sure there was a rash of orders for burglar alarms.

The news had undoubtedly spread that whoever shot the judge had extracted the bullet. She shuddered as she thought of it; it seemed almost worse and uglier than the fact of murder itself. She could hear the speculations, the belief that only someone with surgical or some kind of medical experience would have had the skill to extract that bullet—in the dark, hurriedly but efficiently.

But here the repeated question arose. If the murderer had meant to remove the bullet in order to prevent its identification as a bullet coming from the judge's gun, why leave the gun? If the judge's gun had been fired recently—and the opinion of the police that it had been fired the night the judge was shot was almost certainly accurate—then who, if not the murderer, had fired it? But then why take such pains to remove the bullet?

Almost more important than anything else was the fact that someone had entered the house, setting off the alarm, *after* the judge had been shot—why and what had that person wanted?

She couldn't answer anything, Bea told herself as she turned wearily away from the window. I must try to sleep, she thought—and she did, although troubled thoughts woke her frequently, thoughts of Rufe, Lorraine—and the judge.

Early the next morning the police came to question Cecco. There was an excellent grapevine for news in Valley Ridge. Cecco's presence was known immediately. They talked to him in the judge's study. The whole thing took only a short time, and when they left they were apparently satisfied with Cecco's replies.

Cecco came back up the stairs and met Bea. "Nothing to it," he said airily. "They looked at my passport. Took it away with them. They know when I arrived in New York. They understood my reason for coming to Valley Ridge. They had inquired at the inn. I have an alibi. I didn't leave my room that night. Someone would have seen me. They understood perfectly why I didn't come here until yesterday evening. I didn't hear of the murder until noon, I slept late. And when I did hear of it, I had to debate about coming here. I wasn't sure of my welcome—that's easily understood. But then I decided that my place was at Lorraine's side. Oh, they were most understanding about it. I believe," Cecco added, frowning slightly. But then his face cleared. "However, I do have that alibi. Not that I need it."

Lorraine was standing in the open door of her room, a dress hanging over her arm. "Alibi!" She thought for a moment. "Come in here, Bea. I want to talk to you. You too, Cecco."

Cecco followed Bea into the room and settled down on the chaise longue, languidly. He got out an ivory holder and inserted a cigarette in it. Lorraine gave him an angry glance. "Bea," she said directly, "will you promise me something—"

Cecco said lazily, "I wouldn't, Lorraine."

Lorraine shot a swift look at him. "I can count on Bea."

Cecco lifted his thin black eyebrows. "I wouldn't count on anybody when it's an alibi for murder."

Lorraine didn't quite snort, but almost. "That's all right for you! You can prove that you came out on the eight-ten train, went by taxi to the inn and spent the night and most of yesterday there." Cecco nodded. "But I wouldn't put it past you to sneak out some way and do anything you wanted to do, except"—Lorraine grudgingly admitted—"you couldn't have managed to dig out that bullet!"

Cecco's eyes went to Bea. "I couldn't have done that. She's quite right. I'm afraid of blood. Gives me the creeps. No, I didn't kill the judge. Besides, I had no motive. My wife is divorcing me! Why, even if the judge had left her money or she hoped to get it from her aunt, I wouldn't have profited."

"But you were here," Bea said so accusingly, she surprised

73

herself. It then occurred to her that, oddly, Cecco and Lorraine seemed on slightly better terms. She didn't know why it had struck her and she couldn't be sure of it. But there seemed to her an air of complicity about them, as if they had come to some sort of understanding which neither of them liked but which might be expedient.

Lorraine said, "Oh, that doesn't matter! Nobody is going to blame you, Cecco! But I— Once they know about the judge's will and that Aunt Clara is going to write a new one—"

"Are you so sure of that, darling?" Cecco waved his cigarette gracefully.

"She hasn't said so definitely. Yet. But I'm her only blood relation. She knows the arrangement the judge made her agree to isn't fair. She wants me to stay here. She loves me. Oh, yes, she'll make a new will and she'll put me in it."

"How nice to be sure of that, darling."

"I am sure. I told you—that is—"

Again the notion of some sort of guarded agreement between Cecco and Lorraine flashed across Bea's thoughts. She said, however, "What were you going to ask me to do, Lorraine? You spoke of alibis. I can't possibly give you an alibi. You weren't here. I didn't even know you were in America."

Lorraine bit her lip. "Well, you could try, couldn't you? I mean, couldn't you say—oh, that you'd forgotten but that I was here with you—"

"Oh, Lorraine!" Cecco almost laughed. "Bea has already given her evidence to the police. So have you. Neither of you can change your statement now."

Lorraine debated. "*You* can, Cecco!"

"No," said Cecco.

"Yes, you can. You can say you phoned for me—or somehow got the notion that I would be at the club dance. Yes, that's it. Then you came and met me and we talked. So easy for you, Cecco."

Cecco shook his head. "I've already told the police where I was."

"But, Lorraine, you said you were with Ben, dancing or driving." Bea wished wistfully she and Rufe had been dancing at the club at the time of the judge's murder.

"The fact is, I wasn't. Not all the time. I don't have any sort of alibi for at least an hour and a half. It's all Ben Benson's fault."

74

"Ben's?"

"Because he dances like a cow. I couldn't bear having my feet stepped on any longer. So I pretended to go to the ladies' room and instead I went off and sat in a corner of the veranda, that long one near the bar. I thought somebody might come in the bar, somebody I knew, and would be a better dancer than Ben. But I'd been gone too long. Nobody I knew came, or at least nobody I wanted to get chummy with again. All of them have married and got fat," she said viciously. "I could hear their talk. Nothing but stocks, gold and babies. The window was open."

"But didn't anybody see you?" Bea asked.

"Nobody. I finally gave up and went in and danced with Ben a few times, and when my feet really couldn't take it any longer, I suggested we take a drive in his car. So we did. That much is true. Later—this is true, too—we dropped back at the club for a nightcap and heard the news. Then I couldn't decide what to do, so we drove some more—"

"Until—what time was it?—three in the morning or thereabouts?" Cecco asked, smiling.

"It doesn't matter what time it was, or where we went or—"

"Or what you were doing?" Cecco was still smiling.

Lorraine snapped, "Or what we were doing. Actually, we weren't even talking much. At least I wasn't. I was shocked at the news. And Ben Benson is about as thrilling an escort as he is a dancer. I don't remember. Was he always like that, Bea?"

"Oh, I don't know. Ben's all right. Ben's of the older crowd. But he's almost the only bachelor in town except Rufe and Seth, so he does get invited everywhere."

"Quite a catch," Lorraine said bitterly. "And I've got bruised feet to prove it. Old Mrs. Benson didn't really want me as a guest. I could tell that when I proposed myself. But she gave in. I suppose she thought I was after her darling Ben. Not me."

"Flying for higher game?" Cecco said sweetly.

Lorraine was taking a dress from her suitcase; she whirled around and flung the dress at Cecco, who dodged, gathered it up and eyed it. "You must be more careful of your dresses, darling. I believe this is a Dior—something I couldn't pay for, no doubt. I hope someone paid for it."

"Never mind who paid for it." Lorraine's cheeks had sud-

75

den flames of red. "You go straight back to the inn, or for that matter, go—"

"Now, now, Lorraine. Enough of that!" Cecco dropped the dress over a nearby table and took up a small lacy pillow which he placed under his handsome head.

Lorraine opened her mouth, seemed to think that whatever she had intended to say wasn't sufficiently insulting, and closed it again.

Bea said, "Aunt Clara wants him to stay here. For the time being."

Cecco laughed. "We're all agreed that there would certainly be talk if it were known that I was staying at the inn, clearly unwelcome to stay with my wife. And I'm sure Lorraine agrees too."

Lorraine turned around toward the closet swiftly, as if Bea might catch some expression in her face which Lorraine didn't want seen.

Or am I imagining this? Bea thought. If there is some sort of pact, some sort of arrangement between them, that's their business, not mine. Isn't it? But she wasn't sure of anything any more.

Lorraine said from the depths of the closet, "I don't care what Cecco does so long as he stays away from me!"

"Darling!" Cecco chuckled. "Don't be fatuous. Besides, your dear Ben has certainly by now backed up your story."

With a feeling that in another moment Lorraine was going to hurl everything she could find at Cecco's head, Bea went out of the room.

It was Sunday, but Velda, contrary to her custom, had arrived early, prepared breakfast and a salad for supper or lunch and then apparently gone again. Bea went to the study to find Clara. Through the open door she caught a glimpse of two men in uniform crouched down under the laurels, apparently searching all through the leaf mold of the previous summer. Searching for the missing bullets? Searching for a knife? There were far too many places in the woods to hide either or both.

She found Clara in the library. It was always a dismal room, as the judge had said. It had been furnished at some time with glass-enclosed bookshelves holding volumes of books, enormous chairs and a great mahogany table in the middle of the faded Brussels carpet. The windows were small

76

and half covered with ivy, so there was only a gloomy light filtering through. Bea had loved its seclusion for reading. Clara had loved the room as it was, and when the judge had suggested a change, Clara had turned stubborn. What was good enough for her father and grandfather was good enough for her. Now Clara had the Sunday *Times* spread out and was clipping the judge's obituary with steady little hands. She looked up as Bea came in. "Good morning, my dear. They've made a few mistakes, but not many."

Bea read the clipping Clara held out to her.

Cecco came strolling in and looked at the obituary over Bea's shoulder. He used some sort of cologne, which wafted unpleasantly around him. "I didn't realize the judge was so well known," he said. "That photograph is very fine."

Clara glanced up. "It was taken some time ago. But it is like him—as he once was."

Not as he had been of late years, Bea thought. But he had once been a handsome man and even lately he had a distinguished appearance. Tears came to her eyes suddenly as she looked at that early photograph. Once when the judge had found her in tears over some childhood mishap, he had told her soberly that ladies, even very young ladies, didn't cry. And it was after the incident of Mrs. Benson and the blueberries that he had brought Shadders to her, the long-legged, frolicking Airedale puppy. When the dog had fought his last fight and she had written to tell Rufe, Rufe had said to have him buried on the place, and she herself had dug the grave, down near the pond, below some willows. She wouldn't cry now; she felt almost as if the judge were watching her.

Clara was saying, "It's a good obituary. They left out a club—no, two clubs—and his term as judge of the juvenile court. It was his friend, former Governor Joe Collins, who got him moved to the superior court. Of course, the state legislature always must approve an appointment." Clara took the clipping and started to fold it up.

Lorraine came in then and said, "Aunt Clara, do you have a black dress?"

"Black—" Clara looked stricken. "No! I never thought of that. Why, I haven't got a black dress to my name. The judge liked light colors."

"But you'll have to have a black dress for the services," Lorraine said. "And a black hat, too."

77

Bea thought swiftly through her own clothes. "I have nothing black either. We can't do anything about it today, but tomorrow I'll go to New York and find dresses for us."

"I have a black dress," Lorraine said smugly.

Clara gave her a worried glance. Lorraine added quickly, "Long sleeves, high neck. Quite proper, Aunt Clara."

"Then you can drive to New York with me," Rufe told her that afternoon when she said she was going to the city. "I had my old car tuned up last week. It runs all right."

It was by then late in the evening. After a rather scrambled lunch, which Cecco had unexpectedly helped Bea to serve, both Lorraine and Cecco had disappeared and Clara had gone to her room to rest. Bea was sitting in the study, once more reading the judge's obituary. It stated only that the judge had died suddenly in his own residence. The front page had an account of the murder; and there was a headline: Prominent Jurist Shot. The account was long and was continued on a back page, but there was no mention of Rufe. Bea had looked with a feeling of incredulity at her own name: ". . . the body was found by Miss Beatrice Bartry, a niece and ward of Judge Bartry."

Rufe had come in through the terrace door and taken the paper away from her. "Don't keep reading it."

"Rufe, it didn't mention you. That's good, isn't it?"

"This has nothing to do with my job. My prospective job, I should say."

"Tomorrow will you know more about where you are to be sent?"

"I don't know. It's possible."

Bea thought of her last stormy talk with the judge. Among other things, he had said that Bea would have to act almost as an unpaid servant to, say, the ambassador's wife. "No," Bea had told him hotly, "all that is changed—if it ever happened. The wife of a Foreign Service officer, no matter how minor an officer is at the beginning, is supposed to be a private citizen." There was an added consideration, however. She said now, "The wife of a Foreign Service officer is supposed to behave in every way in a manner suitable to the—the dignity of the United States. Being associated with murder isn't exactly dignified."

"Oh, Bea!" Rufe took her hands. "*You* couldn't help this—

this dreadful thing. Nobody can possibly feel that you have behaved badly. Don't be such an idiot."

"But it means so much to us both."

"Listen, darling, I may be the third undersecretary of the third undersecretary down in the third cellar. I have no dignity or status to maintain."

"But you will have. And this horrible thing! Nobody knows where a murder case can begin or end, and nobody knows how many people can be involved in it."

"You're quoting the judge."

"Perhaps I am. But he spoke the truth. The police even questioned Cecco this morning."

"He was in town. Supposedly at Valley Inn—"

"They checked that. The people at the inn said he was there."

"Those windows are low. He could have simply dropped out and come here—"

"How would he get the judge's gun?"

Rufe sighed. "How would anybody get it? Do you suppose Lorraine has induced your aunt to make a new will yet?"

"I don't know."

"She will."

"Naturally. Lorraine is really her niece."

"Aunt Clara will marry again," Rufe said casually, picking up a cigarette box and looking at it as if it were important.

"Aunt Clara!"

"Why, of course."

"But she was devoted to the judge, she gave in to him about everything, she—"

"She put on quite an act, Bea, of being the cozy little-woman type. In fact, I've always known that she had a will of iron. She's much younger than the judge. She can't be more than fifty or thereabouts—"

"Fifty-two."

"There, you see. Mark my words. She's honestly grieving for the judge and will for some time. Perhaps later she'll travel. She'll do something. And believe me, Bea, it won't be long before she marries again. A good-looking rich widow— Now, don't glare at me like that! It's the natural thing to happen. She'll have time to make a dozen wills."

"But her heart—"

"I'll bet anything you like that her heart is really as good as

79

yours or mine. My father doesn't get very upset about it, believe me. And it seems to me that it's just possible Aunt Clara had a heart attack whenever she wanted to get out of something."

"You're not to speak like that about her——"

"Oh, Bea! I love her. I've always loved her. But I think I see her more objectively than you do. This is all beside the point, anyway."

"Rufe, wouldn't you really rather have a rich wife than a poor one? The judge said that in the Foreign Service——"

"The judge said a great many things. He was an opinionated, selfish old man. Don't quote *de mortuis nil nisi bonum* either. People don't change because they've died. He simply didn't want you to leave him, didn't want to lose all that attention he could count on from you. Let's not quarrel about the judge, Bea. Or about a rich woman or a poor woman——"

Lorraine again showed her talent for appearing at the wrong time and, as far as Bea was concerned, the wrong place. Now she sauntered into the room. "Oh, I wondered where everybody was. I just got back. I took Cecco to Valley Inn to pay his bill and pick up the rest of his luggage. I left the car in the drive, Bea. It's all right there, isn't it? I wasn't sure I could make that curve into the old barn."

"Bea is just going to bed," Rufe said. "We'll have to be up early. I'll toot outside for you about six. All right, Bea?"

"All right."

Lorraine eyed her. "Are you going to Washington with Rufe? What about those black dresses?"

"I'm just going with him as far as New York," Bea said shortly. "Goodnight, Rufe."

He pulled her toward him, kissed her, said goodnight and was quickly off down the drive. Bea wished his kiss had not been quite so brief. But then, Rufe had a strong sense of privacy; he wouldn't have wanted Lorraine—and Cecco, who now stood in the doorway behind Lorraine—to witness any display of emotion.

Feeling let down, Bea arranged the papers on the desk and folded away the account of the judge's murder. When she looked up, both Lorraine and Cecco had gone too.

She closed the terrace door and bolted it. Then she went through the living room and the hall. The front door stood open and lights from the hall were reflected on the shining fenders of the judge's car. He would never have permitted it to stand outside even on a warm spring night.

After a moment she went outside. Lorraine had left the keys in the ignition. Bea started the car, wondering how long she and Aunt Clara would still feel themselves obliged to follow every admonition, every like or dislike of the judge's.

Bea negotiated the abrupt curve into the garage.

It had been an enormous barn; the stalls and feeding troughs had been removed to make space for the two cars, but the ancient beams and the old tack room behind it still remained. Whenever it had to be repainted, Clara had insisted on the original faded-red. There were two doors. Each one was twofold, the leaves latched back. There were bolts on the outside of the leaves fastening them together, but no lock.

She drove as carefully into the slot for the judge's car as if even now he were standing outside, watching her progress sternly. She turned off the engine and lights.

She was getting out of the car when the two leaves of the door behind her swung quietly together.

Eight

The doors had blown shut, of course. Someone had failed to hook back the two leaves. It was very dark, and in the darkness the place smelled so like a barn that she almost expected some long-ago horse to whinny.

She felt her way along the car to the door behind it. She tried to push it open. The leaves rattled but held firm. It was with a sense of shock that she realized they must be firmly bolted on the outside. The wind couldn't have done that.

She pushed and worked at the door; the bolt held. She felt her way to the door behind the small car which she usually drove. It was, as she expected, tightly bolted on the outside, too. She was sure she encountered a cobweb, and brushed her hand on her skirt with an odd tingling of nerves. She tried to calm herself. She had turned off the engine; there would be no chance of carbon monoxide even if she couldn't make anyone in the house hear her.

She had a sudden thought. There was a sure way of making herself heard. She groped her way to the judge's car again, leaned into the seat and found the horn. Its wail echoed wildly in the enclosed space of the old barn.

They made solid barns in the days when this one had been built, solid enough to protect animals from New England winters. But surely someone from the house would hear her. She leaned on the horn until her own ears seemed to rattle.

Clara could have turned on her television, and turned it up very loud, as she always did. But surely Lorraine or Cecco would hear and come to her aid.

Big as it was, it wouldn't be very comfortable if she had to spend the night sleeping in the judge's car. Besides—besides, she didn't like the idea of being alone in the big, dark old barn, accessible from the outside.

Suddenly she remembered that at some time they had put an electric light in the barn. It was rarely used. She felt her way back again to the doors; she had a vague memory that the switch for the light was just inside the doors and that there was one big light hanging on a wire from a ceiling beam.

She found the switch after another unpleasant encounter with a spider web, but no light came on. Perhaps the bulb had burned out and never been replaced; since the judge had retired, no one ever used the garage at night.

She tried the horn again. It sounded deafening to her, but still no one came.

It simply wasn't possible that someone had intentionally shut her in the garage. There was no reason for it. All the same her heart gave a choking leap at the thought. Whatever had happened, she didn't intend to stay there all night. She pressed the horn in a series of furious blasts.

Quite suddenly she felt a current of fresh, cool air on her face. She heard one of the halves of the door swing creakily open. She could see the dimly lighted rectangle behind the car. Someone said, "For God's sake, who's that? Take your hand off the horn."

It was Cecco. She took her hand off the horn. No matter what her feelings about Cecco, at that instant she could have kissed him. "It's me," she said rather faintly.

He flung aside the other half of the door; she could see his

82

tall figure dimly in the gloom. "Do you mean— Is it little Bea?"

"Oh, yes!"

He came closer. "What's the matter?"

"N—nothing. That is—the doors closed." She was recovering a semblance of control. "They must have blown shut just as I was putting the judge's car away."

Cecco came closer; he was between her and the door, and for a brief moment she had a sense of being trapped. A faint odor of cigar smoke came with him and, oddly, steadied her wild fancy.

He said, though, "But, dear little Bea, there's no wind."

"It doesn't matter. It was an accident. Let's get out of here —let's go to the house."

He waited a second and then obediently turned. She took a long breath and followed him out of the garage. Cecco drew the two leaves of the door together. She said, "There's a bolt."

"Yes, I found it."

There was something rather thoughtful, even evasive in Cecco's voice. Bea told herself that she imagined that. Cecco wouldn't have bolted the doors and then after so long a time come back to let her out. Probably the time in the garage had not been as long as it seemed to her.

After a moment Bea said again, but with a strangely tight kind of feeling around her throat, "Accident," and started along the graveled drive toward the house. Cecco said nothing, just walked along with her. When they reached the terrace he said, "Lucky I heard you. I had been out strolling and smoking."

Bea said abruptly, "Where were you walking?"

"I don't know, really," Cecco replied promptly. "There's a kind of path. I could barely see it. It seems to go through the woods. I remembered that there is a lake down there somewhere. Anyway, I only wanted to take a walk. Aren't you glad I released you, little Bea?"

"Somebody would have come," Bea said, and then repented and added, "I'm glad you came. Thank you, Cecco."

He took her hand and kissed it in his caressing way. She said, "Is there a policeman on the place tonight?"

"Why, no. At least I have not seen a policeman. I think it is unlikely—"

83

They walked in at the big front door, which she bolted behind them. Cecco followed after her as she went through the dining room and pantry back to the kitchen door. He watched as she closed it and put on the chain bolt. He followed her back to the hall; she turned out lights as she went. When they reached the hall Cecco said, "Aren't you going to set the famous burglar alarm?"

"Yes." Bea felt him walking softly behind her all the way up the steps and it was as if a very handsome, strong panther were treading on her heels. That was *really* preposterous, she told herself. And again he watched, his gaze bright and lively as she set the alarm.

"I hope Lorraine is in the house," he said. "If not—"

"Oh dear, I forgot Lorraine." Bea went to Lorraine's door and knocked.

Lorraine called out almost immediately, "Cecco, you have the other guest room! I told you—"

"It's not Cecco, it's Bea. I only wanted to be sure you're upstairs. I'm setting the alarm."

"Go ahead. If Cecco gets caught outside, it will serve him right. I don't know where he is."

Cecco laughed. "I'm right here, darling. Don't concern yourself about me." He spoke in melodious tones, as musical as Bea had ever heard outside an opera house.

Lorraine's reply was short. "I'm not concerning myself about you!"

Bea said briefly, "Goodnight."

Clara's door was closed and there were no sounds of the television; apparently she was asleep. Conscious of Cecco standing politely in the hall, waiting for her to close her door, Bea shut it hurriedly and with rather a bang.

Somebody had thoughtfully turned on her bedside lamps and her desk lamp. Clara? It would not be like Lorraine to think of it.

The night was quiet. Yet nobody had heard the horn she had sounded so loudly and so long. Cecco had been in the vicinity; Cecco had heard it. Cecco had come and unlocked the bolt.

Bea went to the closet to get out a dressing gown and remembered with a chill the other gown, stained and blotched with blood, which the police had taken away with them. Nobody had questioned her about it; perhaps its true significance

84

was clear. As she reached into the closet she noticed that dresses were hanging in odd confusion, as if they had been pushed this way and that, all askew.

Lorraine? But Lorraine respected and liked clothes; she wouldn't have shoved them all awry on their hangers. Bea reached out and straightened several of them. Mere curiosity could have led Lorraine to explore while Bea was outside—shut in the garage. Or possibly there was some article of clothing Lorraine merely wished to borrow.

But Lorraine wouldn't have bolted her in the garage for such a reason; all Lorraine would have had to do was say that she forgot to pack this or that.

The question was: Who had bolted her in the garage, and why?

She began to wonder whether Cecco had a perverted sense of humor, enjoyed playing crude practical jokes. Certainly he had been somewhere near the garage. She couldn't avoid that fact.

She had dropped into a tired sleep when something seemed to nudge at her, half rousing her: the thought that her closet had looked as if someone might have pushed aside the dresses in order to hide there.

But why—who? There was nobody in the house who would have reason to do that. The whole thing was like part of an uneasy, troubled dream—but a dream. She dismissed it.

She woke from a troubled sleep well before six o'clock. Sleepily she looked at the little French clock on her bedside table, thought it was six and scrambled out of bed so fast that the small rug skidded over the highly polished floor, threw her back on the bed and jolted her into taking a second look at the time. It was only five o'clock, so she had plenty of time to dress and go quietly downstairs. She made coffee and boiled an egg. Then she sat so long, pondering recent events, that she heard the light toot of Rufe's car before she was prepared for it. She dashed upstairs, snatched up her big handbag and a coat and ran downstairs again. Dawn was cool and slightly misty. They took the winding road across to the main road going into Valley Ridge. They passed the Congregational church with its white steeple pointing skyward; its bell was just tolling the gentle strokes of six.

They had almost reached the wide approach to the Merritt Parkway before Bea could make up her mind to tell Rufe of the unnerving—yet, in the end, harmless—happening of the previous night. When she did tell him, she made it light and casual. The barn doors had been closed, she said. They had been bolted. Cecco had let her out.

Rufe's face took on the closed expression which she recognized as his way of wearing a mask while he was thinking very troublesome thoughts. "There was no wind last night. Besides, that bolt needs hands. So who did it?"

"I don't know. But it really wasn't anything. I put my hand on the horn and held it there, and then, I told you, Cecco came along and let me out."

He turned onto the Merritt. Even at that time of day, there was a stream of cars, speeding toward New York. After a while he said, "I wonder if that could have been Cecco's idea of a rather mean joke."

"I thought of that, too. But he— No, it didn't seem like that. I really think he was just strolling along that path down toward the pond and heard the horn."

Rufe was silent for what seemed a long time. Then he said, "Bea, if there is the slightest thing you know which might give the police an idea about the murderer, you'd better tell them."

"I don't know anything."

"Somebody had to bolt that door. I can't see why unless—to frighten you, do you suppose? That doesn't seem likely. Was anything at all disturbed in the house when you came back with Cecco? Did it look as though anybody had been, say, prowling in the judge's study?"

"No. The terrace door was closed. The front door was open. I bolted it and the kitchen door. Cecco trailed along after me. There wasn't— Well, yes, somebody had been in my room. That is— Oh, it can't be important, Lorraine or Aunt Clara did it, but the lights had been turned on in my room. And the dresses in the closet looked as if they had been pushed aside. Leaving a place big enough for somebody to hide in," she added. "But why?"

"Because someone may have come along the hall, and whoever was in your room didn't want to be seen and have to explain it."

"Only Aunt Clara and Lorraine were in the house."

"The front door was open. The kitchen door was probably

unlocked. Anybody who wanted to could have got into the house. So who?"

"Nobody! There's nothing I know that could hurt anybody."

He considered that for a while, too. "It could be something you don't know you know, if you understand me."

"Of course I understand you but—no."

"We'll tell Obrian about the garage doors. I hope to get back tonight. I'll take the shuttle from La Guardia. If you'll drive back to New York and park behind my club—there ought to be plenty of parking spaces in the early morning—then I'll get back there by, say, four, earlier if I can make it, or if I'm held up until tomorrow morning, I'll send a message. Ask the doorman at the club for it."

There was a shuttle flight to Washington loading when they arrived at the airport. It was still so early by the time Bea reached New York that the stores were not yet open. She parked in the space behind Rufe's club and went to St. Patrick's, and to the lovely solemnity of the Lady Chapel. She sat there for some time, thinking of the judge. His loving kindness over the years seemed to blot out the querulous, erratic man he had become. When she left, it was with a sense of comfort, as if she had said her own private funeral service for him. She couldn't remember much of her own father; his place had been taken by the judge.

It was a curiously normal day. She found a dress for Clara; she found a hat which she was not pleased with but bought because she could find nothing she was sure Clara might like; she found a veil, a thin shoulder-length veil bordered with black ribbon; Clara—or the judge—would have wanted that. She remembered black gloves. She lunched late at a convenient Longchamps, then went back to Rufe's club, where the doorman had a message for her. Mr. Thorne had phoned. He said to tell Miss Bartry he couldn't get home tonight. The doorman relieved her of her packages and added, "He said something else. He said don't go to the garage again. Was that right, Miss Bartry? I wasn't sure I heard him correctly."

"Oh, yes. That was right." She thankfully permitted him to carry her packages out to Rufe's car and get her started on the way home.

Her heart felt like a lump of lead; she knew exactly what

Rufe had meant by saying not to go to the garage. Somebody wanted to harm her. But why? There was no reason for it.

She had hoped to escape the late-afternoon traffic. But early as it was, there were several bottlenecks of traffic. It was almost six o'clock when she reached home. Chief Obrian was sitting in his car watching two policemen who again were searching the lawn down by the shrubbery where the judge had been shot, searching it inch by inch on their hands and knees.

Nobody was at home, he told her, not even Velda. He himself had questioned Willie Griffin again. "He still insists that he heard two shots the night the judge was killed and at about the time he must have been shot. He isn't sure of the time, but it was after ten o'clock, maybe nearly eleven. After the shots, he heard the burglar alarm and then the police car. He says he had gone down to the Ellison gate across the driveway to make sure it was closed. He said that young people had begun to drive in and park there and he was going to put a stop to it. He swears up and down that there were two shots." Chief Obrian eyed the packages beside her, crawled out from behind his wheel and lumbered across to her. "I'll carry these. You looked pretty tired out. I hope you don't mind if I ask you again—but are you sure you didn't hear any shot at all?"

"Oh, I'm sure. But what do you think it all means? Do you think the judge himself shot at somebody? And that's why his gun had been recently fired?"

The chief went into the house with her, deposited the packages on the hall table and chair, sat down and sighed heavily. It was obvious that Chief Obrian was taking the judge's murder very hard; there was a sagging worry in his face; usually, no matter what, he had a cheerful way of looking and speaking. He said, the troubled lines deep in his face, "I wish I could answer all that. The men are down there again, looking for those two bullets. And a knife. Not much chance of finding anything. All these woods around. Well—"

She said thank you as he went out again. After a moment she went up the stairs, thinking of a shower and fresh clothes. At the door of her room she stopped—even at a glance, she could see there was something wrong with it.

Nine

There were several things wrong. She stood in the middle of the room and looked around.

Clara had trained her as a child to neatness and order. The judge had declaimed frequently to the effect that everything had a place and everything should be in that place. The judge didn't subscribe to that notion himself but he expected it of Clara and Bea.

As was her habit, she had made the bed that morning before going downstairs to breakfast. It was now slightly wrinkled and the pillows were not in their usual order: the two plump pillows below, the tiny pillow she actually slept on, on top. Now the small pillow lay at the foot of the bed.

She had seen to the care of her room since she was old enough to do so. Velda would never have touched anything in it.

A drawer in her dressing table was half out, at an angle, as if it had been opened and then closed so hurriedly that it stuck. Objects on her small writing table were just a little displaced; the Irish glass and silver holder for pens and pencils stood at the left instead of the right, as if it had been pushed aside in order to permit someone to examine the big closed box where she kept her correspondence. Her small French clock lay face down on the rug. Someone had been in her room, searching for something. Lorraine? Not likely. Cecco? Not likely. After a stricken moment, she thought of the chief and ran downstairs. He was sitting on the terrace steps. He rose, listened to her hurried story and went swiftly upstairs with her.

He looked about for a few minutes, passing his hand worriedly over his lined face. "Are you sure, Bea? You left in a hurry this morning. Perhaps you weren't as careful as you usually are," he said finally.

"I'm sure. I know everything was okay when I left."

"Well, then—is there anybody who would do this to you just out of spite? Something like that?"

"Somebody shut me in the garage last night! Sunday night!"

He listened again while she told about it, now thoroughly frightened. "And there was something else," she finished. "I told Rufe about it. It seemed unimportant then, but now—"

"What else?"

"When I got to my room last night, after Cecco let me out of the garage, my dresses were pushed aside in the closet. As if"—she swallowed hard—"as if somebody might have hidden there."

Obrian didn't like any of it, obviously. "This Cecco fellow, he let you out of the garage?"

"Yes."

"H'mm. Let's see what Velda Mathers has to say. If somebody was here this afternoon—"

"I know there was!"

"Let's talk to Velda. She doesn't miss much. What's her phone number?"

Bea took him to the extension in the judge's study and listened while he dialed. Presently Velda answered.

"Velda, where is Mrs. Bartry? . . . Where's the rest of the family? . . . Yes, I know, but she's just got home." Velda talked for a long time. Finally he thanked her, hung up and turned to Bea. "She says the parson came to see Mrs. Bartry and then took her to view the—remains," he said delicately and probably in Velda's very words. "Then he was going to talk to her about the hymns for the services and then take her to see that everything is in order in the Salcott lot out at Old Cemetery. Velda said that Lorraine and her husband had gone somewhere in the Mercedes, she didn't know where. She said there had been so many telegrams phoned in, she finally asked Western Union to deliver them instead. Some of them are from people who are coming to the services tomorrow."

"I do hope you'll come back to the house after the services. You've known the judge a long time."

"Thank you," Chief Obrian sighed. "I always liked the judge. Although he was pretty harsh lately, changeable and—well, you know, not himself. But let's get back to business. I don't like what's going on, Bea. But maybe your cousin, Lorraine—"

"No," Bea said positively. "It wouldn't be like Lorraine. If she wanted anything she'd come straight out and ask me for it."

90

Obrian eyed her shrewdly. "Not if it was something person-ally important to Lorraine."

"I have nothing important to Lorraine," Bea said flatly.

"Then what about that husband of hers? He might be snooping around."

"He might be but—— Oh, I don't know, I don't think he'd do it just that way. I mean, he acts and moves as softly as a cat. I think he'd leave everything exactly as he found it. Besides, it was Cecco who let me out of the barn Sunday night."

"How long were you shut in the barn?"

"It seemed ages. But I—— No, I really don't know. Perhaps fifteen minutes. Or longer. I can't be sure."

"Long enough for somebody to get into your room and then hide in the closet if he heard somebody coming. Then this Cecco strolls along and lets you out."

"I suppose it's possible that Cecco heard the horn and just simply didn't come at once to open the door. Oh, anything is possible!"

Obrian nodded, then said after some frowning thought, as though checking out all possibilities, "Mrs. Bartry? No. Velda——"

"No!"

"If somebody *was* there in your room——"

"Somebody was there."

"Whoever it was didn't do a very good job of covering his tracks. So it wasn't one of the state police. Besides, I think I'd have been told."

"I never thought of the police."

"You'd never have known it if they had been here."

"No——" Unexpectedly Bea thought of Seth shambling around in his untidy way, leaving a drawer askew.

She said, "Where's Seth today?"

"Seth!"

"I only wondered . . . I don't know what to think any more. I mean—oh, Seth is careless about things."

"What would Seth want in your room? I think you're imag-ining too much. Besides, he's in Bridgeport. I think he said he was going to do a little fence-mending."

"I just don't see why anybody would search my room," she said wearily.

Obrian sighed. "Somebody must have known the house was empty. I hadn't arrived yet, so no policemen were around and

91

whoever it was took the chance of getting into the house. He must have known which room is yours." He sighed again. "We'd better take a look through the rest of the house. See if he got into other rooms."

Apparently "he" hadn't. Clara's room was neat and fragrant and orderly. Lorraine's was orderly enough and reeked of perfume. Cecco's room was littered with magazines and smelled of cigar smoke and after-shave lotion.

"This is the judge's room." Bea opened the door. Someone, Velda probably, had closed the shades, so it was dimly lit. She snapped on a light. But here, too, there was nothing out of place. It seemed so full of the judge's personality—with its heavy table for books and its pipe rack and jar of tobacco, its heavy mahogany chairs and chests of drawers that had been selected by one of Clara's forebears, but which in this case (as not in the library) the judge had liked—that Bea almost expected the judge to come in and impatiently demand what they were doing there.

"Nothing out of the way here." Chief Obrian frowned. "Looks as if whoever it was singled out your room. To tell you the truth, I can't make any sense out of it at all."

He went out of the room. Bea followed him down the stairs. At the door he glanced down at the men still crouching under the shrubbery, and said, "Lorraine can't like you very much now. At least until your aunt changes her will, as I expect she'll do. But I agree with you, I can't see why Lorraine would hunt through your room or shut you in the barn. Maybe to scare you—but why?" He hesitated; there was an odd look of indecision in his face. Bea had a brief notion that he was debating about something he only half wanted to say. If so, he decided against speaking and got in his car, turned it and called to the men in the shrubbery to stop the fruitless searching. After a short colloquy both of them got into the chief's car. The gravel rattled as it went off down the driveway.

It had turned into the public road and disappeared behind firs and shrubbery when the telephone rang. Bea answered it in the judge's study.

It was Rufe calling from Washington. He wanted to be sure she had got his message, had reached home safely and his old car had not broken down somewhere. He would be home the next day in time for the services. About then he must have

92

sensed something in her voice that wasn't right, for he broke off abruptly. "Are you all right? Has anything gone wrong?"

She decided not to tell him then about the unnerving evidence of a search of her room. There was nothing he could do about it and she had already reported it to Chief Obrian. Also, there could readily prove to be some simple explanation. "Obrian and two men were here, still looking for one of those bullets."

"Yes, I keep thinking about those two shots Willie Griffin heard. I believe him. I suppose the police have covered all the possibilities, But I wonder if whoever killed the judge meant to suggest suicide—you know, firing the judge's gun into, oh, anywhere, into the shrubbery or the woods? Then leaving the judge's gun— No," he caught himself up. "That can't be right; if he had done that he wouldn't have removed the bullet. No, the bullet that killed him must identify the murderer. We can't get around that. Don't go out tonight. Don't go near the garage."

"I won't. Rufe, what about today? What did they want? Is everything all right?"

"Oh, sure. That is—yes. I'll tell you tomorrow."

After she had hung up, the house seemed very empty and subtly threatening. She felt a tingle of something like apprehension. There wasn't a sound, not a footstep, not anything. But nobody could be there! She and the chief had tramped all over the place—bedrooms, kitchen, everywhere.

No, nobody could be in the house. Thinking it over, she decided that there just had to be some small and unimportant explanation for the apparent search in her room. Clara had wanted something; Lorraine had wanted something—

In any event, she began to feel foolish; she had let her imagination gallop away with her. She would go upstairs, ignore the tiny disorder in her room, take a shower, try to recover some semblance of common sense. Clara would be returning soon. The peepers down near the pond were beginning their nightly music.

She went into the hall and stopped at the table where her purchases lay. As she gathered up the packages and her handbag, she glanced automatically at herself in the mirror above the table—and it moved.

It didn't actually move; it couldn't; it was fastened firmly to the wall. Something had moved in it, behind her. She whirled around, her heart thudding like a drum. She faced the open door of the library, shadowy now. There was nothing there.

But something *had* flickered for a second in the mirror behind her, and then vanished.

She should look in the library, she told herself. But overcome by panic, she knew she couldn't do that, not by herself. She had only one thought now—she wasn't going to stay alone in that empty house. She almost stumbled down the steps and all at once she was in Rufe's car, thankful that she had snatched up her handbag with the keys to the car in it.

She'd take the car home and she'd see Dr. Thorne and she'd stay with him until she was sure that Clara and Cecco and Lorraine had returned. She backed and turned and went down the driveway at top speed. She did have the presence of mind to brake before she entered the public road. The stone wall was high; the thick shrubbery shut off the views right and left. The road was empty; she shot across it, down to the Thorne drive and into it. There she stopped and took a long breath. Was she running from a fancy? *Could* someone have been in the library? It had to be. She could still see that shadowy flicker in the mirror.

She got out of the car as soon as she could control an unsteadiness in her knees and took the narrow walk that led from the drive to Dr. Thorne's consulting rooms. There was a bell; she pushed it, over and over again.

She could hear it pealing away somewhere within the depths of the house. It seemed a long time before Miss Dotty came to open the door. She had an apron over her white uniform and a small, very sharp carving knife in her hand. She clearly didn't welcome a caller just then. Her bushy black eyebrows drew together; her mass of untidy black hair, usually neat under a white cap, seemed to bristle. "Oh, it's you! Trouble with your aunt, I suppose."

"No. I just brought back Rufe's car. It's out there in the drive."

"He's not coming back tonight, then?"

"No. He phoned me just now. He'll be home tomorrow."

"Oh—well, thanks," said Miss Dotty grudgingly. "I'll tell the doctor. He's working himself to death. Can't stop him. Can't do anything with him. He's taken the judge's death very hard."

A slight odor of scorching food wafted from the back part

of the house, and Miss Dotty started to turn away from Bea. "I've got to go. I'm frying some chicken for the doctor's dinner. He never sees to himself."

Her martyrlike air stung Bea unexpectedly. Miss Dotty enjoyed her grim authority over the doctor too thoroughly. Bea said, "We really should see to it that the doctor has a housekeeper. Of course," she added quickly as there was an ominous flash in Miss Dotty's black eyes, "you are very good to him, stay after hours, see to most of his meals I expect—"

Miss Dotty cut in savagely, "Your Velda wouldn't do what I do! Naturally! She couldn't! She's not a nurse. But if I say it myself, I don't see how the doctor could get along without me." She eyed Bea with a sudden spark of curiosity. "You look scared. What's the matter?"

"Oh—my aunt is gone and Velda went home and the house —" Under the piercing gaze of Miss Dotty's black eyes she couldn't say that she was frightened and had fled. She said instead, "I'd like to stay here till my aunt gets back—"

Miss Dotty turned around and headed for the kitchen. "Stay as long as you like," she called back over her solid shoulder. "I can't stay here chattering—"

A door closed with a hard bang. So all I've done, Bea thought dejectedly, is nearly quarrel with Miss Dotty and ruin the doctor's dinner.

The door to the patients' waiting room was firmly closed. She didn't dare follow Miss Dotty to the kitchen. As she stood debating what to do, she heard a car coming slowly along the road. She was sure that it turned in at the Salcott place, so she went out again. She took the keys to Rufe's car along with her, however; she couldn't face Miss Dotty again to hand them over to her.

Bea walked down the driveway, under the canopy of old maples which were now beginning to show a thin green foliage. As she reached the drive to the Salcott place, a car was going out, slowly and cautiously. The driver wore a clerical collar and contrived to bow to her with the correct measure of kindness and sympathy even while remaining nervously intent upon his driving. Everybody knew that when the Reverend Cantwell came along in his eccentrically guided car, it was well to take cover.

This time he negotiated the turn into the public road without running into the stone wall, as for an instant seemed to be his intention, and Bea went on to the house to find Clara sitting in a chair in the study, still hatted and gloved. She lifted her head toward Bea and said, "Everything is all right, I think. I couldn't be sure what hymns the judge would have liked; you know he was never much for church, so I selected some of my favorites. They—they made him look so lifelike." She didn't have to say who. "But the judge himself— Oh, Bea, he's gone!" There were no tears in her eyes but there was an acceptance of mortality and a desolation in her face that went to Bea's heart.

"Dear Aunt," she said. "He loved you. You were always so good to him."

"But he's not here," Clara said. Then she braced herself and went on, "Did you get my black dress? I'd better try it on."

There was the sound of a car, the bang of doors, the murmur of voices in the hall. Lorraine appeared in the doorway of the study, carrying a dress box. Suddenly Cecco called sharply from the hall, *"Little Bea—little Bea—"*

There was a note of urgency in his voice. Bea, with Lorraine and Clara close behind her, hurried to the hall. Cecco stood at the library door. "Who got in or out of that window, I wonder?" he said, pointing.

Ten

All three women went closer to look.

Cecco gestured toward the window. "Screen not on yet; I expect it's too early. But the window is open, and see that—" He pointed. Torn strands of heavy ivy dangled along the window sills.

"I don't want to frighten you. But it really does look as if someone got in that window—and went out the same way."

So someone *had* entered the house, and escaped by that window. There *had* been a flicker in the mirror, the suggestion of motion behind her. It just might be, Bea's reason said, that it was a good thing for her she hadn't at that moment summoned up the bravery to explore the library.

96

Lorraine said, "Velda must have been cleaning in here, airing the room. She probably forgot to close the window."

Clara gave Lorraine an impatient glance. "Velda hasn't touched this room or the living room since—since the night the judge died. I meant to speak to her about it. But she's had so much to do."

Cecco's eyes were narrowed in thought. "Perhaps it would be a good idea to close and lock it now." His slender fingers worked at the lock; then he turned with an air of triumph. "There we are! Now then, shall I mix the cocktails, little Bea?"

Bea's nerves snapped. "If you don't stop calling me little Bea I'll—I'll—"

"Drop a pinch or two of arsenic in his cocktail," Lorraine said. "Not," she added, "that it would affect him."

"*Girls!*" Clara was reproving.

They all started up the stairs, quiet now, each seemingly engrossed in her own thoughts. When Clara went into her room, Bea and Lorraine followed her, almost automatically. Bea, unable to contain herself, faced them both and blurted out what was uppermost in her mind. "I think that someone was in my room while I was in town. Was it either of you?"

Clara shook her head and looked hurt at the very thought. Lorraine eyed Bea narrowly. "Do you mean to say you think somebody really got into the house and out again by the library window and was in your room? Did you miss anything?"

"No. But if there *was* somebody—"

Clara took off her hat and pushed at her hair. "I'd better take a look in the safe. That is, if—" Her voice trailed off, as though she did not really want to admit even to herself that the house could have been entered. But she went into the judge's room, where there was an antiquated wall safe. Lorraine and Bea followed.

Clara's little hands moved efficiently over the dial of the safe, opened it and took out, one after the other, her store of rings, bracelets, necklaces—most of them heirlooms, which her grandfather and probably her great-grandfather had presented to their wives. She loved best the jewels the judge had given her, and Bea's throat ached with pity as she watched Clara lovingly, slowly, count over the several rings, the bracelet, the pearls.

Bea glanced up at Lorraine and caught the smug smile on her face as she eyed her own massive bracelet and sparkling rings, far more expensive than anything Clara possessed.

Clara replaced all the boxes. She looked at the few trinkets which belonged to Bea and counted them too. Then she swung back the door of the safe and twirled the dial. "Nothing gone. Whoever it was must have been disturbed before he could work on the safe. Or perhaps there really wasn't anybody."

Lorraine wouldn't let it go like that. "Why did you think somebody had been in your room, Bea?"

"Oh, nothing much. That is, small things. Not in their usual places."

"Is *that* all?"

Bea nodded.

Lorraine thought it over briefly. "I don't see that that is anything to suggest a thief. You and Cecco seem to be trying to frighten us, really. Cecco's talk of an open window. A few things in your room out of place, you say. I don't think we need worry about that, Aunt Clara."

"Please, girls, let's think of other things now," Clara said. "I'll try on the dress Bea bought for me."

"I bought one too," Lorraine said sweetly. "I got to thinking of my black dress and it— The fact is I don't think it would have been suitable for the services tomorrow. It— clings."

Clara gave her an absent but approving smile. "I'm sure you're right, dear. Where did you get the new dress?"

"I took the big car. Cecco went with me, he wanted a haircut. We went to Stamford. It took forever. He spent most of the afternoon at the barber shop. Did you get something for yourself, Bea?"

"Yes. I'd better go now and take it out of the box— See you later."

Once in her own room, she picked up the little French clock and straightened the bed. She believed Clara, she believed Lorraine. She wasn't so sure about Cecco. Had he spent most of the afternoon in a Stamford barber shop?

She hung up the new black dress, washed and changed from her suit into a dress. By the time she went downstairs Cecco was pouring cocktails. He told her proudly that a cas-

98

serole Velda had prepared was heating in the oven. He had put it there himself. If all else failed Cecco, it occurred to Bea that he might enter upon a promising career as a chef.

The cocktails were excellent. However, tonight Bea carefully limited herself and so, she noted, did Clara. Halfway through dinner a boy came from the Western Union office and delivered a thick sheaf of telegrams to Clara, who spent the rest of the dinner hour reading them aloud, telling just who was coming to the services and how many people should be invited to the house afterward. Cecco listened soberly, his fine-featured face intent. Only once did he half smile, and that was when Lorraine's hand, reaching for another helping from the huge casserole, caught Clara's eye. Or rather Lorraine's jewels, blatantly flashing, for Clara said absently, "You really ought to put your jewels in the safe, too, Lorraine. So many of them and so beautiful!"

Lorraine said nothing. Cecco, his face amused yet sardonic, asked Lorraine solicitously if she wished dessert.

The lists occupied yet an hour after dinner; Clara then rose, said she was tired and went to bed. Bea set out to tour the lower floor of the house as usual; Cecco accompanied her again like a sleek, silent tomcat.

Tomcat, Bea thought, panther? In any event, he had stopped calling her little Bea.

Lorraine had disappeared by the time she went upstairs; Cecco waited again while she set the alarm, then said goodnight politely.

There was nothing she could do now about it. However, questions nagged at her; she could see that someone might have entered the house without being seen; there were the woods around the house, some of the pines and clumps of shrubbery were very near the house, especially those which all but covered the library windows. There was the back door which even now Velda rarely remembered to lock when she left. The door had a lock and Velda had a key but locking doors was not—or at least never had been—a custom in Valley Ridge. That habit might be changed now. Someone could have entered the house, even when Obrian and his two men were at the front. Someone could have escaped through the library window; she still felt that she had caught some movement in the mirror. The torn ivy certainly suggested that. She had heard no car leaving the place. But then anyone entering the house could easily have driven a car into the Ellison drive or the Carter drive (more likely the Carter drive since the Ellisons' caretaker lived on the place), and come from there, quickly and easily through the woods, taking advantage of the pines or laurels as shields. He could have escaped by the same route.

It was not altogether necessary for him to have parked a car somewhere out of sight. Lorraine had said that Cecco had "taken forever" at the barber's getting his hair cut. Cecco *could* have taken a taxi from Stamford back to the house; Cecco *could* have pretended to discover the open window in order to shield himself from any questions.

Anybody, knowing the house, could have entered it. Whatever that searcher had wished to find, it had to be something small—small enough to be contained by her box of correspondence or the drawer filled with writing materials. So then what?

She had few jewels, nothing of importance, and what she had was still in the safe. It was Lorraine who had the valuable jewels. Cecco had openly hinted that someone, not Cecco, paid Lorraine's bills; Cecco professed himself to be entirely without money. At the same time there was Bea's curious notion that while they insisted they were enemies, Lorraine and Cecco had come to some kind of understanding. That was only a notion of her own, Bea told herself. There was nothing to substantiate it.

Clara would not like the idea that someone else—Bea put it to herself vaguely—had been buying jewels, clothes, furs, for Lorraine. Naturally, though, that man—if he existed—was the reason for Lorraine's insistence upon a divorce from Cecco. Yet again Bea could not dismiss her impression that somehow, in some way, Cecco and Lorraine were in a guarded agreement.

Through the open windows she could hear, off in the distance, near the pond, the peepers shrilling in the night. She remembered her childhood days, when there were gardeners about the place; one of them, wise in the ways of nature, had talked to her of the peepers. "They come out once, then it turns cold and they go in again. They come out a second time; same thing happens. But the third time they stay out, it's going to be spring."

The next day Rufe arrived home in the morning but Bea did not see him until he came slowly down the church aisle along with the pallbearers, Joe Lathrop, Ben Benson and the others. There was Tony, too, almost unrecognizable in his sober dark suit.

The church was filled mainly by old friends; murder was one thing and terrible, but the death of a well-known and respected friend was quite another thing. If there was a special something in the air, a kind of tension and half frightened anger, Bea sensed it only in the utter silence of those around her. She doubted if anyone at all had come to the church from motives of curiosity. Everything was done as the judge would have had it. In Old Cemetery the rites were also orderly and dignified. Clara was completely composed; Dr. Thorne stood at Clara's side with her black gloved hand on his arm. Seth stood just behind her.

Dr. Thorne was very neatly dressed, unusual for him. Suddenly, even at this inappropriate time, Bea was again assailed with suspicion. The doctor knew Bea's room. He was one of the closest of the judge's and Clara's friends. Could he have been too close a friend of Clara's? Could the judge's murder have been the drastic climax of an elderly, but sad and now tragic romance?

The cool breeze touched her suddenly hot face and swept away her speculations. Not the doctor. Not Clara. She was thoroughly ashamed of her ugly, baseless thoughts. She took Rufe's arm as they left Old Cemetery.

The First Selectman, James Castleton, came to shake hands with Bea and say a few words of sympathy. He fell in beside Seth. "Good to see you at home, Seth. I expect you're busy politicking." He gave a decorous little chuckle. "You've always had my vote. Far as I'm concerned you'd be a good President! Why stop at the Senate!"

Seth gave a deprecating murmur. Mr. Castleman added, "Mrs. Bartry is holding up well. Of course the doctor is a great help to her."

He disappeared, and as Bea watched the doctor help Clara into the waiting car, a sudden and devastating notion flashed into Bea's mind. The judge's shabby old jacket had been left in his study. True, it was a warm night; he might have removed it and flung it over the desk himself. She had rarely seen the judge—a formal man—without a jacket, although if

101

the doctor had happened in and taken the judge's blood pressure, the judge would have had to remove his jacket.

She could not help noting the solicitude with which the doctor settled Clara into the car. Again she felt a kind of hot wave of shame at the course of her own galloping doubts. No, she said to herself. No! Seth folded himself into the car with Clara and the doctor and managed to knock his hat off in doing so. Rufe picked it up and handed it to Seth.

The house was filled with people; Velda had known precisely what to prepare; coffee and tea with sandwiches and tiny cakes in the living room but drinks in the judge's study. The governor had arrived a little late; he was obliged to leave early for the drive back to Hartford. The state's attorney, his eyes alert, but questioning nobody, went with the governor. When they had gone, other people drifted away. Bea was aware of Rufe's helping with tea cups or drinks, as indeed did Cecco, looking all the time very intent, even fascinated by this evidence of American custom. She had no chance to speak to Rufe alone until everyone had left; Clara had gone upstairs and Velda was noisily gathering up glasses and plates. The house was too full of flowers and their sweet odors. Bea started out the back door, intending to walk down to the pond, through the woods, her favorite walk. As she left, Rufe called to her, "Wait, Bea. I'm coming too. Gosh, the air in there is like an oven. I thought people would never stop shaking hands and leave. Cecco is helping Velda with the dishes."

"Rufe, how did things go yesterday?"

Afterward it struck her that her question brought for the first time the faintest hint of some change in Rufe. At the time, though, he said, "All right. It was a—general sort of conference."

"Was anything said about the judge?"

"Yes. In a way. Nothing to worry about, Bea. Really." He hesitated. "Old Upson spoke of him, too. I had dinner with him. He was very shocked about it. He'd known the judge."

Upson was a congressman who had given Rufe a fine character reference. But there was something about Rufe that seemed, all at once, evasive and not like him.

They had reached the shallow, swampy edge of the pond. She said bluntly, "There's something wrong, Rufe. What did they say about the judge's murder?"

Rufe walked on for a few steps. "Oh, nothing much. That

102

is, of course they had known of our coming marriage. That's the way things are. They had read the news of the judge's murder in the New York papers."

"They asked you just how much I might be involved in his murder!"

"Oh, Bea, forget it!"

"They don't want you to marry me. At least until this—this thing is settled and it is proved that I had nothing to do with his murder."

"I think that I am of more interest to the police than you just now," Rufe said shortly. "Oh, Bea, let it alone."

"No." They both walked on among the shadows of the pines. Finally Bea said, "We'll not be married until the police have found the murderer. If they ever do," she added.

He swung around. "Bea—"

"No." She meant it. "I'll not marry you and put any kind of doubt or smear on your name."

"Our name," Rufe said. "You didn't kill the judge. Neither did I."

"But it's got to be proved. We can't start out on your career with a—a—"

"Blot?" Rufe said with a short and rather grim laugh. "Don't worry, Bea. Things will straighten out. It's been only a few days."

Again, though, in spite of his words she sensed an evasiveness. Either his interview with his superiors had effected some change in him or—or perhaps Lorraine. Lorraine?

They turned back, past the willows, yellow now; past the thickest of laurel and pines toward the house. Rufe said suddenly, "These memoirs of the judge's. You say you typed all of them?"

"Yes. He would dictate and then I—"

"I know. Bea—" He stopped to face her. "Was there anything about my father in them?"

"Your father! Why, no! I'd remember."

"They're all in those filing cabinets?"

"Yes!"

"The police would have found something by now," Rufe said, as if to himself. "But still, if the judge put it in veiled language—"

"Rufe, what *are* you talking about?"

"A suit for malpractice."

103

"A suit—you mean, your father was sued!"

"And somehow the judge fixed it."

"But he—no, I'd have guessed! If there was anything like that in the memoirs I'd have recognized the circumstances."

They passed the big old barn. Lights were appearing in the house. Finally Rufe said, "How were those memoirs filed? Under what headings?"

"Oh, the usual. Childhood. School. University. Opening his law office. Then his term as judge of the juvenile court. His term as judge of the superior court."

"Nothing else?"

"Yes, there was one he facetiously called Extracurricular Activities."

"Personal affairs?"

"Yes, in a way. They were personal anecdotes, mainly things he did *ex officio*, so to speak. As you know, people still came to him when they wanted friendly advice, even after he closed his law office."

"Nothing about my father?"

"No! That is, not by name, Rufe. I'd remember that. But— your father! I can't believe it. A suit for malpractice!"

"Miss Dotty told me this morning when I got home. She had to make it quick but I think I've got the facts. There was some sort of accident on the road. My father happened to drive past, and of course he stopped and tried to help. The ambulance came and took the man to the hospital. He was unconscious. Something went wrong and in the end the injured man sued my father."

Bea swallowed her astonishment; if Miss Dotty had told Rufe, it was all true. "When did this happen?"

"Years ago. I was away at school. The point is everybody in Valley Ridge seems to have heard about the judge's memoirs. Miss Dotty got it into her head that the judge might have mentioned this—if not by name then in such a way that anyone reading it could guess quite accurately the facts. I don't know how the judge got Pa out of the thing, but he did."

Bea thought for a long moment. "We'd better look at the files."

"There's another consideration. Remember how the judge has been lately. Suppose all at once, after all this time, he got it into his head that Pa shouldn't be allowed to practice or that he ought to let people know about the malpractice suit. Remember how he was about the Ellison boys' still?"

She remembered all too well. The Ellison boys, as a lark, had built a still in the Ellison woods. The judge had sniffed it out, probably; in any event, he had reported it to the police. Mrs. Ellison had managed to get the still destroyed and the boys off to school, but after that, she refused to speak to the judge.

Bea said soberly, "People have gone. Let's look at the files now. The suit would be in his Extracurricular business."

Velda was still working furiously in the kitchen. She gave them a sharp look and said they were to have a cold supper. "Funeral baked meats," she added with gloomy relish. Velda had ways other than current slang to express herself.

When they reached the study they found that not only was his Extracurricular file gone but also the file on his juvenile court term. "But they ought to be here! Right here!" Bea held the long drawer open so Rufe could see they were indeed missing.

Rufe sighed. "I suppose the police have them. Is there anything else gone?"

"No. But really, there simply wasn't anything in either of them that would interest the police." She paused, then said, "Rufe, I didn't tell you over the phone. Last night, I mean yesterday afternoon, when I got home somebody had been in the house and in my bedroom."

The curiously remote expression settled in his face which was in reality, she knew, an extremely sharpened interest. "Take anything?"

"No. But I'm sure that my room was searched." She told him what she knew. Obrian had been there, and had seen no one. But there was nothing she had which anyone else could possibly want. Later she had seen, or thought she had seen, a movement in the mirror; she had gone to Dr. Thorne's and talked to Miss Dotty. When she returned and Cecco and Lorraine arrived, Cecco had pointed out the torn vines and the open library windows.

Rufe sat for a long time on the edge of the desk, looking at the floor. "And somebody shut you in the barn Sunday night and might have given your room a quick search then. There must be a reason. And somebody took those two files. If it wasn't the police it was someone who had good reason to think there was a secret between him and the judge. Of course, Miss Dotty would do anything at all to protect my father. She's had considerable experience as his assistant."

"Rufe! She didn't dig out that bullet!"

"I don't think so either. I only meant that she could have done it. My father could have done it for that matter. But he didn't. Let's have some of those funeral baked meats Velda warned us about."

Clara came down; she had changed from her black dress to a blue silk with a touch of white at the throat and a diamond brooch. She *was* attractive, Bea thought suddenly; she was very attractive. She had been deeply, sincerely devoted to the judge; but she was much younger than the judge, and Bea was beginning to get glimpses of that will of iron.

Lorraine, who had done her hair up neatly in a smooth roll for the services, came down too. Cecco joined them in time for more cocktails.

Supper was eaten in what struck Bea as a cold if exhausted silence. Afterward she had her second real shock of the day, for Ben Benson came to see her.

She had walked down the drive with Rufe and it occurred to her this time more forcibly that there really was a subtle change in Rufe. It wasn't owing to the story Miss Dotty had told him; he had been perfectly open about that, trusting her, telling her the whole of it. Whatever made an odd kind of barrier between them had nothing to do with his father. But it was there all the same. Was it a threat to his career? Or Lorraine? He kissed her goodnight in an absent way and started across the road. At that moment Ben Benson drove up, stopped his car, leaned out and spoke a few words to Rufe. Then Rufe went on; Ben drove toward the house and saw her, standing at the edge of the drive.

"Bea?"

She came forward. "Yes. Do you want to see Lorraine?"

Ben was a lawyer; he was the youngest member of the legal staff for a large city corporation. He had been born discreet, but had now grown pompous. He turned off the engine of his car. The dashlight shone upward into his plumply stolid face, which, though usually pink, seemed pale and flabby in that light. "The fact is I want to talk to you, Bea. You see—well—it's the judge's memoirs," Ben said in a burst.

"The judge's—" Did all of Valley Ridge know of the memoirs?

Ben said in another burst, "My mother—she's afraid everyone—she's afraid somebody—the police or— She knows that you typed them for the judge. She wants them back—that is, the part that relates to her."

"Ben! Your mother!"

Ben's stubby fingers grasped the wheel. "She—the fact is— there was a time when—" He removed one hand from the wheel and brushed his forehead. "She was a kleptomaniac," he said desperately. "She was caught. The judge fixed things for her."

Eleven

She stared at Ben's face; to her horror a wave of almost hysterical laughter caught her. Mrs. Benson a shoplifter! She had to get control of herself. She mustn't even let her voice quaver.

But then speculations began to whirl through her mind and her suppressed giggle suddenly vanished. Bea imagined her walking through the woods to the back door of the house in such a way that Obrian and the police would not see her. It was almost easier to fancy Mrs. Benson in the role of a kleptomaniac than to envision her crawling in and out the library window and searching Bea's room.

Bea said, "I can't believe you!"

"I'm afraid—yes, it's true. You see—" Ben gulped and went on, "My mother told me all about it last night. My father—well, not many people knew it; I didn't know it, although sometimes I wondered—but I was away at school and —" He seemed to realize that he was incoherent. He took a long breath. "My father was a periodic drunk. My mother did everything she could to stop it. She went through a time of terrific nerve strain. Somehow, nobody knows about these things; maybe a psychiatrist understands, I don't." He stopped himself, wiped his forehead on the back of his hand again and said unhappily, "Anyway, she began to—to shoplift. She said

107

she didn't want the things she took, she had plenty of money to buy anything she wanted but— Anyway, to make it short, somebody caught her in the act. She got hold of the judge, and he fixed things up. Then he got her to go to a good psychiatrist, and he cured her—he and, I'm afraid, my father's death. It's all in the past, long in the past, but those memoirs—you see, the judge had changed so much he might have told the whole story or—oh, for God's sake, Bea, what am I going to do?" He checked himself abruptly as a car turned into the drive behind them. It puffed up the slight slope and stopped. "Hello, Bea," Seth said from the car. "Oh, it's you, Ben. Clara told me to come back tonight."

"She's in the study, I think."

"All right." Seth edged past Ben's car and went on to the steps. His car door banged. The shadows under the old maples and along the stone wall seemed heavy and quiet. Ben said, "You didn't answer me, Bea. What am I going to do?"

Bea replied flatly that she didn't know. "But I can't remember anything at all in the memoirs, Ben, that could possibly connect with your mother, ever!"

Mrs. Benson! Bea still couldn't really believe Ben. Mrs. Benson served on every philanthropic board in Valley Ridge, and was a respected elder of the church. Yet, Bea mused, if at one time she had been so out of balance as to indulge in stealing, could her imbalance have returned? Or—and this was more likely—could the judge have got into one of his moods of setting the world right and threatened to expose her? Could Mrs. Benson—Mrs. Benson!—possibly have shot him?

She'd have had to come to the house, get the judge's gun somehow, and dig out the bullet. Suddenly Bea remembered that at one time Mrs. Benson had taken a course for volunteer nursing; but as far as Bea knew she had never practiced. Still, in a return of imbalance and fear of the judge's disclosure, she could have steeled herself to dig out the bullet, and then entered the house in order to find the memoirs. And it would have been simple enough to discover which cabinet contained the memoirs. The judge himself in one of his Jovelike moods, thundering down denunciation, might have told Mrs. Benson or anyone. It was altogether within the realm of possibility.

Ben said, "Are you sure, Bea?"

Sure? Her thoughts had made so swift a journey of conjecture that she had to think back to his question. "Oh, yes, Ben, I'm sure that there was nothing, ever, that could suggest your mother's name. Besides——" Besides, the Extracurricular file was gone. She decided not to tell him that.

"There's another thing, Bea. I don't know what to do about it. I don't think my mother would want me to——but right is right," Ben said, again with something like desperation in his voice. "It's about Lorraine; and the murder. One of the police questioned me Sunday. The point is Lorraine was not with me at the time they said the judge was murdered."

"I know that. She told me."

"She told you!"

"She said she didn't really have an alibi."

"But she didn't tell the police that. She told them she was with me. So of course I backed her up. But I got to thinking —well, it's a murder case. If it comes to the grand jury, as it will, I'll be a witness. But she did disappear at the dance. I thought she'd gone to meet Cecco. So I left too. I knew Cecco was at Valley Inn. I went there, but since Cecco wasn't there at the time, he doesn't have an alibi. Neither does Lorraine."

"Ben——"

"Oh, I know. I ought not to tell you about it. But I *don't* know what to do. I went to Valley Inn, because I knew that Lorraine was thinking of a divorce. I'm a lawyer, and I knew she ought not to be seeing Cecco or——"

"How did you know that he was here? At Valley Inn?"

"Cecco had phoned me that evening just before dinner. Nobody heard him but me. He said he hadn't any money, and then he waited for me to invite him to stay with us; but, of course, I couldn't. Not with Lorraine there and——everything," Ben said miserably.

"Your mother wouldn't have liked it."

Once Ben broke down his own inhibitions he spoke freely. "Mother wouldn't have liked it at all. She never liked Cecco. She doesn't like Lorraine either, but when Lorraine called and talked to her from New York——"

"Go on."

"It doesn't seem possible that——I mean, Lorraine is so darned attractive. I'm not her kind of man. She's used to a different kind of world. More"——he hunted for a word and came out with it—"glamorous. So I just thought I'd tell the police, yes, she had an alibi, me. I could see the police might make things uncomfortable for her. Because of the judge's— Clara's money."

"I know what you mean."

"Naturally. If I could help her— But I never dreamed she was at the club. I looked for her."

"Did you look on the veranda, that end that's just outside the bar?"

"Why, I really don't know. I just got it into my head that she'd gone to meet Cecco."

"The police inquired at the Inn. Cecco was—at least he was supposed to be in his room."

"He wasn't. Nobody saw me at the Inn. I just walked in and no one was in the hall or at the desk so I went up to Cecco's room. He had told me the number. It made me think that perhaps he expected me to call him or get in touch with him."

"But he wasn't there?"

"No. He could have gone down and out the door without being seen, I suppose. But also, you know how the Inn is built, right along the ridge, so some of the second-floor windows are only three or four feet from the ground. Cecco's room was one of those. All he had to do was open the window and step out. He could have returned the same way."

"But where did he go then?"

"I don't know. I told you, I'm a lawyer," Ben said virtuously. "I hope I have the sense to keep quiet about other people's affairs."

Bea sighed. "You didn't keep very quiet about all this tonight. Really, as far as you know, neither Lorraine nor Cecco has an alibi for that night."

"Lorraine wouldn't kill the judge!"

"And you think Cecco would?"

"I think Cecco would do anything he made up his mind to do. As long as it suited his purpose. And by that"— Ben was suddenly quite forceful— "I mean money. The fact is he asked me for a loan. I refused Cecco— Why, it was nothing short of blackmail."

"Blackmail!"

"Well, you see, when we were both young and Mother sent

110

me on a trip to Europe—well," Ben said unhappily, "I wouldn't want my mother to know much of that trip. But all the same I refused to lend Cecco any money." Then he added, "If I tell the police that Cecco was not at the Inn at the time of the murder, then I have to tell them that I was lying when I gave Lorraine an alibi. On the other hand, if Cecco killed the judge—" Again Ben wiped his forehead. "It's a matter of conscience."

"You'll have to make up your mind, Ben. It'll be hard to admit to having lied."

Ben almost groaned. "Yes. But on the other hand if Cecco—"

"Do you think he killed the judge?"

"I don't know what I think. Except," Ben said, suddenly very firm, "I want to keep out of it. The judge is dead. Nobody can bring him back. I see no purpose served in giving the police a reason to dig into Cecco's past."

He meant his own past.

"You must have really kicked up your heels when you and Cecco traveled around Europe."

"Bea! What a dreadful thing to say! All right then. I'll keep quiet about Cecco."

"Perhaps they ought to know," Bea said seriously, thinking it over.

"I'll think about it. Meantime you'll not tell them. I don't want to get involved. And I'm sure my mother wouldn't want to get involved in anything."

"I don't think your mother should have much to object to about Lorraine—considering . . ." Bea said.

"But that was so long ago. My mother wasn't responsible for her own actions—dreadful, of course. But as long as nobody knows about that—unhappy period of her life—"

"Ben," Bea said forcefully, "why don't you marry Lorraine?"

"But my mother—"

"You're a man. Tell your mother to keep out of your affairs. Good Heavens, Ben, don't you see—"

Ben glared at her through the dim light from the dash. "Really, Bea, I confided in you because I thought you were reliable. Now I'm not at all sure I've done the right thing."

Bea interrupted. "You confided in me because you wanted

111

to make sure that there was nothing in the memoirs that could injure your mother. Oh, for Heaven's sake, Ben, grow up!"

She turned away, boiling with a curious kind of wrath. Mrs. Benson had no right to object to Lorraine. No matter how Lorraine had got her jewels and clothes, Bea was sure she hadn't stolen them. Ben's car started up and backed away down the drive.

But then, thinking of Cecco, Bea had a flash of insight. Cecco had hinted, so broadly that there could be little mistake about it, that Lorraine's jewels and clothes had not been paid for by Cecco; it seemed likely that a man had been buying them for her. This could be the reason for her desire to divorce Cecco; but if Clara knew it, Lorraine might feel that it would alter Clara's affection for her and endanger the prospects for a new will. In effect Lorraine might have promised to share with Cecco any money Clara would eventually leave her. In other words, Cecco could be blackmailing his own wife. Although it was in a sense a reasonable hypothesis it was nonetheless based entirely upon Bea's notion that there was some kind of complicity between Lorraine and Cecco.

She went on into the house; the door to the library was open and she saw Clara and Seth there. "Your aunt wants you to hear about her new will. I have notes about it here." He gestured with a yellow, lined tablet in one hand. "I'll have it drawn up properly tomorrow and then Clara can sign it, put it away and forget all about it."

Bea entered the library. Clara was sitting in the armchair near the enormous writing table where she had sat Sunday morning and read the judge's obituary. The lamp on the table had a green shade so everything in the room was slightly tinged with green. Lorraine was leaning against one of the glass-enclosed bookshelves; Bea thought that she was trying to control her emotions even though her eyes were blazing.

Clara said placidly, "Lorraine has already heard it all but if you will, Seth—"

Seth put on horn-rimmed spectacles, which made him look very studious. "There's no use in reading all of it. In a nutshell it's this, Bea. There are a few small bequests, something to the church, something to Velda Mather—if she is still in your aunt's service—" He smiled slightly. "A not unusual provision. Then there's a scholarship fund for the judge's law school. That's a rather large bequest."

"The judge would have liked that," Clara said firmly.

Seth nodded. Lorraine's hands clenched up against her skirt as if she'd like to tear something apart. Seth continued, "The residual estate—and it is a large one—is to be divided equally between you and Lorraine. I think that's all, Clara."

"Yes." Clara rose. "I love both my girls. They have been like children to me. I am grateful to both of them. However," Clara said with decision, "I intend to live for a very long time."

She took up a packet of envelopes, held together by a rubber band. "Here are the cards that came with the flowers. Will you answer them, Bea?"

Bea took the bundle of cards and went to the study where she left it on the judge's desk. When she came back into the hall, Clara had apparently gone upstairs. Bea went to her aunt's room and found her there holding a photograph of the judge in her hands. She turned to Bea. "My new will is right. You should have half. That's fair. You are not to talk to me about it. It's a weight off my mind. When I die you'll be provided for. Lorraine won't have to take what she can get in— any way she can get it."

She must have seen a flicker of question in Bea's face. "Good Heavens, Bea! Don't you think I can see things. Where would Lorraine get such things as—as a sable stole? Jewels. All those clothes. Cecco has no money. Don't look so surprised. I'm not a child!" She smiled unexpectedly. "Goodnight, my dear. We'll not talk of this further."

It was a definite dismissal. Bea was back in her own room when she remembered all the doors and windows to be checked and went back to the hall below. Seth and Lorraine were standing just outside the open door, and Seth held Lorraine in his arms. She was nestling close to him; his head was bent over her. "Don't cry, Lorraine."

"But it's all wrong! *Half* of it to Bea!"

"Never mind now. Your aunt will have time to change her will a dozen times."

"Not," said Lorraine, "if she should die tonight."

113

Twelve

Bea went out to the terrace. Seth looked up, embarrassed. Lorraine snuggled closer into his arms. "Lorraine is upset about Clara's will," he said.

"Aunt Clara is not going to die tonight," Bea said.

Lorraine's head moved against his shoulder. The light from the hall streamed out upon them and reflected itself, gleaming, against his car below the steps.

"All right, Lorraine," he said, "even if she shouldn't change her will later you'd have plenty to live on."

"But not what I ought to have." Lorraine's voice came out murmuring sadly but stubbornly. He gave her a little—but gentle—shake. "Now, Lorraine! There's nothing you can do about it tonight."

Lorraine's face jerked around toward Bea. "*You* did this! *You* wormed your way in here! All you ever wanted was to get my aunt on your side. She's my aunt, not yours!"

Seth intervened. "I've been wanting to talk to you, Bea. Rufe told me about that thing that happened in the garage—"

"What thing?" Lorraine cried.

"Nothing," Bea said. "The garage doors blew shut. Go on, Seth."

"—and he told me about your room being entered Monday afternoon. I talked to Obrian about it."

"Obrian was here."

"So he told me," Seth said. "He said he searched the house. But then Rufe told me that you thought you saw somebody."

"No, I didn't. I mean yes, I thought there was a movement behind me. I saw it in the mirror. But then it was gone. Later Cecco found a library window open."

"Didn't you have any idea who it was?"

Lorraine was suddenly as still as a cat at a mousehole.

"No. I went across the road and waited."

"That's what Rufe said. Was anything gone? Money or jewelry or anything?"

"I never carry much money. I had only a little in my hand-

114

bag and I had taken that with me to New York that day. Aunt Clara keeps what jewels I have with her own. The safe was closed. Nothing was missing. I don't know what anybody could possibly want. Unless to—well, to frighten me and that makes no sense."

Lorraine said suddenly, "It might make sense! If Cecco has anything to do with it! He could have shut the garage doors. I take it you were inside and—yes, he could have done that—"

"He let me out."

"But not till he'd given you a good scare. Am I right? You needn't answer. I know Cecco."

"But why would he do that?" Seth asked.

"There doesn't need to be a reason for Cecco's doing anything he decides to do! Seth, you will get me a divorce at once."

Cecco appeared from the shadow below the terrace. "Not as soon as all that." He smiled, and his white teeth gleamed.

Seth said peaceably, "I ought to do a little more fence-mending tomorrow. I'll send Joe Lathrop around with the will. Goodnight."

"Seth, wait. Could this—this murder injure Rufe? I mean, his career," Bea began.

Seth shook his head. "No. There isn't the slightest real evidence against Rufe. No jury would believe that one or both of you murdered the judge merely because he opposed your marriage. There was nothing in the world to prevent your getting a license and marrying. In my experience the average jury is very clear in its collective mind about reasonable arguments. And remember, Bea, that if someone really was in the house Monday afternoon, it couldn't have been Rufe. He was in Washington that day."

"There was somebody," Bea said stubbornly.

"Then Obrian ought to have seen him. Don't worry, Bea. Get some rest. It's been a very hard day for all of us."

He contrived to move away from Lorraine's clutching arm, and got into his car. Its red rear lights had gone down the drive and turned toward Stony Road before Lorraine sighed. "He's certainly distinguished-looking."

Cecco laughed. "Get your divorce first, Lorraine. You can't marry anybody until you've divorced me."

"Wait till you hear what Aunt Clara—" Lorraine checked

115

herself. Cecco's smile vanished. His eyes narrowed. Bea said bluntly, "I want to close up the house."

Both Cecco and Lorraine followed her again as she made the tour of doors and windows, and watched again as she set the alarm.

But she had the talk with Ben in her mind. Suddenly she decided to face Cecco with the part of it that effected him. "Cecco, the night the judge was murdered you were not at the Inn as you told the police."

Lorraine grasped it at once, her eyes glittering. "Who told you that?"

Bea ignored the question. "Where did you go, Cecco? Why?"

"I didn't come here and kill the judge." But Cecco, too, was sharply curious. "Who told you that I wasn't at the Inn?"

"It doesn't matter. Where did you go?"

"There is no reason why I should tell you. But I suppose you'll go to the police with this—". Cecco's slender hands made a deprecating gesture. "If you must know, I simply walked out of the Inn and started toward the Benson place to see Ben. But I had forgotten the way. I must have walked miles on these winding roads. Finally I found the way back to the Inn. Nobody saw me leave or return. I did *not* come here. As long as the people at the Inn thought that I was there all the time, why should I tell the police any different?"

Oddly, it sounded true. However, Lorraine's face seemed to tighten with speculation. Cecco saw that. "No, darling, you can't frighten me. I was *not* here. You can't make some neat little plan to suggest to the police that I had anything to do with the judge's murder so—" Cecco smiled but there was cruelty in that smile. "I don't advise you to try it."

Lorraine seemed to think that over. Then she said, "I don't believe he did come here, Bea. He would be afraid of the judge."

Bea, too, believed Cecco. She went into her own room, aware that both of them stood watching her as she closed the door. There was an air of poise in their stillness, as if they were only waiting for a real quarrel—over Clara's will, over Cecco's lack of an alibi. Over anything.

They did quarrel, immediately after entering Lorraine's room. Bea could hear their voices; Lorraine's at first was cool and composed, while Cecco's became angry. This seemed to

116

arouse a like explosion in Lorraine. At last Bea went into the hall, afraid they would wake Clara. She was about to knock on the door when she heard Cecco say, loudly, "—resident! So what do you think of that?"

Lorraine didn't reply for a long moment. Then she said loudly, too, *"How do you know?"*

"I hear things. It may be only gossip. Your aunt and Bea seem to know nothing of it. But—" Cecco's voice lowered.

Resident, Bea thought. Could some question of Cecco's possible one-time residency in America have arisen? The police might have arrived at a fact about Cecco which none of them had known. If so, they were putting the lives of everybody associated with the judge through a very fine mesh of inquiry. She didn't like Mrs. Benson. She could see now why, although the judge had assisted her, he had never seemed to like her. All the same Bea hoped that the police would not discover the long past shoplifting phase. But if Cecco had in fact lived for some time in America, perhaps in New York, what could that have to do with the judge's murder?

Both Lorraine's and Cecco's voices had fallen into an angry kind of murmur. Just then Clara opened her door, saw Bea and beckoned to her. "What are they quarreling about?"

"I don't know. I was about to tell them not to wake you."

Clara listened. The voices were now very low. She sighed. "Let them quarrel. I suppose it's something about my will. But I really couldn't include Cecco. Not after the way he's treated Lorraine. Oh, I suppose she hasn't treated him very well either. I think they've quieted now." She turned without another word and went back into her own room and closed the door. Bea was still standing in the hall when Cecco flung Lorraine's door wide open.

"I thought I heard someone! Listening at keyholes, Bea?"

"I couldn't help hearing some of it. Please let Aunt Clara have some rest."

Cecco's handsome face with its arched eyebrows and high cheekbones seemed, in the dim light of the hall, more than ever like a portrait of some old-time Spanish grandee—about to give orders to send somebody to torture, Bea thought briefly. "What did you hear?" he demanded.

"Nothing much really. I only knew that you were quarreling."

Lorraine appeared behind him. Cecco's dark eyes gleamed.

117

"You think you've got your aunt's new will all arranged, Lorraine. So now you cast me off. You promised to share her money with me."

"I promised you nothing," she retorted.

"Ah, but you did. And you know what happens to anybody who breaks his word with me. I'm going to tell your aunt all about the man who gave you those jewels, furs, clothes. *I* couldn't give them to you. But when she hears about him—"

Bea broke in sharply, "Aunt Clara knows."

Cecco's face went stony with surprise. "And yet she is making Lorraine a co-heir to all her money? I don't believe it!"

"It's true. She is nobody's fool. That's one of the reasons she wanted to make sure that Lorraine would have enough money so she wouldn't feel that she had to—take money from anybody."

Lorraine's mouth had opened and stayed open. Cecco seemed to retreat within himself. After a moment Lorraine gave a triumphant giggle. "So what about it, Cecco? What can you do?"

He turned to face her. "I think there may be something I can do. Yes, I think there's something—" He went off toward his room without looking back.

Lorraine watched him now soberly. She looked even a little frightened. "When Cecco acts like that he's got something in mind. I don't like it."

Bea felt that she had had all the emotional storms which she could survive that night. "I'm going to bed."

"Wait a minute." Lorraine followed her into her room and carefully closed the door. "Is it true? Does Aunt Clara know all about Benito?"

Another Ben, Bea thought wearily. "She doesn't know his name. She just knows that there had to be somebody. Are you going to marry him?"

Lorraine's eyes opened wide. "Marry him! Good Heavens! Why should I?"

Bea said in spite of herself, "There must be good and sufficient reasons."

"Reasons? Because we were good friends," Lorraine said smoothly, "for so long? It was a great bore."

Bea stared at Lorraine. Somehow way in the back of Bea's mind an image of a dramatic, all conquering love affair had built itself up.

118

Lorraine giggled. "Don't look so stunned. Oh, we liked one another after a fashion. He is a brilliant man, too. Knows all sorts of important people. Not that I got to meet many of them. We had to be very discreet. There were two very good reasons why we didn't marry. First, Benito's wife's family is very influential: a divorce is still not looked on with favor in Italy. It might have cost Benito his position; besides, his first interests really were his wife and children. But the other reason is, the whole thing became a great bore. Actually, it was a bit of a bore from the beginning, and in the end we were both so tired of all the nonsense of making excuses and trying to keep—our friendship a secret that both of us were thankful to break it off. He was always very generous. Gave me a nice little sum so I could come back home. It was an easy way out for both of us. Dear old Benito! But marriage. My dear, what an idea!"

"Cecco knew about it."

"Of course. As a matter of fact I expect a number of people knew about it. Benito was important in his way. He was also more than a match for Cecco. I've never known for sure, but I've always suspected that Cecco tried to get money out of Benito—if he did, Benito didn't tell me. It would have been too humiliating to me. Benito was always kind— You needn't look so surprised, Bea. You know only the Valley Ridge world, not the world Cecco introduced me to. Maybe sometimes," Lorraine said with one of her moments of candor, "I wished I hadn't known that world. However, the point is, Cecco agreed to keep quiet about Benito if I would borrow on my expectations and give it to him when Aunt Clara made a new will. But tonight, when I heard the terms of her will—that I was to get only half of her money—I decided I'd have nothing to do with Cecco's scheme. The will is to be signed tomorrow. I don't think Aunt Clara is going to write another one, putting me out of it entirely. At least—well, of course, the way she acts she may write any number of wills. But I—" Lorraine frowned. "It was a poor idea of Cecco's. He had me frightened for a while. But when I thought it over I decided I wouldn't go along with him. So I told Cecco I didn't feel bound by any promise to him. He was very angry. He thought he had quite a firm hold over me. But as you see, he hasn't. Aunt Clara has eyes in her head," Lorraine said with a touch of admiration. "I really thought she was rather an old fool."

"She isn't," Bea said.

But Lorraine went back to Cecco. "When I married Cecco I thought I was getting money, a title, a social position, a fine home, all that. The judge saw through Cecco. He may even have inquired about him somewhere. I don't know. I was a great fool. But honestly, Bea, I don't think Cecco killed the judge. He really is a coward. Oh, he'll do small, mean things, anything for money, but he would never actually face the judge, get his gun away from him, induce him to go down to the wall and shoot him. Not Cecco. So I see no reason to tell the police about the fact that Cecco has no alibi for the time of the judge's murder. Is that all Ben told you?"

"He said you weren't with him for an hour or so."

"Is he going to tell that to the police?"

"I don't know. He was trying to make up his mind."

Lorraine chewed a little on her lower lip. "It'll put Ben in an odd position if he tells the police he was lying for me."

"I don't think he will. He doesn't want to get involved."

Lorraine gave a sudden giggle. "I'd like to see his mother's face if he did that! Goodnight, Bea."

She strolled away.

The house was all at once too quiet. It had been a strange, long day. Somehow, among all the images her memory of the day presented to her, Mrs. Benson—a shoplifter—came first.

She sought in her memory for that portion of the judge's memoirs which he had called Extracurricular Activities. These were rambling dissertations about courts of law, about his quarrels or disagreements—always victorious as the judge told them—with other members of the various boards or trusteeships of which he was a member at one time or another. In some of these memories the judge broke his rule of discretion and named names. There was the library board, the school board, a bank trusteeship, and almost every philanthropic enterprise in Valley Ridge. But even though Bea would leave blanks for the judge to fill in later when his words ran together on the dictaphone, she was sure there had been no mention of shoplifting; she'd have remembered that.

However, amid all the faces of the day, Rufe's became the important one. There was that small, indefinable difference in him. She was dismally afraid that something had been said by his superior concerning her own possible involvement in murder. So it was impossible to marry Rufe until the murderer

120

was convicted. Lorraine would certainly want another husband. She had nestled her head close to Seth, a senator. But Rufe had once been in love with her.

In the morning Rufe and Lorraine disappeared together. Velda saw them, and when Bea came down to breakfast she told her, "They went off together in Rufe's car. I don't know where they were going. I took your aunt's breakfast up to her. She's tired, and no wonder. All that, yesterday. She says young Joe Lathrop is to bring a new will for her to sign some time today. She told me to remind you about those cards that came with the flowers and all those telegrams and letters."

The telegrams were on the judge's desk along with the bundle of cards. Bea spent most of the day writing thank-you notes. Rufe and Lorraine did not return. Sometime after lunch, which Bea had on a tray in the judge's study, Cecco lounged in, watched her for a moment and then settled himself gracefully in a chair. There was nothing about him to remind her of the sense of threat which she had glimpsed in his narrow face the previous night. All the same she wished he would leave; it was as if a slender and elegant spider were sitting at ease but curiously thoughtful and quiet, as if waiting for a chance to strike. She forced herself to keep on steadily writing notes which had by now acquired set phrases.

During the afternoon she heard Clara trotting around overhead in the judge's room. She had promptly seen to her will. Now probably she was working at the next chore, sorting the judge's clothes and belongings, what to be given away, what to keep. Late in the afternoon Lorraine returned, breezing up across the terrace and in the study door. Cecco rose lithely and without a word went out. Lorraine lifted her eyebrows. "What's he doing?"

"Nothing, as far as I know." Bea rubbed her tired hand.

"You can never tell about Cecco." Lorraine flung her hair back in her habitual and this time triumphant gesture. "I've been out with Rufe all day. He's as much in love with me as ever. Of course, being the man he is, he'll expect you to release him from his engagement to you. He wouldn't ask you himself."

121

Thirteen

Bea leaned back in the judge's chair. Lorraine slid down into the chair Cecco had left. "I hope you'll take it sensibly, Bea. Although of course I've got to make up my mind. Rufe—after all he's no great catch. But he adores me."

Like a fresh breeze through the room Bea's common sense operated. To her own surprise she laughed.

Lorraine sat up. "Don't you believe me?"

"Not a word," Bea said cheerfully.

Lorraine thought for a moment, her green eyes bright. "Why not?"

"Because it isn't true, that's all. Why are you lying to me like this?"

Lorraine shifted her position and leaned over so her hair almost hid her lovely face. "I was only thinking that—if you really want him, I'll see to it that you get him. But I want—"

Bea eyed her. "Money?"

"Why not?"

"But I have no money . . . Oh"—a wave of enlightenment came to Bea—"you're thinking of Aunt Clara's will."

Lorraine nodded.

"Aunt Clara is alive and well. She's much sturdier than you seem to think." Bea borrowed from Seth. "She'll have time to make a dozen wills." It was not really hard to find a way through Lorraine's tortuous reasoning. "Are you thinking of a bargain with me?"

"Bargain?" But her voice was entirely too innocent.

Bea didn't even have to grope her way; she spoke, however slowly. "A trade, I suppose. Is that it? You give up Rufe and I try to influence Aunt Clara so she changes her will—"

Lorraine lifted her head boldly. "Of course! Perfectly simple! You talk Aunt Clara into giving me a larger share of her money, and I'll give up Rufe. Of course, I don't mean that you should be cut out of her will entirely but—"

Bea interrupted. "No! For one reason, Aunt Clara is no pushover. She thinks out what she intends to do and then she

122

does it. And another reason is— Oh, Lorraine, how can you be so silly! You can't give up Rufe. He doesn't belong to you to begin with!"

Lorraine thought for a long moment. "But the little money Benito gave me—that is, it was very generous of him of course and all that—but it's not going to last me very long."

"Rufe has no money either. Even when he gets his appointment it will be a minor one. It'll take years—"

"Yes, I thought of that." Lorraine had one of her waves of candor. "He may rise in his career and he may not. I can't exactly see myself waiting around for him to advance and in the meantime doing all the things the wife of a Foreign Service officer is supposed to do."

Bea replied, as she had once said to the judge, "If that kind of thing ever existed it's in the past."

"It's like being the wife of a low-rank officer in the Navy or the Army."

"No. Not any more. The wife of a Foreign Service officer is a private citizen, Lorraine. You don't want Rufe anyway. Why don't you marry Seth?"

"Suppose Seth comes to nothing! Suppose he has to come back here and take up life as a small-town lawyer again."

Bea stared at Lorraine. "You really have thought of everything, haven't you?"

"Not quite," Lorraine said. "Wouldn't you like to know what Rufe and I did today? I'll tell you. We drove and drove in Rufe's old car. We stopped at places where we used to go. On the way home we had a drink at Cobb's Mill. Then we stopped at the Westport Playhouse. It was still closed for the winter, of course, but we looked around. Do you think Rufe would take me on such a drive if he didn't want to?"

"I don't know."

But Rufe wouldn't have taken Lorraine on a long and apparently sentimental journey if he didn't want to, that much was true. Bea bent over her notes again and Lorraine gave a short laugh and went out of the room.

Bea was eying a letter absently when Obrian came. He brought her, wrapped in brown paper, her dressing gown. "They didn't see any need for keeping this," he told her. "It was natural for you to lean over the judge and try to help him."

123

She took the package. "Does that mean they don't think I —I shot him?"

Obrian's face took on a guarded and unnatural expression; as a rule, he was good-natured and frank. "I don't know what it means or what they think. Bea—"

He sat down at her gesture, crossed his legs one way, then the other way. It struck her that he was embarrassed, so she braced herself for his next question. It wasn't what she expected. "Bea, that file of the judge's memoirs—"

"Yes—"

"You transcribed them, didn't you?"

"Yes."

"To tell you the truth," he burst out, "I've been kind of worried about them."

"*You*—"

"He may have said something about me!"

Did *everybody* in Valley Ridge at some time or other ask the judge for help and now expect to find himself in his memoirs! Bea was caught again by an almost hysterical mirth.

"I couldn't do anything about them," Obrian said. "I had to just wait and see if the police or those detectives found anything. I'll not say it was easy for me. It's been hell, waiting. Now they've apparently finished looking through the memoirs and nobody has said a word to me so— But if I could be *sure* there is nothing . . ."

Bea choked back her helpless laughter and said, astounded, "What did you *do?*"

He stopped looking embarrassed and turned pale. "I took a bribe."

"*You*—I can't believe it!"

"The judge gave me the money. That is, it wasn't his money. It was from somebody else. I was in a situation that —well, I had just bought a house. I had a heavy mortgage on it. My wife was ill. I was desperate for money or I wouldn't have considered a bribe. The judge didn't like offering it to me either. But he said it would help."

Bea's thoughts made a convincing leap. "Mrs. Benson!"

"So you did find that in the memoirs."

"No, I didn't. Ben told me. He was upset about it. His mother had told him."

"Oh." Obrian studied her face. "She'd been picked up for shoplifting and asked the judge to help her. I felt sorry for her. The judge—she gave him money, she said, to show her appreciation if"—Obrian swallowed with a gulp—"if I let her off. Quietly. So nobody knew about it. I expect she paid off the jeweler; she'd picked up some trifle, I don't remember what. But the judge put it to me so forcefully! He explained her shoplifting to me. She promised to go to a psychiatrist. The judge told me it would be all right, she wouldn't do anything of the kind again. And she didn't," he ended with an air of relief.

"There was nothing about that in his memoirs."

"Are you sure?"

"Unless he told it in such general terms that even when I transcribed it I didn't think of Mrs. Benson. Or you."

He looked around at the cupboard where she kept the used tapes. "What about those dictated tapes? Could he have said something there?"

"No. I typed every one of them. Then I used them for French practice. After that, when we'd get to the end of the supply we'd start over again."

"The state police have them, haven't they?"

"They're perfectly worthless." But she went over to the cupboard. "Yes, the police must have taken them. But I had used each one. I'd do French verbs or read something and then listen to myself and correct my pronunciation whenever I could."

Obrian said thoughtfully, "They'll get somebody who can understand French to read them, I suppose."

With another quiver of mirth Bea thought of somebody sitting down and intently listening to her fumbles over verbs or her faulty reading of "La Dernière Leçon" or "Le Voyage de M. Perrichon." She wondered if they would get hold of a native Frenchman who was likely to have some hysterics of his own, listening to her. A student from Yale was a possibility; what he would make of them she couldn't guess.

"The memoirs were all arranged in sections. Childhood, school days, university—" She stopped abruptly. There was the Extracurricular file. Obrian had had a chance to enter the house Monday, when no one was at home. But that was wrong. The detectives had looked through the files on Saturday. Almost certainly the Extracurricular file had to be gone before Saturday, that and the Juvenile Court file, for the police had neither returned them nor inquired about them. Further, if Obrian had helped himself to that particular file, he wouldn't now be talking of it. "You must have felt horrible," she said. "Why didn't you just tell the police?"

He heaved an enormous sigh. "You don't know what you're talking about! Even now, after all these years, the taking of a bribe—no, no, I couldn't tell anybody. I just had to wait it out. There was nothing else I could do. I wish Mrs. Benson had taken to shoplifting in some other town."

Bea came back to the judge's desk. "So do I." She hesitated and then decided. "I'd better tell you that there are two missing files. One is what the judge called his Extracurricular Activities."

Obrian stared at her. "Oh, my God."

"I typed them all. I don't remember much that was in that file but there was nothing"—she searched back in her memory—"really *nothing*, Mr. Obrian, that seemed to refer to you."

"Who took the files? You said two are missing."

"Besides the one he called Extracurricular Activities there was one about his term as judge of the juvenile court, and I don't know who took them. Perhaps the state police. I didn't know they were gone until last night."

The experienced police officer abruptly came forth in Obrian. "How did you happen to look in the files last night?"

She thought swiftly: He doesn't know about that suit for malpractice which the judge fixed. "I just happened to. I wondered if they were all there," she added rather lamely.

Obrian seemed to detect her hesitation. "Had the judge fixed things for somebody else?"

"Please, Mr. Obrian."

He rose. "You're not going to tell me who."

"But it—but I—" She took a quick breath. "It's not important."

"The judge was quite a fixer, wasn't he? But the people trusted him. Everybody went to him with troubles. Of course, lately he'd changed. If he got something on his mind that he thought ought to be stopped he'd try to stop it." He brooded for a moment and added, "But he knew I didn't like that bribe from Mrs. Benson. He always trusted me."

She wondered who next would turn up to accuse himself of appearing in the memoirs. Obrian straightened up. "Anything else you haven't told me?"

Anything? Why, yes! He didn't know that after he'd gone Monday, she'd been sure that someone was in the house. She told him quickly.

He listened, all police officer now, and shook his head. "But what could anybody want? I can't make anything of it unless someone else thought he was in the memoirs. By the way, this husband of Lorraine's. Our state police have been in touch with the Italian police, Lieutenant Abbott told me. But there doesn't seem to be anything very revealing so far. Cecco seems to have spent money but didn't have a steady income, not that anybody knows about. There was a hint that he might have been involved in drug rackets but nothing factual enough to make a case of it. He seems to have managed to get fast cars, maybe fast women. Too bad Lorraine didn't take the judge's advice about not marrying him. But Lorraine was always headstrong and somehow everybody in Valley Ridge got the notion that Cecco was rich and had a fine place in Italy." Suddenly Obrian turned a rich red. "They had some things to report about Lorraine, too. Oh, nothing criminal. That is—well, it seems she was the friend—the special friend —of a man there who is very rich. A guy—I can't pronounce his name—"

"His first name is Benito."

"Huh?"

"She told me. That's all over."

"Don't let your aunt hear about it."

"Oh, she knows. That is, she guessed. Lorraine has such good clothes and jewels and—she guessed."

Obrian sighed. "I always said your aunt had more sense than anybody gave her credit for. Furthermore," he said with unexpected perspicuity, "she had the good sense not to let the judge know that she has a good head on her shoulders. He had to be the authority. Of course, lately there was no telling what he might get into his head and worry himself about and — Try to find those missing files, Bea. Especially the— What did he call it?"

"Extracurricular Activities. But it's only a string of anecdotes. Not even very interesting to me as I typed them up. Truly, Mr. Obrian, your name isn't there. As a matter of fact —" Bea was struck rather vividly by that recollection— "I don't think he used many names. He was too cautious of libel

127

or slander. But writing, or rather dictating, kept him entertained and busy."

"Entertained," Obrian said thoughtfully. "I'm not sure I like that idea. The judge was a good man, respected. But lately he could be mean, you know. Headstrong and—mean."

Without another word Obrian went wearily away. Bea listened for his car as it went slowly down the drive. He wouldn't be easy in his mind until the missing file was found; neither would Mrs. Benson if she ever learned of its disappearance.

She pushed back the notes she had written. It was getting late; the afternoon sun sent a rosy glow over the terrace. She heard footsteps on the gravel of the drive. Rufe came along the terrace and looked in the door. "Bea? Can I come in?"

He entered and sat down wearily, then stuck out his long legs and stared at his scuffed loafers. "I didn't accomplish much," he said.

"You took Lorraine for a very long drive." She couldn't help saying it, but Rufe didn't even look up.

"Oh, sure. I was backing out of our drive when she saw me and before I could say anything she hopped in and said she wanted a drive. On the way home we stopped at places she wanted to see again. That was after I had visited Millwood."

"Millwood!" Millwood was a correctional institute for minor offenders.

"I keep thinking that Cecco simply must have been here in America during his childhood. He couldn't possibly pick up such a natural American idiom and pronunciation otherwise. The Juvenile Court file has been taken. I'm sure the police don't have it. If they did have it and kept it for some kind evidence I think they would have questioned you and Aunt Clara or—oh, somebody.

"And then, you see, Cecco mentioned the time when you had braces on your teeth. How did he know that if he had seen you only when he first knew Lorraine and you were in your teens? You'd stopped wearing braces by then. Perhaps Cecco had lived somewhere near here before, and he could have come up before the judge and been sent to Millwood. It would have been a long time ago. The names of minors are never published. Cecco could have felt himself entirely safe. But that may have been the reason the judge was opposed to Lorraine's marriage."

"I'm sure I never saw Cecco before he started coming to see Lorraine," Bea said after long thought. "Wouldn't Aunt Clara know about it if he'd been sent to Millwood?"

"I doubt it. She's often said that the judge never talked to her about his cases. Of course, there may be nothing to know. It's only Cecco's American way of talking, the braces on your teeth, and the missing file."

"But what could a minor, a boy of sixteen or under, do that would make him an undesirable husband for Lorraine years later?"

Rufe shrugged. "You knew the judge. Anything at all."

"Did you find any records at Millwood referring to Cecco?"

"No. That is, in the first place they were very cagey about giving anybody a look, even at old records. Quite right of course. However, in the end I got hold of an old-timer who knew the judge, told him why I wanted to know if anybody who might have been Cecco had been in the place years ago. He had a very clear memory. He went through records of more than thirty-odd years back. He said it wasn't proper but rules were made to be broken and kind of smiled at me. He connec over everything. There were some boys with foreign-sounding names, but not Cecco di Pallici. Usually the offenses were breaking and entering. He said that he remembered the judge took a great interest in all the boys he had sent to Millwood, tried to get them onto the right course, used his influence about getting them into schools, all that kind of thing. The judge was young then. Only in his mid-thirties. In his day," Rufe said with real respect, "he was a great man."

"But there was nothing about Cecco?"

"Nothing."

"Where was Lorraine while you were at Millwood?"

"Watching a movie." Rufe grinned. "I told her I had to look up something in the Millwood library and it would take a while. She couldn't fancy herself just sitting in the car waiting."

"Sometime you'll really be a diplomat."

"I'll try," Rufe said with a grin.

Just then Lorraine, with her customary flair for entering the room at the most inconvenient time, came in. She had changed to a thin green wool dress.

"Rufe! Did you tell Bea what a lovely ride we had today?"

Rufe paid no attention to that. "Lorraine, when did Cecco first come to America?"

"After you'd gone to Vietnam, Rufe. And then Cecco and I fell in love and were married. That is, I thought I was in love. I was wrong——"

"How did he happen to come to Valley Ridge?"

"Why, he knew Ben Benson. They had met somewhere, in Paris I think. Maybe in London. I don't remember. It was during a trip Ben took while he was still in the university. Anyway they seem to have become friends. So when he came to America and I met him, the Bensons had invited him to stay with them. I don't think," Lorraine said in her candid manner, "Ben's mother liked Cecco much. She didn't really want me to stay with them for a few days when I came home Wednesday and phoned them from New York. I could tell. Her precious Ben."

"The Bensons are very rich," Rufe said rather dryly.

"Oh, yes. But Heavens! That Ben! I have never in my life seen anybody so pompous. The girl who gets him won't have an easy life of it."

"She'll have money."

"Yes." There was now a trace of wistfulness in Lorraine's voice. "But how would anybody pry money out of Ben? Besides it was all left to his mother and she'll live to be a hundred. Oh, Ben is no catch."

"So he knew Cecco."

"Oh, yes."

"You're sure that was Cecco's first visit to America?"

Lorraine shot a swift glance at Rufe. "Ask Cecco. I don't know everything about him. It's almost time for dinner. I'll see about cocktails, Bea."

She sauntered out nonchalantly.

Rufe said, "Doesn't know or doesn't want to answer. I've got to get home for dinner. Miss Dotty will take a knife to me if I don't." He heard his own words and looked all at once rather white. "I didn't mean that."

"No, I know. We used to laugh and call her——"

"Madame Defarge. But she—I'll see you." He left.

He was not changed at all, Bea told herself, and yet knew that there *was* some difference, something too deliberately calm and yet tense about him. She couldn't analyze the dif-

130

ference but it was there, like an intangible wall between them. Yet he seemed as frank and open with her as ever.

She took the package Obrian had returned to her, uneasily aware of her stained dressing gown, then thought of Lorraine and Rufe—and suddenly became suspicious of Miss Dotty. But Miss Dotty, devoted though she was to the doctor, would not have shot the judge. The fact of the malpractice suit was buried in the accumulation of years.

But Dr. Thorne couldn't be more than in his middle fifties. He had every reason to look forward to many years of practice unless somebody or something checked his activity. A malpractice suit, even though it had happened years ago and had been covered and kept a secret, would, if it were known, throw mud, and a little mud always sticks. Miss Dotty would have protected the doctor in any way she could. She was quite capable of probing for a bullet.

Bea put the dressing gown in her bathroom laundry hamper, hating to touch it, and changed her dress.

When she went downstairs again, Clara had not yet come down. Lorraine was apparently still in the pantry mixing cocktails. Only Cecco sat in the living room and eyed Bea with a trace of malicious mischief in his dark eyes. He rose gracefully. "Dear Bea, I hoped for a moment alone with you."

"You sat in the study with me most of the afternoon."

"Oh, well, what I have to say didn't occur to me then. The point is, are you going to let Lorraine take your young Rufe away from you?"

"No," Bea said bluntly.

Cecco's slender eyebrows rose. "Dear child! You are so sure of yourself."

"I'm sure of Rufe, if that's what you mean." But in her heart she wondered again—was she really so sure?

Cecco eyed her. "Men have long memories, dear child. Now that Lorraine and Rufe have seen one another again—"

Bea interrupted sharply, "Cecco, when were you first in America?"

"My dear Bea! You know that. It was when I met your cousin Lorraine and fell in love with her."

"That was the first time?"

"In America or the first time I fell in love?"

"You know what I mean."

"I came here to stay with the Bensons, at Ben's invitation. I met Lorraine. She had a notion then that she was in love with this young Rufe Thorne. That didn't last long."

"Lorraine said that you knew Ben Benson in Paris. Or London."

"You asked her? How unimportant. But, of course. We met —let me see—in London. When we were both very young."

"How did you happen to meet?"

Cecco sat forward, his black eyebrows now drawn into a frowning line. "What are you getting at? There's no dark secret about our meeting. Although"—his eyebrows went up again and he smiled—"his mother might not like to hear about it. We met actually over a roulette table."

No, not even the former shoplifter would like that. Cecco went on, his eyes dancing again with a certain malice. "As I say, we were both young. But I had seen something of the world. Ben hadn't. I rather gathered that his mother kept him tied to her apron strings. However, she had released a generous sum of money to permit him to enjoy the culture of Europe, he told me. So we enjoyed European culture, on Ben's money. Horses, gaming clubs—"

"So when you came here to America at that time you intended to see Ben and—"

"Get more money out of him? Why, Bea, what a naughty thought."

"*Did* you get more money out of him?"

Cecco sobered. A reflective look came again into his mobile face. "I thought I did. I was wrong."

"You mean Lorraine."

"Naturally. He introduced us. Here was her rich aunt and Lorraine, I understood, had fine prospects."

"Was Ben glad to see you?"

"I wouldn't say glad. But he invited me to stay with him. Introduced me to his friends. However, Ben had changed. Grown stodgy, adult, had a position in some law firm in the city by then. Possibly," Cecco said delicately, "he really didn't want reminders of his youthful—not excesses but certainly impulses. However, he invited me here."

"And you exercised a neat little blackmail to get him to do that."

"Blackmail! Why, Bea! Truly a naughty thought doesn't become you."

"A naughty thing like blackmail doesn't become anybody," Bea said shortly. "Mrs. Benson must have had some notion that you and Ben had gone about together in Europe."

"I really don't know whether Mrs. Benson knew anything of those tiny blots on her Ben's spotless soul. She wasn't very nice to me. But Ben did take me around and I met Lorraine. And if you want to know why she wishes a divorce, it's because she intends to find another husband."

Fourteen

Lorraine, lovely in her pale green wool, carried the cocktail tray into the room. Cecco sprang up to assist her.

Clara came in, and Cecco served cocktails. Lorraine chattered of her long drive with Rufe that afternoon. "And coming home we stopped at Cobb's Mill and had drinks. Nothing had changed much. The same old swans."

"The same old you?" Cecco inquired, smiling.

Clara frowned a little but said nothing. Clara took her place for the first time in the judge's big chair at the head of the table. When she saw that, Velda's eyes popped. Halfway through dinner the telephone rang and Velda, having answered it, relayed a message. "It was Joe Lathrop. He says he's got your new will typed up and ready for signature, Mrs. Bartry."

"Good," Clara said. "Ask him to bring it here now."

Lorraine and Cecco were both very, very still. Clara said, "We'll have coffee, Velda."

Rufe came with Joe Lathrop. "I stopped and asked him to come along," Joe said cheerily. "We need some witnesses to your signature, Mrs. Bartry."

Again both Lorraine and Cecco became extremely quiet.

Clara suggested that they move into the judge's study. "The big desk there," she said and led the way. Joe sat down opposite her and pulled papers from the briefcase he carried.

133

Clara slowly read every word of the document. There was only the sound of the few pages turning. Finally she reached for the pen, signed her name to the will and to the copy. "Joe?"

Joe leaned over to sign his name as a witness to Clara's signatures. She nodded and said, "Rufe?"

Rufe was eying something on the desk rather closely; he shoved the mass of letters, blotters, writing paper aside and signed the will and the copy.

"All right. Now what do you want me to do with these, Mrs. Bartry?" Joe was being very businesslike.

"I'll put one of them in my safe-deposit box as soon as I can get into it. Do you know when the appraisers will be through with it, Joe?"

Cecco sat up alertly. "Appraisers?"

Joe glanced at him. "It's the law. A safe-deposit box—Mrs. Bartry and the judge used a joint box—is sealed until the appraisers have had a chance to go through it."

"Why?" Cecco said blankly.

Joe allowed himself an unprofessional frown. "For the inheritance taxes of course. Every item in the box must be examined; everything belonging to the judge therefore belongs to his estate and is taxable as such."

Clara eyed her copy of the new will. "The appraisers can take their time. It's not urgent for me. But, Joe, do you know anything about the inquest? When it will take place, and where?"

"No, Mrs. Bartry. But it may be, oh—some time before they get around to it."

"Why so long?" Cecco asked.

Joe was annoyed and frowned. "Several reasons. The medical examiner has made his statement, all that is on record. But one very good reason for not requiring an immediate inquest is that the people concerned are—sometimes, I mean—in an emotional state and their evidence may not be entirely accurate."

Cecco did not look convinced. Clara said, "I wish they'd get it over with. Meeth killed him. No doubt of it." She took the original draft of her will. "Keep the copy in your office safe, will you, Joe?"

"Certainly." Joe had two large envelopes, each with the

legend Last Will and Testament in ornate black letters. Clara took her envelope. Joe said, "I think that's all. Feel better about things, Mrs. Bartry?" Young Joe assumed an experience in legal affairs he couldn't possibly have had. "People always do, you know. As if a load had been taken off their minds."

"I expect we ought to have some port on such an occasion," Clara said.

Bea thought rapidly and was about to say, there isn't any, when Joe thanked Clara and said he had to leave. Rufe and Joe said goodnight and left together. There was still in Rufe's pleasant glance something that disturbed Bea, something that seemed to divide them.

Clara had gone calmly away, clasping her copy of the new will. Lorraine had disappeared with her. Cecco sat back in a lounge chair gazing off into space. Bea bent over the desk to rearrange the oddments, which had been shoved out of the way to give space for signing the will. As she picked up some envelopes and a blotter she saw the judge's gold cigar case below them.

She knew it well. She could almost see the judge's gnarled hands turning it over and over. He did not use it much, he complained to Bea privately, saying the cigars dried in it. But Clara had given it to him, so he carried it all the time and pretended to make use of it. The case had not been there during the day. In fact, she could not remember seeing it at all after the judge's murder. So who had had it? Who had placed it on the desk and then neatly covered it with papers, envelopes and blotters?

Joe had shoved aside some of the papers to give a clear space for Clara and again for himself when he signed the will as witness. Rufe had done the same thing, rather swiftly. But Rufe could not have had the gold cigar case.

"What's the matter, Bea?" Cecco said lazily, yet with the sharpness in his eyes which Bea was beginning not only to dislike but to fear.

"Nothing." She put the cigar case in a drawer and rose.

As usual Cecco walked lithely behind her as she made the tour of the house. He laughed softly when she locked the kitchen door. "Velda doesn't seem to think it necessary to lock a door."

135

"It never was necessary—until lately."

He followed her up the stairs, and watched as she set the alarm.

She was almost asleep when the telephone rang. Clara apparently answered with the extension in her room. A moment later she came to Bea's door, said, "May I come in, Bea?" and entered.

She had wrapped her plumply pretty figure in a pale blue dressing gown. As usual her hair was netted. Yes, Bea thought, remembering Rufe's observation, Clara was a very attractive woman.

"That was Seth on the phone," Clara began. "He's just got back from Bridgeport, and wanted to know if Joe Lathrop had brought the will around. I asked him about Meeth. The police don't seem to be sure of their case against Meeth. I don't see how they can be so stupid. Nobody—*nobody* else would have killed the judge. He was a good man."

He was also a selfish, domineering and obstinate man, Bea thought, in spite of herself.

"I just thought I'd tell you." Then suddenly she asked, "When are you and Rufe going to get married?"

"I don't know."

Clara's eyes sharpened. "You sound undecided. You can't mean that Rufe is letting himself be taken in by Lorraine!"

"Oh, no!" Bea cried, lying. "No, no. But we—that is he—well, since the murder things have been so hurried. I mean—"

"You mean," Clara said, "that the circumstances and publicity of the murder may reflect upon you or Rufe. You mean you're afraid it would damage his career or even put a stop to it if you marry before the police have found his murderer." She waited a moment, thinking. "Dear Bea, they'll find out that Meeth did it. That will put everything in the clear. Nothing can possibly affect Rufe or you."

"No."

Clara was still not satisfied. "Don't let Lorraine grab him," she said firmly, and then unexpectedly veered from Rufe to his father. "I don't think I've seen Rufus, I mean Dr. Thorne, since Tuesday after the services. It seems strange he doesn't come to see how I—that is, how we are getting on."

"Rufe says he's very busy." Yet it struck Bea, too, that it would have been a normal thing for the doctor to drop in frequently and keep an eye on Clara.

Clara sighed. "Yes, I suppose he is busy. All his patients suddenly getting symptoms so they have to see him—and pump him all they can about the murder."

Her cynicism surprised Bea. She swallowed her shock as Clara waved a hand, said a pleasant goodnight and went away.

Apparently the police were still not sure that Meeth had murdered the judge. She wondered what they were doing.

The next day she found out a part of what they were doing, for Detective Smith came to see her and Clara. He brought with him the boxes of dictated tapes. Clara invited him to sit down. "Those tapes are just what you said they were, Miss Bartry," he said with half a smile. "We got a French teacher from Yale down to translate. He didn't seem very interested himself. I thought that one of those plays, the one about the man who did the favor for Mr. whatever his name was—"

"Perrichon," Bea said.

"Maybe. Anyway, the man who wrote that knew human nature. We always like people we've done a favor for and dislike somebody who does a favor for us. Too bad. But human."

Clara said, "What have the police been doing? I hope not favors for Meeth."

The detective blinked at the sharpness of her voice. "Well, it's still early, you know. A murder case is very serious."

"You needn't tell me that!"

"No, Mrs. Bartry, of course. But we've been busy. The trouble is we have too much work. We can't just drop everything and concentrate on one case although we'd like to. There are other problems, other investigations."

"Not murders, I hope." Clara was still sharp as a little angry bird.

"No," the detective said seriously. "Now, I do want to ask you some questions about the judge. For example, take the day before his murder. Thursday. What did he do that day?"

Clara gave Bea a helpless look. "Well, he was very nervous. I mean—oh, I can't describe it—"

"I thought he was working himself up to a real storm about something," Bea said flatly. "He was not rational, really. I de-

137

bated calling Dr. Thorne. But then the judge didn't do anything that was uncontrollable."

Clara sighed. "We didn't speak of it, Bea and I, but I could see that he was unusually upset about something."

"Didn't you try to find out why he was acting so peculiar?"

Clara shrugged. "No. We never made a point of questioning him. It would only have made him worse. No, the only thing to do was to wait until he cooled off."

"But you think that this irrational attitude was worse than usual."

Clara bit her lip. Then she said honestly, "We couldn't have sent him to a sanitarium. We couldn't have done that. We always just rode out whatever his moods were."

"But this attack," said the detective kindly, "was worse than usual."

"Yes," Clara said.

Bea nodded.

"And the next day, the day he was shot, he was no better?"

"Worse," Bea said. "But truly we didn't neglect him. We only tried to weather whatever that particular storm might be. We always did that."

"I see. Well, tell me his usual routine."

Bea replied, "In the mornings he would dictate letters or work on his memoirs. Afternoons I would take him for a drive or he'd work in the garden. We lead a very quiet life."

"We looked thoroughly through his files and found nothing that seemed of any special significance. Except, of course, what we took to be his account of Meeth's threats. But he did not mention Meeth—or anybody for that matter—by name."

"No. He avoided actual names as a rule," Bea said.

"Afraid of libel? Surely he didn't expect these rambling anecdotes to be read by anybody."

"It gave him something to do." He had not mentioned the two missing files. Bea debated for an instant and then told him, "Mr. Smith, two of the folders are missing."

His gaze brightened. She could feel Clara turn around quickly to look at her. "Do you mean that we didn't see all of the memoirs?" Mr. Smith asked.

"You should know. I looked through the folders. There was one he jokingly called Extracurricular Activities. There was another referring to his term as judge of the juvenile court. Both of them are gone."

The detective waited as if seeking back in his memory. "But those two folders were not in the cabinets when we examined them. I'd remember."

"They're not here now," Bea said flatly. "You can look if you want to."

"Oh, I believe you." The detective got out a pencil and chewed on it thoughtfully. "When did you discover that the folders had been taken?"

"Tuesday night."

"Why did you look at the files?"

Why indeed? To make sure that neither Dr. Thorne nor Mrs. Benson had been mentioned even by implication. "I just happened to," Bea said.

"The two folders were *not* there on Saturday morning. So someone, presumably the judge's murderer, came into this room after that man Griffin heard the shots. You found this door open. Did you have any impression that whoever had entered the house had gone near the filing cabinets?"

"I don't know. I didn't look at the cabinets or anything, really. I was intent upon finding the judge."

The detective gave a brief nod. "Yes. That would be natural. But if the murderer came into the room and got out those two folders, first he'd have had to know they were there. He'd have had to know that he might have been mentioned in an"—he paused and then brought out the word—"in an opprobrious way by the judge, a dangerous way. The fact is, the two folders were not in the files the morning we went through them. When did you last see them?"

"I really cannot remember."

"It would help if you could remember."

"I'll try. But just now—no, I can't remember."

"The point is, either they were removed at some unspecified time before the judge's murder, or they were removed the night of his murder while young Thorne and that boy of Obrian's, Tony, were presumably keeping an eye on the files and the house." He paused again. "It seemed to me that Tony and young Thorne are good friends."

"They wouldn't conspire to remove anything from the files."

His face expressed skepticism. She said quickly, "There was a time when they were not in this room at all. They went to the kitchen and had coffee and pie."

139

"You mean someone could have entered this room and got hold of the folders and gone away without being seen or heard by two ex-soldiers, who were supposedly guarding the room?"

"I think it's possible."

"Well," he said abruptly, "then it wasn't Meeth. We had him that night."

"It was Meeth who killed the judge," Clara said stubbornly.

The detective didn't even look at Clara. "Well, I'll talk to young Thorne and Tony. They'll stick up for each other, but I'll have a try. Meantime, we'll have to search for those folders. They may have been destroyed. Now what about the day *before* he died when you first noted his mood?"

Again Bea scurried through her memory. "That's the day the lawn boys were here. They came to cut the grass and work on the garden. My uncle usually followed them around. It interested him." She thought briefly and sadly of the judge's not always hidden bitterness and regret over his retirement, voluntary though it was.

Clara, sitting now with her hands folded but listening hard, spoke. "Oh yes, he did do something unusual that day. I remember now. He had one of the lawn boys take him out in the car. I don't know where they went. But all that day the judge was very, very upset."

Fifteen

"The lawn boys, I have their names. Which one was it who drove for the judge that afternoon?" Detective Smith asked.

Clara didn't remember. "I'm not sure. I only saw the car leaving and I knew that Bea wasn't driving and I thought it was unusual."

"Did you know he had taken the car, Miss Bartry?"

"I didn't then. Later, yes, of course. The judge told me that the car was in the drive and asked me to put it away. He said that he didn't trust Bob Forrest—I think it was—to drive into the garage. The entrance is rather narrow."

"I'll talk to Bob. Why do you think the judge would leave like that without telling either of you where he was going?"

Clara shook her head. The judge did as he pleased. I never questioned him."

"He didn't hint to you that he had something special on his mind?"

Clara shook her head. "He never talked to me of anything that bothered him. Never. He got into the habit while he was judge. He never talked of his cases. He said it wasn't fair, that I just might bias his opinions, something like that. He was always scrupulous."

"But he did seem remarkably disturbed that day?"

Disturbed was not quite the word, but both Clara and Bea nodded.

Bea said, "He had these moods. Especially when he felt he had to do something he really didn't want to do. Like seeing the doctor. That is, he liked Dr. Thorne as a friend. But he hated to go to his office for a checkup."

"My husband was an unusual man," Clara said promptly but rather absently. "Most of that week before his death he was deeply troubled about something. It was as if he had to do something he didn't want to do. It made him"—she paused briefly—"rather difficult. I'm not sure I can make you understand this. But my husband was an extremely conscientious man. Lately though, he—this trait seemed to grow more decisive. I mean—well, once he saw somebody speeding in town and got the number of the car and reported it to the police. He'd do that kind of thing."

The detective looked puzzled. Finally his face cleared. "You mean the kind of person who writes letters to the *Times*?"

"Well, yes," Clara said doubtfully. "But I don't think he ever did just that."

"He didn't," Bea said positively.

Clara went on, "But he did report things that seemed wrong to him. Like the time the Ellison boys made a still in the woods. I understand that poor Mrs. Ellison had a hard time getting the boys off and paying fines."

"Where is she now? I thought that place was closed."

"It's closed. She's in New Mexico. The boys are now in school. They meant no real harm by that still, you know. It

141

was only a boyish kind of—trick," said Clara, running out of words.

The detective seemed to think that over. At last he said, "In other words, the judge still felt himself, in a way, dedicated to upholding the law?"

"Oh yes! He couldn't stand by and see lawbreaking or anything he thought wasn't honest going on. He'd have tried to stop it." Her eyes filled with tears. She leaned forward. "Do you think that could be why he was murdered? I mean, suppose he knew something that somebody wanted to keep him from telling or— Oh, I don't know what I mean!" She flung out her hands and rose. The detective sprang up. "Thank you, Mrs. Bartry. You've been very helpful."

"I don't see how," Clara said in almost a wail. "I don't understand how anybody could hurt such a good man." She went out of the room, her head held high.

The detective shook his head as if he felt sorry for her, and then reached for the telephone book which lay on the desk. Bea heard him dial and ask for Robert Forrest. He talked for a moment, then hung up. "He's not there. He's working over at Dr. Thorne's. I'll talk to him later. I really would like to know where the judge went Thursday afternoon. But now, before I go, you're sure that aside from his mood, there was nothing unusual about Friday. Phone calls, say?"

"There might have been some that I didn't know about. Fridays Velda and I usually do some extra chores in the kitchen. I remember I took the car early in the morning and did our grocery shopping. Then Rufe got home and came to tell me the good news. He had passed all the tests. I didn't see much of the judge that day. But that night, after dinner, I decided that I had to tell him about my coming marriage, whether he was in a good mood or not. So I did and—"

"Yes, I know about that. But you think then that he had something else on his mind? That is, something he was determined to make a fuss about?"

"I didn't think of it at the time. It occurred to me only now, when you asked."

The detective picked up his hat. "Think about it. Oh, by the way, Mr. and Mrs. Di Pallici's passports will be given back to them. The dates correspond with the information both Mr. and Mrs. Di Pallici gave us. It was only a question of confirmation."

Bea risked a question. "Do you think there's a suspect besides Meeth?"

The detective evaded that neatly. "We don't know who killed him." He went away, driving a small inconspicuous car, headed toward the Thornes'.

He had barely gone when she found the files. She had sat down on the sofa and found its cushions packed down and needing to be shaken up; she took up one of the cushions to pummel it and discovered the two missing folders beneath it. She riffled through the pages of both folders and found they were all in order, precisely as she had paged them. There was not a sheet missing.

Thinking of Rufe's surmise about Cecco's boyhood, she sat down and went through the notes of the juvenile court file. There were records of a few individual cases but none that seemed to apply to Cecco.

Most of the youthful offenders had been sent to Millwood for such offenses as car stealing, vandalism and breaking and entering; she found nothing involving a more serious charge such as murder or manslaughter. Clearly he was proud when one of these minors showed himself not only repentant but on the way to becoming a worthwhile citizen. He appeared to keep in touch with some of the boys, as if he were in effect a guardian. At last she shoved the unrevealing pages together and put them in the file where they belonged.

Then she addressed herself to the folder labeled Extracurricular Activities. There were occasional, long-winded dissertations about the place of a judge in the law; the power of the judge; the necessity for strict justice. He quoted from Blackstone, Chief Justice John Marshall and Justice Brandeis. He went off into long anecdotes about his quarrels with various board members. But there was nothing even remotely referring to shoplifting or to being the middleman for bribery. That ought to relieve Mrs. Benson and Obrian.

She finally closed the folder and put that away in its proper place, too. Unless the president of the bank had shot the judge for objecting to a change in interest rates, unless the librarian had shot him for insisting that certain books were pornographic and should not have been bought, unless indeed the Reverend Cantwell had shot him because the judge disapproved of a new surface for the parking lot behind the church, then there was absolutely no clue.

143

She must tell Rufe that the folders had been found and what they contained—or rather what they did not contain. It was, however, an odd place to find them. The only reasonable explanation was that someone had contrived to get at them, but was unable to return them to the cabinet, and so hid them.

She sat at the judge's desk for a long time, thinking of the curious impression which the detective had so gently probed out of her memory. The more she thought of it the more she became convinced that the judge had had a certain air of reluctant but unrelenting decision. He *had* looked as he did when he reported some infraction of the law.

And then there was always the troublesome fact that the judge's gun was found beside him. He wouldn't have permitted anyone to take it; it would have had to be taken without his knowledge and fired. Then possibly the murderer had used his own gun to kill the judge and had left the judge's gun beside the judge as deliberately as he had extracted the bullet. Perhaps whoever had entered the house and set off the alarm had come into the study in order to secure the judge's gun, to leave it beside the judge as he made his escape!

She thought of that for a moment and saw the flaw; the judge's gun had been fired *before* the alarm sounded. If after, she and Clara would have heard the gunshot. Probably the police had come to that conclusion long ago.

She was still sitting at the judge's desk when Clara came back. "Has that detective gone?"

"Oh, yes. Long ago."

Clara sat down. "Bea, the police will find that Meeth killed the judge. This dreadful tragedy can't affect Rufe's career. I want you to be married."

"Not now, Aunt Clara."

Clara leaned forward. "Are you thinking of Lorraine?"

"No. But I don't want Rufe unless I'm sure he wants me."

"What makes you think he doesn't want you?"

Bea replied slowly. "I don't know. But there's something— different. I can't explain it."

"I'll talk to Rufe myself."

"*No!*"

Clara's face was suddenly stern. "Lorraine goes after anything she wants and usually gets it. You've got to tell Rufe

144

that you'll be married as soon as it can be arranged. Of course, we can't have the wedding I had planned for you, a church wedding and a reception and all that. We couldn't do that so soon after the judge— But we can have a quiet little wedding right here in the house. I'd like that." She broke off, listened and said, "There's somebody coming."

There was the familiar sound of gravel in the drive. Bea went to the terrace door; it was a state police car. As she watched, two troopers in smart uniforms got out; between them was another man, a stranger to Bea. The troopers must have seen her in the doorway, for each touched his hat in a formal way as the three approached her. One trooper said, "Miss Bartry, this is James Meeth. He insists that he must talk to your aunt. I hope this is convenient."

"Why—why, I—" She turned toward Clara, who had risen, looking very set and firm. "Let him come in," Clara said. "The troopers, too."

Meeth came in first. He took off his hat, disclosing dark, very short hair; his face was pale with thin lines and a weak chin. He wore a suit which looked new but didn't fit, and new but rather clumsy-looking oxfords. One trooper slid his revolver from its holster and held it closely to his side. The quiet action gave Bea a tremor of fear.

"All right, Meeth," the trooper said. "Say your piece."

Meeth opened his thin lips and then just stood there, turning his hat in his hands. Finally he said to Clara, "Mrs. Bartry?"

"Yes." Clara stood as firm and unyielding as a rock.

"I came to tell you I didn't mean to hurt the judge. I'll never hurt anyobdy ever again. I did kill my wife but I hadn't intended to. I didn't mean it when I said I'd kill the judge."

"You said you would," Clara said coldly.

He swallowed so hard that Bea could see his throat move. "Yes, I know I did, ma'am. I was furious. I'd only killed my wife because—I was mad. But that's in the past. I threatened to kill the judge, yes, but I was wild and scared and—but then later I knew I never would try to hurt him. You see—the past years have—they make a mark on anybody and I—" He had the air of a frightened and desperate child.

"But you came here the night the judge was killed." Clara's eyes were intent.

145

"Yes, I did. But all I wanted to do was give him a piece of my mind. He wasn't fair to me. The jury wouldn't have given the verdict they gave if he hadn't been against me."

"My husband would never have directed a jury, not in a case like yours."

"No, ma'am. But—" Meeth swallowed nervously again. "That's the way it seemed to me. So I had to get it off my chest. I had to tell him. But there were lights in this room that night and I could see the judge through that door there. It was half open and a young fellow was talking to him. The judge was talking so loud and—so furious that—I guess he scared me. So I left. All at once I decided I'd been wrong to come. It wouldn't change anything to talk to the judge. I'd be just the same, a man on probation. Maybe he'd make it harder for me. It's all the truth, everything I told the police. But I had to see you, ma'am. I had to tell you that I wouldn't have hurt you or the judge, not really. I'm sorry I came that night. I'm sorry I threatened the judge. But I didn't really mean it."

Bea, thinking of her talk with Rufe about the judge's term on the juvenile court, entered the conversation. "Mr. Meeth, did you know the judge? I mean before your case came before him in court?"

He turned faded and rather hopeless gray eyes toward her. "No, miss."

"You never even saw him?"

He shook his head, puzzled. "No, miss. Not that I remember."

"Then," she said directly, "were you, when you were young, ever sent to Millwood?"

Both troopers seemed to stiffen. Meeth merely continued to look puzzled. "Millwood? That's like a reform school for boys, isn't it? No. I was never in any sort of trouble, not even for speeding until—"

He stopped abruptly. There was a short silence. Clara's face was troubled. Then Bea said, directly again, "How did you manage to get the police to bring you here? I thought you were being held as a material witness."

Meeth looked at his hands, still seeming like a frightened child. The trooper with the revolver in his hand said, "He insisted on seeing your aunt. We thought—" He cleared his throat.

146

Clara looked at him and said, "You thought he might tell something that would add evidence against him?"

The trooper blushed slightly. The other shifted his weight from one foot to the other and said, "We don't know what our superior officer thought."

"I do," Clara said unexpectedly, and turned to Meeth. "What did you do before you went to prison?"

"I drove a truck."

"Do you have a driver's license?"

"Why, I—why, yes, ma'am. That is, I did have."

Clara turned to the troopers. "This man did not kill the judge," she said. "So who did kill him?"

There was a short silence. Meeth's face was childish again in his surprise. The troopers looked bewildered at Clara's abrupt and defiant change of opinion. She said firmly, "It's your duty to find the man who murdered my husband."

Sixteen

Clara's abrupt reversal not only bewildered Bea, as it did the troopers, but also frightened her. She had known that Meeth could neither have entered the house on Monday and searched her room, nor have shut her in the garage Sunday night: he had been held as a material witness. But Meeth had always been a kind of buffer between questions she did not want to consider; he had provided a ready-made answer to murder. If he didn't kill the judge, it left too narrow a field of possibility, and, in a dreadful way, too urgent a need for inquiry.

"Thank you both for bringing him here," Clara said suddenly. "I am sure he is telling the truth. Mr. Meeth, when the police let you go, let me know where you are to be found. Thank you, gentlemen. Thank you, Mr. Meeth, for coming to see me."

James Meeth's face brightened, as if a gleam of hope had reached him.

"Come on," a trooper said to Meeth. "We've got to get you back."

147

Meeth gave a kind of half bow; both troopers said good afternoon. Clara sat down and said mildly, "I was all wrong. I was sure he had shot the judge. He didn't. Not that man."

"But, Aunt Clara, this could be nothing but a device to help clear himself in the eyes of the police."

"He's not got sense enough for that," Clara said. "And he didn't murder the judge."

"You can't know that. You can't be sure."

"I've lived long enough to know a few things about people."

"You feel sorry for him, Aunt Clara! He managed to get around you."

"You felt sorry for him, too," Clara said shrewdly. "I could tell. Why, that poor man wouldn't intentionally kill a fly!"

"He killed his wife." Now that she had seen James Meeth, though, it was hard to believe.

"They said it was really manslaughter, something not premeditated. Done in a rage or—I don't remember and I don't care, but I've no doubt his wife deserved what she got."

"You are completely—" Bea began, and Clara finished with a gleam of laughter in her eyes, "Unreasonable? Indeed I am sometimes. But I know what I want right now, and that's your marriage."

"But, Aunt Clara, if Meeth didn't kill the judge, then who did?"

"That's the obvious question. Poor Meeth has been a scapegoat, and I helped to make him one."

"But that isn't all—"

"Naturally not. It means that whoever shot the judge must have been somebody he knew. Nobody else could have induced him to stroll down to the wall. Although, of course, if the murderer managed to get hold of the judge's gun—say the judge was threatened and pulled his gun out and the murderer got it away from him and forced him outside the house, far enough away so he hoped nobody would hear the gunshot— oh, yes, I quite see all these possibilities. The murderer might even have known that Meeth was going to be paroled and hoped the blame would fall on Meeth." She thought that over and became less certain of herself. "Of course, that was known by almost everybody. I believed it was in the papers. So that knowledge doesn't narrow the number of people who might have killed him."

Bea said slowly, "The judge would not have gone outside the house if he had felt himself in danger. He'd have done something—fired his gun right here so we'd hear it—even shout for help."

Clara nodded. "Probably. Although you know how stubborn he could be. Remember how violently he objected to having that alarm installed?" Clara's eyes filled with tears. "I wish I hadn't gone upstairs so early. I wish—it's no use wishing now."

There was a light knock on the door. It was the detective again, and when Bea opened the door he came in rather hesitantly. "I met the two troopers with Meeth as they were leaving. I understand that you now think Meeth did not kill the judge, Mrs. Bartry."

"I know he didn't," Clara said simply.

He went on quickly, "Well, I'm sorry to bother you again, Mrs. Bartry. I've been talking to Bob Forrest. He said that he drove the judge into town, and the judge got out at the library steps and told him to meet him there in a half hour. Bob waited, but the judge didn't return for almost an hour and a half. He was positive about that because his working hours for the day were up and he wanted to get the judge home and then go home himself."

"The judge must have been in the library," Clara said. "He was on the library board."

"No. I talked to the librarian and the girls there. No one remembers seeing him in the library at all. Bob says the judge walked up the street but he didn't see where he went. I thought perhaps you might remember something he said which would indicate his errand that afternoon."

Bea shook her head. Clara just looked at the detective, who sighed. "I see you don't. I thought that what Bob told me might jog your memory. But you've been very helpful." Both Bea and Clara looked puzzled; the detective added, "I mean about the judge's behavior. When you said that he was especially disturbed and must have had something on his mind that upset him. Thanks once again." The detective nodded and went away. They heard the closing of a car door and the departure of his car.

"What do you suppose the judge did that afternoon?" Clara said worriedly. "If he didn't go to the library or the bank, where did he go?"

Bea thought it over. The extent of the police inquiry, the fineness of its net, was beginning to impress itself more and more clearly upon her. "If the police have to question everybody in Valley Ridge they'll find out."

"But it seems to me if there was anything important about where he went, then somebody would have come forward by now and told us. Or the police." Clara rose and came over to the desk. "Where did he keep his gun?"

"Here—" Bea opened the drawer; she didn't remember placing the judge's cigar case in the drawer.

Clara saw it and seized it. "Why, Bea! I'm so glad you found that. I haven't seen it since a day or two before the judge was killed. I gave it to him you know. Long ago. Actually he didn't like it much but he pretended he did and constantly used it. But I knew." She took up the gold cigar case and pressed it to her cheek. Tears came to her eyes.

"It was here on the desk. Last night."

"I didn't see it!"

"It was underneath some of the papers that Rufe and Joe had moved to give space for signing your will."

Clara frowned, still smoothing her cheek with the cigar case. "I can't understand—oh, of course Velda found it somewhere and put it here." Clara walked out of the room, holding the cigar case in her hand. Bea sat down again at the desk.

It had been a long morning, yet she was surprised when Velda came in with a luncheon tray, saying, "It's very late. I knew those policemen were here and that man Meeth, so I didn't bother you with lunch then, but you'd better eat. Mrs. Bartry had hers on a tray. Lorraine and Cecco are gone somewhere. I'll not bother with them. When they get back they can fix themselves something."

"Thank you, Velda."

As she was eating, the appraisers arrived along with the other detective, Whipple.

Clara came down to meet them and to escort them to the safe in the judge's room. That was a simple bit of routine; the appraisers kindly overlooked the jewelry belonging to the judge. Shown the Mercedes and looking at the canceled check which Bea had found for them, they also concluded that since Clara had paid for the car, it was not a part of the judge's estate. Clara went with them, then, in the appraisers' car to the bank. When they returned Mr. Whipple opened the car door for her with a certain awed respect.

Clara explained it when all of them had gone. "You see, the judge really didn't have much of an estate. He always insisted on paying most of the household expenses. He had a few bonds. They searched through our safe-deposit box but found nothing that could have anything to do with his murder. It held mainly records of my own property and some insurance policies, that's all. I don't think the inheritance taxes will amount to much. I'm going to rest, Bea. It was a tiresome affair, although the bank president couldn't have been more polite. He let us use that little private office of his own."

She went upstairs. Probably the appraisers and the detective had been more or less astonished at the amount of Clara's property, Bea thought. Obviously whatever inheritance taxes there might be would not seem great to Clara.

Bea sat down again at the desk to write some more thank-you notes, vaguely wondering where Lorraine had gone, when Cecco came in whistling a rather merry little tune as if he were pleased with himself. "Still at it?" he said. "It's taking you a long time."

"There were people here."

"Police? Detectives?"

Bea did not want to be led into conversation with him. She nodded and picked up her pen.

"Don't want to talk, is that it?" Cecco's voice was intent and full of interest. "Did they have any news?"

"No," she said flatly.

He sat down and eyed her, but almost as if he didn't see her and was actually intent upon some inner calculation.

Bea suspected that he would not be quite so debonair if he knew of the dossier the police had received from Rome. Still there was apparently nothing in that dossier which proved criminal activities on Cecco's part.

After a while he said, "Do you know where Lorraine is now?"

"No."

"I suppose she is trying to decide where her best chances are. Your Rufe, Ben Benson or Seth. Or perhpas she'll wait and find somebody more promising or more amenable."

"That's her business," Bea said shortly.

"In fact, I saw her coming along the road toward Seth's

house on Stoney Road—isn't that what you call it? The same road the Bensons live on."

"Perhaps she went to see Mrs. Benson."

It was more likely that Lorraine had gone to exercise her wiles upon Seth. "When did you see her?"

"Not long ago. Half an hour or so. She was coming from the direction of the Bensons'. Probably making up to Mrs. Benson just in case she decides on Ben. Now I know just where their house is. I can't imagine how I happened to get lost the night the judge was killed." He eyed his glistening oxfords. "My feet hurt. I went for a long walk. These country roads."

Bea addressed an envelope. Cecco said softly, "It's an odd thing about small towns. Gossips, especially the barbers. But in a place like Valley Ridge or Stamford, where I had a haircut Monday, they know all sorts of things. And talk about them."

"They like to entertain their customers." Bea put down her pen. "What are you getting at, Cecco? What particular gossip did you hear when you went to the barber's?"

"Oh, this and that," Cecco replied airily.

On an impulse Bea decided to question him directly. "Cecco, how did you know that I wore braces on my teeth when I was young?"

"You're still young, dear."

"I mean when did you see me wearing braces?"

Cecco's eyes widened merrily. "But I didn't. Lorraine told me. She said once that you were—forgive me, Bea—that you were a beanpole of a child with braces on your teeth. Permit me to say that you look very different now. Not at all like Lorraine's description of you."

"Oh," Bea felt rather flat. It was a reasonable and somehow, she felt, a true explanation.

"Anything else you want to know?" Cecco asked, and as she shook her head he walked out of the room.

So that answered the braces-on-her-teeth question, yet there was about him an aura of mingled calculation and satisfaction. It was nothing tangible, but it struck Bea that he might look like that if he were considering a bet on a horse. Then she called herself fanciful and went back to writing.

Rufe came in half an hour later and flopped wearily down

into a chair. "I've been talking to a detective. The police got onto the fact that I'd driven up to Millwood, and then asked about the boys the judge sent there."

"How did they know?"

Rufe shrugged. "How do they know anything? They're extremely efficient. I understand they brought Meeth here this morning."

"Yes. Did they tell you that?"

"The detective named Smith did. He explained that Meeth had something he must say to Aunt Clara, so I suppose they brought him in the hope that whatever he was determined to say would constitute some sort of evidence."

"It did in a dreadful way, Rufe. Now Aunt Clara is sure he didn't kill the judge."

Rufe leaned over, his head in his hands.

"Oh, and Rufe, I asked Cecco when he had seen me wearing braces on my teeth. He said, never. He said Lorraine had told him."

Rufe eyed her thoughtfully. "Did you think he was telling the truth?"

"Well, yes, I did." Lorraine's description of her, as quoted by Cecco, sounded very like Lorraine. She said, "Rufe, I found the two folders that were missing and read them very carefully. There's nothing in them that I can see would be dangerous to anybody."

"Where did you find them?"

"Right here. Under the cushions of the sofa. Anybody might have put them here."

"When?"

"Maybe right after the murder, or it could have been later during the night you and Tony were here. They were not in the files the next morning when the detectives went through them."

Rufe shook his head. "Pull yourself together. I didn't take them. Tony didn't."

"But you were in the kitchen part of the time."

"Meaning a phantom intruder could have got in and taken them. We weren't gone long enough for anybody to read them. Besides we'd have heard anybody in the room."

"He could have come in very quietly, couldn't he?"

Rufe sighed, lifted his head and shoved his hands in his

153

pockets. "I suppose so. I'm beginning to believe almost anything. The wildest sort of ideas—nothing of real evidence. May I see the two folders?"

"Of course." She took them from the cabinet. Rufe settled down to read.

He read rapidly but thoroughly. She had almost come to the end of her letters when he finished, rose and carefully returned the folders to the memoirs file. "Nothing," he said to her inquiring look. "The judge was too cautious about names or even circumstances which would indicate anybody in particular. Except of course his quarrel with Reverend Cantwell. And the banker. And the librarian and— No, there's simply nothing there that could endanger anybody. The page numbers are accurate too, so nothing has been removed."

"No."

"Well— Oh, Lorraine!"

Lorraine, of course. She came in breezily. "I've been driving. That's a beautiful car. Do you think Aunt Clara might give it to me? She can't drive."

"You don't have a driver's license, do you?" Bea asked and thought dismally: Can't I behave just a little more enticingly, more like Lorraine?

Lorraine danced over and sat on the arm of Rufe's chair. "Guess where I went."

"Cecco thought the Bensons'," Bea said.

"Right. I went to call on Mrs. Benson, a duty call. And do you know the strangest thing happened. She actually asked me to stay for lunch. Can you believe it! She talked to me, she asked me about the judge's murder, not that I could tell her anything she didn't know. She even talked about his memoirs. It seems everybody in town knows he was writing his memoirs. She asked if they were interesting."

Bea's hands tightened. "What did you say?"

"Why, I said yes. They were interesting indeed. Especially things about people here in Valley Ridge."

"But, Lorraine—" Rufe began.

Bea said, "Did you read the memoirs?"

"Heavens, no." Lorraine made her habitual gesture of tossing her head gracefully so her black hair fell away from her face. "Do you think I'd be so silly as to plow through all that stuff! But I told her yes, I had read them word for word.

154

What else could I say?" She opened her eyes wide and innocently.

"What did she do then?" Bea asked after a moment.

"Oh, what didn't she do! Honestly! Made me stay to lunch. Even gave me a thimbleful of sherry. Talked about Ben all the time; made me look at his baby pictures, school pictures, graduation pictures—all that. I was never so bored. I thought I'd never get away. All the same I thought I'd sort of butter her up—"

Rufe grinned. "You mean Ben?"

"There *is* all that money and to tell you the truth she acted as if she really wanted me for a daughter-in-law. Can you imagine that nice old woman carrying on over me that way?"

I can imagine it, Bea thought; she thinks Lorraine knows about a shoplifting episode. She'd rather have Lorraine for a daughter-in-law, obliged to keep quiet about it, than to have it known all over Valley Ridge.

Lorraine shook back her hair again. "On my way home I passed Seth's place. He was just getting into his car, so of course I stopped and he invited me in and offered me a drink. We chatted, you know. He is so attractive!"

"Seth? Well, of course, he's a senator," Bea said dryly. Then she thought, in pride or something she couldn't account for: Leave her to Rufe. Leave them alone. If Rufe wants her he'll only have to say so.

She gathered up her letters, said something about seeing to dinner and walked out. She could feel Lorraine's green eyes following her. She didn't go to the kitchen. Instead she went to her own room where she paced restlessly up and down, trying to talk herself into some common sense. Suddenly she wanted a cigarette. She had practically stopped smoking after the judge made one of his violent scenes about it a year or so ago. Yet surely there must be some around—dry perhaps but still cigarettes.

She looked in the drawer of the writing table; there was none. There might be some in her handbag, for it was a big utility bag, designed to carry everything from grocery lists to hairbrushes. She glanced through the odd items—change purse, billfold, handkerchiefs, scraps of paper that somehow got in the handbag and were never removed until she had a grand clearing-out day, even a few half-used match packs—

but no cigarettes. There were two large pockets with zippers on each side of the handbag. She opened one pocket, feeling a bulge. The bulge was not an ancient package of cigarettes; it was one of the judge's dictated tapes.

It surprised her; yet she must have taken the tape in order to practice French, or perhaps it was one which she had already used for French and had absently put in her handbag and forgotten. She was holding it in her hand when Lorraine strolled in without knocking. "Rufe's gone and— What's that?"

Lorraine's eyes were even greener and more brilliantly set off by the dark-green turtleneck sweater she wore; the clinging black slacks displayed her lovely legs.

"This? It's only an old tape of the judge's. Have you any cigarettes?"

"No, I—no, I don't think so." Lorraine turned and looked out the window for a moment. Then she said, "Oh, I nearly forgot. Aunt Clara wants all those letters put out in the mailbox tonight."

"All right." Bea shoved the used tape back into her handbag. Lorraine went with her into the hall.

Bea went downstairs and into the study, took the letters she'd been writing and brought them down the drive toward the mailbox at the entrance to the road. She drew some letters from the box, mainly notes of condolence, magazines and junk mail, and trudged up the drive again. At the terrace steps she paused. She didn't want to go into the house. She'd been sitting at the desk all day; she needed exercise, and wanted to clear her head of the doubts about Rufe's love for her. She put the assortment of mail on the top step and strolled around the house.

Lights shone from the kitchen windows. She caught a glimpse of Velda adding something to a mixture in a bowl. She went on. The garage doors were closed and bolted on the outside. The evening air was growing chilly, and the tree frogs were starting their musical whistles. The path toward the pond invited her; she thought of old Shadders stalking beside her when he was not diverted by some promising scent. The pines were blue with dusk. She had almost reached the pond when she saw a man's figure. It was Cecco standing at the very edge of the pond, almost concealed by a thicket of laurels. He was simply standing there, gazing down at the pond.

He heard her approach and turned swiftly. In almost the

same instant he gave a hoarse gulp and fell backward, half into the pond. She heard the gunshot. It rocked the world. She stumbled and fell herself, heavily, behind the laurels. This saved her life, for there were immediately two more gunshots.

Some birds whirred up, frightened, from the trees.

Seventeen

Somebody was running through the woods. Then there was a heavy splash as though something had been thrown into the water. She could see one of Cecco's shining oxfords at the edge of the pond.

Rufe came plunging along the path out of the sudden evening twilight and found her. He caught her in his arms and then made her crouch down again behind the laurels. He went to look at Cecco. "I think he's dead. Come——"

She was on her feet, Rufe's arm supporting her. "I saw the mail on the steps of the terrace. I guessed that you had come this way, it was always your favorite walk. Hurry, Bea. Shall I carry you?"

She must have said no. When they reached the house it was blazing with lights. Velda met them at the front door, eyes popping. "I heard the gunshots! Is she hurt?"

Rufe shoved her at Velda and ran for the telephone. Clara came from somewhere out of the whirling darkness around Bea. Velda led her firmly to a chair and then stood wringing her floury hands. Lorraine appeared. Bea shook her head dazedly; she was not fainting, yet everything was moving around her. She leaned against somebody who proved to be Lorraine. Lorraine told Velda to get whiskey. Velda went in a flurry out of the room.

"Rufe said it was Cecco. Is that right?" Lorraine asked.

Bea nodded.

Lorraine was sitting on the arm of her chair, one arm around Bea. "Who killed him?"

"I don't know. It happened just as Cecco turned to speak to me. He heard me coming and then he gave a kind of—— scream or something and fell over."

157

Clara came out of the confused dizziness around Bea; she had two glasses. "Drink this," she said. "Here's one for you too, Lorraine."

Lorraine took the glass, downed the whiskey, and half choked as it struck her throat, for neither Velda nor Clara had diluted it with water.

Lorraine said, "He was no good, Cecco—but still—"

"There, there," Clara said in a calm and soothing way. But she had not stood in the evening dusk beside the laurels and seen Cecco topple over into the pond. She had not heard the gunshots so close, so near. She had not dropped down behind the clump of laurels. Bea thought dully: He was shooting at me, too! Then she thought quite clearly: It must have saved my life, stumbling into the laurels. Why would anybody try to kill me?

It was like a nightmare which took on substance. Rufe came back from the study and went to Bea, looked at her, touching her arms, her hands, assuring himself that she was not hurt. Lorraine sank down into an armchair. Clara said, "They're coming. I hear the sirens."

They did come. It was a repetition of the night of the judge's murder.

There was the medical examiner, called from an early dinner, and Obrian, directing Tony and two other policemen. After what seemed a short time the cars carrying the state police arrived. There was Lieutenant Abbott again with some of his men as well as Detective Smith. The police lieutenant showed Clara a search warrant. "Certainly, yes, I understand," she said.

Nobody, however, really understood. Someone repeated what seemed to be a stock formula about willingness to answer questions. Bea was questioned first. How many shots were there? She thought three. Anything else? With a great effort Bea replied, yes, she thought that something had splashed in the pond. What something? She didn't know. Could it have been a gun? She didn't know.

Lorraine sat close beside her all the time they questioned her; Lorraine's dark green turtleneck sweater and her smart slacks looked strangely out of place in a world that had spun off its axis. Dr. Thorne arrived and Bea heard him tell the police that she had had a shock; they must not question her further that night; she had told all she knew.

Seth backed him up. Bea hadn't known that Seth had come, but he was there, telling the police that she couldn't talk to them any more that night. Dr. Thorne took her upstairs.

By then, she realized dimly, it was late. The doctor helped her into bed and put a stethoscope to her chest. Then he tucked an eiderdown around her. Rufe opened the door and came in. "Bea, are you really all right?"

"No," Bea said with truth, "I feel terrible."

"She wasn't hurt though," Dr. Thorne said.

He handed her a glass of water and two capsules, which she swallowed obediently. "I'll go down now and see to Clara. Stay with Bea, Rufe, until she goes to sleep."

Rufe nodded and sat on the edge of Bea's bed, simply holding her hand in his own and asking no questions.

"How about Lorraine?" Bea said presently.

"Okay. Go to sleep."

"Sleep! What are they doing?"

"Same things they did when the judge was shot. Searching all over the place."

Bea opened her eyes to look at Rufe. There was something in his voice that seemed to withhold information. "You're not telling me something. What?"

"I don't know who shot Cecco, if that's what you mean. Not very many people here even knew him."

"Ben Benson knew him."

"Can you imagine Ben lurking behind some shrubbery and shooting somebody?"

"Mrs. Benson might." Bea gave a breathless giggle which she herself recognized as near hysteria.

Rufe eyed her worriedly. "Now, please, Bea, it's been a shock but—" He broke off as Seth knocked and then opened the door. "Rufe, they want to question you again."

"I've told them everything I know! I didn't see who shot Cecco. Do I have to talk to them again?"

Seth replied shortly, "You asked for my advice when you phoned and told me that Cecco had been shot. So here's my advice, take it or leave it. Don't talk too much. Don't say anything that could be—" He checked himself; Rufe finished for him. "Incriminating? I won't."

Bea sat up. "Rufe, do be careful. I mean people can twist words around—"

159

Seth smiled. "Relax, Bea. Rufe has good sense."

"Don't let them say that Rufe did it."

"I can't tell them what to say, but there's not a chance in the world they'll accuse Rufe. What on earth would be his motive?" Seth's long face sobered; he said suddenly, "Are you thinking of Lorraine? Rufe's getting rid of Cecco because he was Lorraine's husband? Really, Bea—"

"*No!*"

Rufe at the door whirled around. "For God's sake! Lorraine! Get rid of Cecco because he was Lorraine's husband? A motive for murder? Lorraine doesn't mean anything to me!"

Bea's heart gave a leap; new life seemed to flow all over her.

Rufe looked merely angry and incredulous.

"Of course not. Your girl is right here, Rufe," Seth said good-naturedly. "I was about to scrape up something for dinner when you phoned. Will you ask Velda if she can manage a sandwich or anything to eat?"

"If I can find her. Last time I saw her she was in the kitchen moaning, threatening to leave forever."

Bea sank back on the pillows. "Go with Rufe, Seth. He has a right to have a lawyer present, doesn't he?"

"Well—yes. But I don't think it's come to that. However, I'll go with him. The house is full of people," Seth told her comfortingly. "Nothing for you to be afraid of."

He went out after Rufe and closed the door against a kind of background of sounds, voices from both inside and outside the house. There were cars coming and going.

Dr. Thorne would see to Clara, Bea thought hazily after a while, but how about Lorraine? She must have cared for Cecco once. It seemed to her now that some of the background noises were dying away. Her capsule-induced languor was abating, too. She disentangled herself from the eiderdown and went into the hall. There was a steady murmur of voices from below. Lorraine's door was open and she was sitting at the small writing table with a tray set before her. She nodded at Bea, chewing. "Want a sandwich?"

Bea eyed the large plate of sandwiches which was covered neatly with a dinner napkin. "Did Velda fix those?"

Lorraine nodded, still chewing.

"I thought she was having hysterics, threatening to leave."

Lorraine swallowed. "Oh, she did that, all right. Got all the attention she could get. But believe me, she's not going to leave. She's having the time of her life. Here, the chicken ones are best. There's a little salad, too. Coffee? I'll get my bathroom glass."

Bea took a sandwich, discovering with surprise not only that she could eat but that she was very hungry. When Lorraine came back, she stuck a spoon in the glass to prevent it from breaking and then poured hot coffee. Bea said, "What about Aunt Clara?"

"Oh, she's all right. I tried to get her to come upstairs but she wouldn't. Funny," Lorraine said, "it's as if she got a new lease on life since the judge was killed. Different woman altogether. Used to be so mousy."

"I don't think she's changed at all. I think she was always like this. Lorraine, did Cecco tell the truth about where he was the night the judge was killed? I mean when he had gone from the Inn and Ben couldn't find him?"

Lorraine took another sandwich, bit into it with vigor and nodded. "I think so. Probably he felt sure that if he actually saw Ben he could"—Lorraine shrugged—"get something out of him. Money or— Anyway, Cecco always wore tight shoes. His feet began to hurt so he gave up. Yes, I believed him."

"Did the police question you tonight?"

Lorraine's eyes opened wide. "Question me! You were there! Didn't you hear them? Good Heavens, you'd have thought that I got a gun from somewhere, followed Cecco, and took a pot shot at him. Then more shots at you for fear you had recognized me. But I didn't," she said flatly. "Sugar?"

"No, thanks. But, Lorraine, they let you come up here."

"Oh, certainly. I had to do a bit of carrying on—stage weeping, you know. Cecco was my husband. We had our disagreements, but here we were staying in Aunt Clara's house. Sure they let me leave. Bea, didn't you see *anybody* down there at the pond? Besides Cecco, I mean."

Bea shook her head. "I saw him fall. I heard the shots. I scrambled down."

"Yes, I know. I heard you tell them over and over. What does Seth advise?"

"He told Rufe not to talk too much. That's all."

"Bea, do you really think *I* killed Cecco?"

"Do I think—*no!*"

"Well," Lorraine said coolly, "Cecco did try to hold me up for half my share of Aunt Clara's money. I told you all that —his idea of borrowing on what he called my expectations. He really believed that Aunt Clara has a bad heart. But I changed my mind. And after you told me that Aunt Clara knew about Benito there really wasn't anything Cecco could blackmail me about."

Rufe came to the door and saw the plate of sandwiches. He made for it. "Aunt Clara is in her room. I told Velda to take her some soup. The police are still at it. I asked Obrian to let Tony stay around the house tonight. I'll stay too. Any more coffee?"

"I'll rinse out my cup." Lorraine took it to the bathroom. Bea thought suddenly that perhaps Benito was not Cecco's only hold over Lorraine. Perhaps there were other things Cecco could have employed for blackmail. Suppose he knew something which was in fact so damaging to Lorraine's further prospects in life that she had to silence him!

No!

Yet Lorraine *could* have followed him from the house. She could have concealed herself in the clump of pines. Why, she is even wearing colors for concealment, Bea thought, horrified at the swift course of her own reasoning: the dark green sweater, the dark slacks wouldn't have shown in the dusk!

But what about a gun?

Rufe ate voraciously. "I hope I'm not robbing you girls, but I'm starved. They're going to drag the pond tomorrow. I could tell them that the pond has a muddy, swampy bottom. They're not likely to find the gun—if that was what you heard splash in the water, Bea."

"I don't know. I just know there was a splash."

"Bea—" Rufe shot a quick look at the bathroom door; Lorraine was still rinsing the cup. He said in a low voice, "Do you remember that jacket of the judge's? The night he was killed. There in his study."

"Yes. It was on his desk. But then later it was on a chair all folded up."

"When I first came it was just tossed over the desk, as if the judge had thrown it there."

"I suppose the police found it and had gone through the pockets."

Rufe did not look convinced. "Maybe. There's an odd thing. Somebody did pass me as I crossed the road. The lights were full on me. But nobody has come forward and told the police about seeing me. Why?"

"The driver could have been somebody from out of state or—"

"Not on this road. Unless he was lost. Of course he could have been Meeth, not wanting to admit it and place himself on the scene of the murder so close to the time of the murder. It was only later that he talked very fully to the police."

Lorraine came back and Clara appeared in the doorway. She nodded. "It's a good thing to get something to eat. I'm sorry about Cecco, Lorraine. Naturally I know that you were not on good terms but still—"

"Have a sandwich," Lorraine said.

"I've just had about a quart of soup. Velda stood over me." Clara had the judge's gold cigar case in her hands. "I do think it's strange that I didn't find this case sooner. Where has it been all this time?"

Rufe looked steadily at the rest of his sandwich. Seth came to the door. "May I come in? Or is it a family conference?"

"Come in," Clara said. "Sandwiches?" Lorraine asked.

"Velda fed me. I think the police are leaving. Lorraine—" Seth leaned against a chair, his elbows on the back of it. The move brought his face into the shadow of the lamp on the table and again, oddly, there was a teasing, fleeting resemblance to Cecco, although in fact, Bea thought sharply, there was no resemblance at all. He said seriously, "Did Cecco know who killed the judge?"

Lorraine shook her head. "I don't know. If he did he didn't tell me. Cecco—" Lorraine was again overtaken by one of her disarming moments of candor. When she chose to lie, Bea thought, she could lie with the best of them, but when she chose to tell the truth she withheld nothing. "Cecco," Lorraine said, "was by nature a chiseler and a blackmailer. He did it in mean but small ways. He wouldn't have had the courage to blackmail a murderer." She finished calmly and sat down on the bed, looking very lovely. "No," she said decisively, "he wouldn't have had the courage to do anything so dangerous."

Rufe said abruptly, "Why did he go to the pond?"

There was a complete silence. Then Rufe said, "He must have gone to meet somebody."

"And that somebody shot him and shot at Bea?" Seth considered it. "Sounds possible. Unless Cecco just liked to walk and happened to make a target of himself."

"He said he'd been strolling down that way the night I was shut in the garage," Bea said, and then caught Clara's look of inquiry and said quickly, "It wasn't anything, Aunt Clara. An accident. The doors—blew shut and Cecco heard me and let me out."

Rufe bit into another sandwich. "Cecco seems to have been around at odd times. He might have known something."

Seth nodded. "Certainly whoever killed him had to have a reason. People in Valley Ridge don't just go around shooting one another for the fun of it."

"Seth! What a way to talk! I'm going to bed," Clara said firmly. "You girls go to bed, too. It's late."

Seth arranged it so Tony could stay in the house that night. Rufe and Seth stayed, too. Dr. Thorne had gone long ago. Miss Dotty had telephoned for him, saying that there was an urgent call. Gradually the house became quiet. Bea did not set the alarm that night. Tony advised her not to. "You see, we may be out and around the house tonight."

He and Rufe and Seth stood together in the hall. Bea saw Clara to her room and said goodnight.

Bea looked at her watch with incredulity. It was very late. It was also dreadfully like that other night when the judge had been killed. The difference was that she loved the judge; she had never liked, certainly never trusted, Cecco. She tried not to think of Cecco's startled face, his backward plunge, his shining oxford turned at an outrageous angle on the edge of the pond.

She tried not to wonder who had killed him. But it couldn't have been proper stolid Ben Benson and she couldn't imagine why she kept thinking of Ben.

Eighteen

She was still thinking of him the next morning.

Everybody came down late, but this time Velda did not object beyond uttering various threats about leaving a house where murder happened. "Seems as if there's murder right here in the house somewhere," she muttered. Bea felt much the same way.

But she kept on going over in her mind every possible reason for Cecco's murder. She thought about Lorraine, then about Ben. Obviously he had not welcomed Cecco's arrival; if Cecco had been, as Lorraine said, a blackmailer, would correct and proper Ben Benson actually have killed him to prevent Cecco's telling some story of youthful indiscretions? Bea could not seriously accept that as a hypothesis. Yet Ben seemed to be putty in Lorraine's hands. Could he have thought that in killing Cecco he was removing an obstacle to his marriage to her? That didn't seem reasonable either. The troublesome point was, again, that so few people knew Cecco. One must know someone very well or fear him very much to bring one's self to murder.

She didn't see Clara until noon. Lorraine came down as Bea was sitting at the table eying a cup of cold coffee. Police, Velda told them, were dragging the pond. Lorraine shook her head. "They'll never find anything in that pond. Are you going anywhere this morning, Bea?"

Bea replied, "No, I expect the police will be here sometime——"

"The drive is already full of photographers and reporters." Lorraine snapped off a grape and swallowed it whole apparently. "It's like the time when the judge was killed. Only worse. I suppose I'll have to give some sort of interview."

Rufe came in as she spoke. "Don't do that, Lorraine. You're the widow, remember. Doesn't do you or anybody any good to go posing in front of cameras." He sat down wearily.

Velda came bustling in. "You haven't had any breakfast and it's almost time for lunch!"

165

"I wanted to see how my father is doing. He's getting too old to work so hard. Needs a younger man to help him."

"Huh—" Velda said scornfully. "He'd never consent to that. I'll get you something to eat." She bustled off again. No, Velda wouldn't leave in spite of her mumbled threats; her eyes were agleam and excited.

Rufe fiddled with a spoon. "There are some policemen down at the pond now. Cecco—" He glanced swiftly and rather apologetically at Lorraine, who said, "Of course, they'll do an autopsy. I agreed to that last night. They'd have done it anyway. They'll find the bullet that killed him. But if it was a gun that splashed into the pond I doubt if anybody can ever find it."

Rufe frowned. "Things have been hurried. I didn't ask you, Lorraine, if there were relatives in Italy who ought to be notified. I mean, any cables you want to send. Or you could phone."

Lorraine shook her head, brooded for a moment and suddenly chose to explain Cecco's American accent. "There's nobody now. His mother was a New Yorker. She was separated from his father ages ago when Cecco was a boy. I didn't learn this until after I had married Cecco. She died."

Rufe said quickly, "Then he lived there as Cecco di Pallici?"

"Oh, no," Lorraine replied airily. "His mother gave him another name."

"What?" Rufe asked sharply.

Lorraine seemed to think back. "I really don't remember. Something that sounded American. Her maiden name probably. I think it was something like Brown or White or Johnson. When she died Cecco went back to Italy. I don't know what happened to his father, probably he came to no good end. I didn't tell you that Cecco was brought up in New York because I—oh, I was afraid you'd connect him and me with the judge's murder. Cecco couldn't have been a very nice boy. I didn't know, I was afraid that some time he had been in this vicinity and had come up before the judge and that that was why the judge didn't want me to marry him. Well, to tell you the truth I was afraid somebody would take a notion that Cecco and I were working together to get rid of the judge and to get Aunt Clara's— Never mind that." Lorraine's typical burst of candor seemed to relive her. "But now, you see, Cecco couldn't have killed the judge. No, there's really nobody to notify. He's to be sent to Italy to the family mausoleum. It's hard to tell the difference between his so-called *palazzo* and a mausoleum, but the mausoleum exists and they can make room for Cecco. I arranged all that with the police last night. They searched Cecco's room and all his luggage. Did you know that?"

Rufe was looking very thoughtful; probably, Bea thought, he was searching his memory of the records at Millwood and trying to discover any connection between a White, a Brown, a Johnson—or even a quite different name—and Cecco. If it existed, it would be necessary to trace Cecco's mother's residence in New York, his own residence there and countless details.

Rufe did not seem to hear Lorraine's question for a moment; then he nodded. "Apparently they found nothing of any special interest. Except a few bills, not paid."

"They'll never be paid as far as I am concerned," Lorraine said coolly. "No letters from any of his dear little friends?"

"I don't think so. In any event I don't think one of them would follow Cecco here and kill him. Do you?"

Lorraine's green eyes widened. "I never thought of that."

"I don't think it likely," Rufe said and Velda returned with bacon, eggs and toast. "Enough for a regiment," Rufe said. "Thank you."

He absently ate his meal in brooding silence, finished, said thank you and left, his shabby loafers flopping along the hall and out.

The day went on. Bea occupied herself by replying to the letters she had found in the mailbox and left on the terrace steps. She wondered, coldly, what would have happened if she had not left the stack of mail on the steps, and Rufe had not come along.

She had read all the letters and made a list which required replies when Clara came down. Clara was fresh and neat, her hair done carefully, her eyes as blue as her favorite blue suit. She said mildly, "It's odd but there have been no phone calls about Cecco. I wonder why."

As she spoke, Lorraine came in. "Darling, nobody here knew Cecco."

"But the idea of the tragedy! I should think somebody would phone me."

167

Nobody had. Ben was the only person to whom Cecco's death might have a personal significance. Unless, of course, Seth had actually fallen in love with Lorraine at once . . . But that was absurd. Bea was appalled at the extent of her own speculations; the next thing she knew she would be mentally accusing Velda, Miss Dotty and again Dr. Thorne.

Clara peered up suddenly over her glasses. "I don't think a single one of us had an alibi for the time of Cecco's murder. I don't have an alibi. I was in the judge's room, just sitting there thinking of him."

Lorraine came to the desk and perched on the edge of it. That day she wore almost flagrantly bright colors as if she defied the role of widow, as by law she certainly was. Her dress was a tangerine-colored wool. A jade-green sweater was slung over her shoulders. The tangerine dress was so well cut and simple that it must have cost a great deal. Bea thought of Benito, who had supplied Lorraine with money and from whom she had parted with apparently no regret on either side.

"I was taking a shower," Lorraine giggled. "Nobody saw me there naturally. When I heard Velda yelling her head off I just dashed into the sweater and slacks I had taken off and ran down to see what was going on."

"We have answered everything the police asked us. It does seem really too dreadful." Clara sighed. "Lorraine, are you going back to Italy with Cecco?"

Lorraine stared at Clara. "No!"

"But there must be— Things have to be done."

"There is nothing at all for me to do there and I don't intend to go back."

Clara sighed again. "Well, as you wish. I do think it would be more becoming, but then we can always make some excuse."

"There's a very good excuse," Lorraine said flatly. "I loathed Cecco."

"Lorraine, don't speak like that! Or—" Clara said prudently, "don't let anyone else hear you speak like that."

Lorraine recovered her sweet and loving manner. "Darling, don't you think I have any sense. I'll be the grief-stricken widow if you insist but it'll be hard."

"Bea," Clara said, looking rather shocked. "What about meals? Do you think Velda—"

"I'll talk to her."

In the kitchen Velda was muttering gloomily again. "A funny thing! Nobody has come. Nobody has phoned."

"Nobody knew him," Bea said placatingly.

"Somebody," Velda said darkly and truthfully, "knew him well enough to kill him. Well, we'll just have to hang in. Can't cop out on Mrs. Bartry. I'll see to meals, don't worry. We'll skip lunch; breakfast was too late. Will Rufe and Tony or the senator be here tonight? If so, I'd better make something for them to eat." Velda's bark was always worse than her bite, although, if put to it, she could bite, too.

"I don't know. I hope so." Bea did indeed hope so. Three women alone in the big house with murder in the woods, murder down by the stone wall, murder!

Velda said, "You're scared. I don't blame you. Honestly, now didn't you see whoever killed that Cecco?"

"No! I didn't see anybody. I just heard the shots."

Velda stared at her for a moment. "Well, I was only going to say if you *do* have some idea about the murderer, you'd better tell the police right away."

"But I tell you I *don't* know." Bea went back to the study and Clara's letters.

The day went along with what seemed remarkable quiet. The telephone did not ring and nobody came to call. Rufe did not return. Nobody questioned them. Once Bea thought she caught sight of Detective Smith walking slowly past the garage and down toward the pond.

If the men dragging the pond found a gun or anything else of any significance, Bea knew nothing of it. As dinner time approached the one remaining police car departed. The rosy spring twilight fell softly as though there were no such things as murder and fear in the world.

Seth came in after dinner. "Have you heard?" he asked. He looked angry. When Clara cried, "Heard what?" he told them. "Joe Lathrop! In my office! Knocked out, gagged and bound up with tape."

There was a silence. Lorraine recovered first. "Did they get Aunt Clara's will?"

"Oh, no. No reason for that! Besides the safe was closed. Only Joe knows the combination—Joe and I. So far I haven't discovered anything missing."

"But doesn't Joe know who——" Clara began.

Joe had said that he didn't know; Seth had found Joe about

169

five o'clock. He had stripped off the tape and got out the gag —a hand towel from the office washroom. Joe said he'd been bending over a bookshelf near the door but with his back to the door. It had opened quietly and as he began to turn he felt a smashing blow. When he became conscious again, he said that he could neither move nor yell for help. He didn't know how long he had remained unconscious. Seth had called Obrian. "He and a couple of his men are going through the office now for fingerprints. I took Joe home. He said he had a headache but that was all."

He wouldn't have coffee, he was tired, but he'd come back and spend the night in the house if they wanted him. Clara summoned the courage to refuse. "Get some rest, Seth. We won't need you tonight."

Seth offered a vague protest, but then went on home.

Rufe still did not come or telephone. Velda left after warning them, unnecessarily, to lock the house. A moment later Obrian pulled up to the front door and came in for a moment. "If you're afraid, I'll try to get somebody to stay here. I don't know who but somebody. We're so short of men."

Clara refused. "It's all right, Mr. Obrian. We'll set the alarm and nothing will happen to us. I have the phone right beside my bed."

Seeming somewhat relieved, Obrian left.

After Clara had set the alarm and said goodnight as calmly as if it were any night, and the key in the door of Lorraine's room had clicked, the house seemed very quiet.

Too quiet, Bea thought after a long time; she wished for some normal and customary sound. She also wished she could stop going over and over again all the known facts of the judge's murder—and Cecco's murder. It struck her suddenly that she—all of them—appeared to have taken it for granted that whoever had murdered the judge had also murdered Cecco. Perhaps this was simply because murder is unusual; it did not seem likely that there were two murderers, one intent upon killing the judge and the second on killing Cecco. It did seem likely that Cecco's murder was somehow linked to or even a result of the judge's murder. She hadn't heard the police say that; it was only a reasonable hypothesis.

According to Lorraine, Cecco had never hesitated if he happened upon an opportunity to indulge in a little blackmailing. Yet if he knew anything of the judge's murderer it would have been a very dangerous kind of blackmailing.

It *had* been dangerous; Bea remembered Cecco's startled face and the way he had plunged backward. Yet he couldn't have been such a fool as to place himself, like a target, down by the pond.

Nobody could get into the house that night without rousing the three women and giving Clara time to use the telephone. There was no reason for anybody to attack Lorraine or Clara or Bea herself. Yet reason couldn't conquer instinct. Bea did eventually drop into a troubled sleep, struggled out of its uneasy darkness and knew that someone was in the room. It was Clara, whispering. "Bea, wake up. The judge is talking. I can hear his voice."

Nineteen

The judge *was* talking. His rasping, rather harsh voice came clearly, yet distantly up the stairwell. It was eerie, unnatural, not quite lifelike; yet it was the judge's voice. Clara held Bea's wrist tightly; Bea could feel her hand tremble. The voice went steadily on, but there were no distinguishable words. Then all at once there was merely the cadence of a word or two and Bea's common sense came back. "It's the dictating machine," she whispered. "Somebody is running through one of the judge's dictated tapes."

"Are you sure?"

"Oh, yes. I heard him say, 'Paragraph here, Bea.' I'll turn off the alarm and go and see."

The alarm was already turned off. Clara said, "You'll not go down there! Use the phone in my room. Call Rufe. Seth. Anybody. Be quiet though."

She trotted into Bea's room and came back with a dressing gown, which she draped over Bea's shoulders, as Bea dialed the Thorne number; there was a repeated buzz, then a woman's voice said sleepily, "Dr. Thorne's wire."

It was his answering service. Bea said, "Did he go out or did he tell you not to call him except in an emergency?"

The woman apparently debated; finally she said, "Who is this?"

Bea told her. "I don't want the doctor. I want to talk to his son."

"Is it serious?"

"Yes. Hurry, *please*."

She rang and rang; finally a voice said drowsily, "Dr. Thorne."

"Oh, Doctor, it's Bea. I want to talk to Rufe."

The doctor seemed to pull himself together and awaken. "Rufe, why, yes! Certainly. Hold on. I'll call him."

As she waited she could still hear the judge's voice from below, so lifelike and yet subtly unlifelike, droning on and on. After what seemed a long time the doctor came back on the telephone. "Rufe's gone. He's not in his room. His car is gone, too. I looked. Do you want me to come?"

Bea debated for a second and said, "No, thanks. But if you hear Rufe come back will you tell him I phoned?"

"Yes, certainly. But why? Is Clara all right?"

"Yes. I'm sorry I wakened you."

His voice was dull with drowsiness. She put down the telephone and as she did so the faraway drone of the judge's voice from the study simply stopped.

Just then Lorraine came swiftly up the stairs. "Bea! Aunt Clara!" She reached the hall and paused for a moment; there was the swish of silk, then she came to the door. "Oh, there you are!"

Clara said, "You were downstairs. Why?"

"I thought I heard someone talking in the study. It was like the judge's voice. I had to go down and see who—but I remembered to turn off the alarm. When I got there whoever it was had gone."

This time Bea couldn't tell whether she was lying or telling the truth. Obviously she had no reel of tape in her hand. Besides, the used tapes which the police had heard had none of the judge's dictation, not a word of the judge's voice, only her own— But those weren't all the tapes!

That memory was like a dash of cold water in her face. She herself had a reel in her handbag. She still couldn't remember putting it there, pushed neatly down into the zippered compartment, yet she must have done so, absently, in-

172

tending to use it again. But that reel just might be a recording that the judge had made and she had not transcribed. Suppose that was the reel somebody had been listening to, on the machine in the study. Suppose there was something on it which could give information about the judge's murder.

Lorraine had seen her, surprised, with the reel in her hand. She ran back into her own room. Her big black handbag stood on the table. She opened it swiftly. The reel was gone.

Clara and Lorraine had followed her. "What is it?" Clara asked. "Bea, what—"

Lorraine didn't ask. Lorraine knew. Bea was now sure that the reel was the reason for the search of her room Monday when she was in New York—her handbag with her. Lorraine couldn't have searched her room. She had been away that afternoon, shopping for a black dress. Cecco—yes, Cecco could have returned by taxi from Stamford, searched Bea's room, then left to return again later, with the excuse that he had had to wait for a haircut. But Cecco himself had been murdered. He couldn't have found the reel, for she had it with her. So he couldn't have used it for blackmail. All that shot through her mind like a series of pictures in fast motion.

However, someone had taken the reel and was curious enough about it to run it through the machine. Since Lorraine had admitted she turned off the alarm, Bea had to ask, "Lorraine, did you take that reel of tape from my handbag?"

Lorraine blinked. "That thing you had in your handbag? Heavens no! Why should I?"

"Bea—" Rufe shouted from the hall below. "Anything wrong?"

Everything was wrong, Bea thought dismally. Clara turned back into the hall. "Rufe, we were phoning to you. Your father said you weren't at home."

"I wasn't." Rufe ran up the stairs. "I was out in the drive. Parked my car and intended to stay there all night. I didn't like the idea of you three women left alone. Why did you phone me?"

Bea told him briefly. "Someone was in the study, running a tape through the dictating machine. There was one reel of the judge's dictation in my handbag. I didn't know it. I don't remember putting it there. Now it's gone. I don't know what he said on the tape. Lorraine saw the reel when I found it."

173

Lorraine interrupted. "She's going to tell you that I took that tape and tried to hear what the judge had said. She's going to accuse me of Heaven knows what!"

Clara said, "Why did you come in, Rufe?"

"I saw the light in the study. Then it was turned off. I didn't see anyone and the light made me wonder what was going on. I tried the front door but it was locked. The terrace door was open so I came in that way. Bea, where did you last see the tape?"

"Yesterday afternoon, late. I told you Lorraine saw it."

There was a flash of mischief in Lorraine's green eyes. She put out her arms toward Rufe. She was wearing a flesh-colored silk dressing gown, her blue-black hair tumbled over her shoulders and she looked stunningly beautiful. "Don't you want to search me, Rufe?" she said, smiling.

"I don't see how you could have a reel of tape concealed anywhere about you." Rufe's voice had a slight edge to it but he looked amused, too. Then he sobered. "I suppose there just could be something on the tape which would supply evidence about the judge's murder, even a motive. Did you hear anything important, Lorraine?"

"Why, I told you I didn't touch that reel! I don't think you believe me!"

"I don't think I do," Rufe said bluntly. "Lorraine, if you have that tape it might be very dangerous to you."

She smiled. "Darling, I told you. I don't have it!"

Rufe said abruptly, "I'm going down to the study."

Without a word, moved by a shared impulse, the three women followed him. There were lights in the study. Miss Dotty sat on the sofa; she wore her white uniform under a gray coat; her nurse's comfortable shoes were planted firmly on the floor. Madame Defarge, Bea thought irresistibly, although Miss Dotty had no knitting. Miss Dotty looked at Rufe and it seemed to Bea that there was a flash of some intelligence between them. If so, it was so fully understood by both that neither of them spoke. Clara cried, "Why, Miss Dotty!"

Miss Dotty simply sat and said nothing. Lorraine came nearer, looking puzzled. "But you weren't here when I came down."

"No," said Miss Dotty.

"Well, why did you come?" Lorraine said in a burst.

174

Rufe walked behind Miss Dotty and the sofa to the judge's desk. He put his hand on the dictating machine and nodded. "It's still warm. Well, Lorraine, where's the tape?"

"Stop asking me that!" All at once Lorraine turned sharp and angry.

Rufe looked at Miss Dotty. "When did you get here?" he asked in a casual way, which seemed to Bea a little too casual.

"Just now. Door was open. Thought I'd wait." Miss Dotty vouchsafed that much and stopped, looking stolid and completely immovable.

The telephone rang. Rufe was nearest it, but his proximity didn't quite account for the dash he made for it. "Yes, it's Rufe. I see. Right. Well, hold it. Right."

Miss Dotty looked at the floor in a remarkably knowing way. Lorraine, Clara and Bea stared at Rufe, who had suddenly grown rather pale. He sank down into the judge's chair. After a long moment he seemed to become aware of the unspoken questions hurtling around him, for he said, "Wait— I've got to think—I've got to—"

"Who was that on the phone?" Clara demanded in a tone that brooked no evasion.

"Joe."

"Joe Lathrop! But how did he know where to find you?"

"He thought I might be here."

"You mean you told him you'd be here! Why?"

Miss Dotty said, "I'm going," and rose.

Clara turned a distracted face to Miss Dotty. "Where— why—" Miss Dotty started on a plodding but determined way toward the open terrace door.

Lorraine watched her, then looked at Rufe and snapped, "I don't know what Joe had to say at this time of night but he must be out of his head to call here."

"I think I'm out of my head." But Rufe seemed to make a decision, that or Miss Dotty somehow had made up his mind for him. He rose. "I'll take you in my car." He addressed Miss Dotty's solid back.

"My bike," Miss Dotty said over her shoulder.

"I'll put it in the back of my car." Without another word, without even a look at the three women, he followed Miss Dotty. She reached back to hold the door open for him. They disappeared into the dark spring night. There was the barest sound of their footsteps outside. Bea went to the terrace door and closed it.

"What are they up to?" Lorraine demanded. "That Miss Dotty and Rufe are in cahoots! Anybody can see that. But what has Joe Lathrop to do with it?"

"I'm going back to bed," Clara said. "It was a shock, you know, hearing the judge's voice and—I'm going to bed."

She went slowly but with resolution. It had been a shock to Bea, too. She turned to Lorraine. "You *did* take that reel of dictation! You did run it through the machine. What was on it? What had the judge said?"

"I told you I didn't take it."

Bea thought for a moment. Clara wouldn't like it, but she went to the telephone.

Lorraine came up beside her. "What are you doing?"

"Calling Obrian. I'm going to tell him about the tape and somebody running it on the machine."

"Aunt Clara will be very upset. Call Seth. That's better. He'll know what to do. I'll call him. What's his number?"

"I don't see what he can do. But—all right." Bea told her the number and Lorraine dialed quickly. There was, however, a repeated buzz at the other end of the telephone. Lorraine put down the receiver with a bang. "Line's busy. Wouldn't you know it! Well, we can wait."

"No. Aunt Clara looks too tired. Let's go upstairs. I'll set the alarm. Tomorrow we can talk to Obrian and Seth and Rufe."

"Do you think you can make Rufe tell you what's on his mind? I don't." Lorraine waited while Bea turned off the lights. They went up the stairs together, and then Bea made sure that the alarm was set again. Lorraine suddenly seemed to listen. "I don't know why," she said in a whisper. "But somehow it's as if—oh, I don't know. The house feels wrong."

"Wrong!" Bea's heart gave a disconcerting jump.

"As if somebody is in the house."

Someone had been in the house Monday afternoon and had slid out of sight, a mere flicker in the mirror. Lorraine said quickly, "But there can't be anybody here!" She went to her room and locked the door emphatically. Clara's door too was firmly secured.

Nobody could get into the house or come upstairs without

176

rousing the whole place. Bea hoped though that Rufe had deposited Miss Dotty at her small apartment and driven back home across the road. The house was so still she could have heard the faintest motion anywhere. She sat for a long time, staring at nothing until at last she dropped over onto the pillow.

After a while it seemed she must have begun dreaming, for the pillow suddenly reversed itself. It pressed so hard she couldn't breathe. Then she knew that somebody's hands held the pillow over her face, smothering her. She kicked; she struggled; she clutched into the darkness with both hands, yet someone evaded her and pressed even more relentlessly. Darts and flashes of light seemed to shoot across her eyes. The eiderdown seemed to hold her as if it too had hands.

But suddenly the pressure was gone. There was a flurried scramble and hard thud on the floor near her. She pushed the pillow aside, took a great breath of air and reached automatically to turn on the bedside light. Seth lay, sprawled on the wrinkled rug, rubbing his head.

"Seth!"

"He got away." He struggled awkwardly to his feet and rubbed his head. "He knocked me down. Half killed me—"

"But you—I didn't know you were here."

"Oh, sure. I couldn't let you three women stay in the house alone. Didn't want to alarm you either by insisting on staying with you. The terrace door was open so I came up the back stairs and just sat in that little bedroom. Must have fallen asleep. But then all at once I thought I heard someone here. I grabbed for him."

"Who?"

"I couldn't see. He knocked me down and—he's got to be somewhere in the house or near—" He rubbed his elbow this time. "Damn near broken. I'll call Obrian."

"We tried to call you. Your line was busy."

"Call me? Why?"

"I'll explain later. Call Obrian."

"Right."

"Oh, Seth." Her senses were returning. "Rufe may be outside in his car. Get him first."

"Rufe! Why, all right—all right." Seth went out, half running.

So Lorraine had been right, Bea thought. Someone had been in the house, hidden himself, but had not reckoned with Seth.

There was a sudden sound which ought to be familiar. It *was* familiar. The alarm was shrieking.

Twenty

Somebody turned it off. The silence was like a blow. Then she could hear voices in the house. She didn't know who and didn't care. But the door swung open, light streamed in from the hall and Rufe ran to her and caught her in his arms.

She clung to him; she would never let him go. He pushed back her hair, he turned her face toward him and said, "Bea, Bea——" over and over again.

"Somebody was here—the pillow—Seth took it away. He went to call you——"

"We were watching and broke in. That started the alarm. I turned it off."

"We——?"

"Joe and Tony and Miss Dotty."

"You mean all three of you were out there watching the house?"

"Sure."

"But—but Joe——"

"Oh, he's all right. I knocked him out this afternoon, you know. He insisted. I made it gentle and then wound him up in office tape. Tony has put in a police call. He had his radio car down there in the entrance of the Ellison place. The police will be here. They'll find the tape. I think that may explain it."

"*Who——*"

Lorraine said from the doorway, "Here's the tape, Rufe. I hid it in the linen closet after taking it from Bea's handbag. I ran it through and heard enough to——" She gave the tape to Rufe. "Perhaps I picked up some hints about blackmailing from Cecco. So I decided to keep it in the event of— Oh, never mind. Here come the police."

178

The police siren was wailing. Cars thudded up the drive. Lorraine, her head held high, led the way down to the judge's study. Seth leaned on the judge's desk, a red blotch showing up now on his temple. Clara sat like a pretty little statue, her hands folded around the judge's gold cigar case. She looked up as Bea, Rufe and Lorraine came in. "Is that the tape?" she asked.

Rufe nodded. "Put it on the machine, will you, Bea?"

Bea adjusted the tape in the machine and turned it on. Clara flinched a little as the judge's voice came out, but then she leaned forward, listening intently. Obrian came in as they listened. Unexpectedly Ben Benson stuck his head in the door and came in. He looked weird in a raincoat over pajamas. He mumbled something about hearing the police car and then he, too, listened.

The judge said from the machine, "Now take this down, Bea, exactly as I say it. But you must never never tell anybody at all what I'm saying. This is a solemn order. You must never tell even your aunt. I think it will work out all right. Not many people here in Valley Ridge know of it. We so seldom get out and see people. I only happened to hear a rumor of it a few days ago when I was in the bank and was asked my opinion. I was deeply shocked. Seth cannot run for President. He cannot become President."

Clara cried, "President! Seth! Is that true, Seth?"

Seth smiled, shook his head and rubbed his elbow again.

Rufe stopped the machine. "I heard a rumor of it, too, when I was in Washington, Seth. Old Upson told me when I had dinner with him."

Lorraine said coolly, "Cecco heard it, too. That afternoon he went to the barber shop in Stamford for a haircut. He told me. That's why I— Never mind," she said again and might as well have said that she had thought of just possibly becoming a President's wife—with the help of the tape.

Suddenly Bea remembered when Cecco had told Lorraine; Bea herself had heard it. Rather she thought she had heard Cecco say only "resident" and had taken it to refer to something of his own or Lorraine's affairs. He had actually said "President." She was sure of it.

Seth didn't even look at Lorraine. "Go on with the tape, Rufe."

Rufe started the machine again; the judge's voice went on

179

inexorably. He was working up to one of his irrational moods of what he would have considered justifiable anger. "I must consider my duty as a lawyer and former judge.

"I'll begin at the beginning. Seth was brought before me on a breaking and entering charge while I was judge of the juvenile court. I had to send him to Millwood but I was interested in him. He did very well; he always learned rapidly. His name was kept out of the papers because he was a minor. When he came out of Millwood his father and I determined to keep his presence there a secret. That is, the man we thought of as Seth's father was his stepfather. He gave Seth his name. Seth was born in Spain of Spanish parents; his mother married old Seth Hobson when Seth was a child. Seth's real name was Juan Perez. But some time or other Seth trumped up a false birth certificate. He admitted that yesterday. I went to see him in his office. He showed it to me but I know that it is a forgery. He had sent Joe Lathrop out on an errand so I was there alone with Seth. I told him I couldn't stand by knowing that a law might be broken.

"Paragraph here, Bea."

Paragraph here, Bea. It was the familiar cadence of the words which Bea had recognized. At the same time a fleeting recollection nudged her; she had felt once or twice that there was a resemblance between Cecco and Seth; now she knew what that was. Cecco, though Italian, had reminded her of portraits of Spanish grandees. Seth had almost the same kind of long, slender face; she had thought it a New England face; but it was Spanish.

Clara was sitting very straight and implacable. "Is all this true, Seth?"

Seth shrugged. "Some of it. My foreign birth. Sure. There was no point in advertising the fact, either that I had served some time at Millwood when I was a youngster or that my stepfather had adopted me and given me his name. No point at all. The judge agreed."

Clara insisted. "But are you going to try to run for the Presidency?"

"Certainly not!"

"But the rumor the judge heard—"

Seth sighed. "I can't help it if some of my friends start up such talk. I've made a good record in my years in the Senate. They need a candidate. I suppose it's natural that they should think of me. But I had no intention of ever becoming a candidate. The judge—well, we know how he was recently. Go on with the tape, Rufe."

The judge coughed and went on. "I am giving Seth till tonight to make up his mind. I realize that this is too lenient, but I have followed Seth's career with pride. He became a senator because he was brilliant. He has made a fine record. There is nothing in the Constitution to prevent his acting well as a senator. No one knew anything about his background. No one questioned it. But he can't be President. He was not born in the United States. His forged birth certificate shows premeditation. He'll be here tonight and promise to withdraw from the candidacy which he hoped to get. I'm sure of this. However, it's a very—" There was a long pause as though the judge were trying to think of a suitable word; finally it came out, "a tremendous temptation to any man, especially an ambitious man and Seth is ambitious. He is also ruthless. I may be obliged to use strong measures to persuade him. Of course, a gun— No, that can't be necessary—yet Seth will not give up easily. If I show him that I mean what I say—"

The judge's voice was harsh, which Bea recognized as the prelude to a fit of anger. He went on in disconnected phrases. "I know—I'll get out my gun and show him that if he gets mean." His voice began to take on a rasping, frenzied note. "I must defend the Constitution. I'm the only person who knows the fact about Seth. He knows that only I can accuse him." He seemed to pause here and consider. He mumbled into the microphone; then his voice became louder, almost incoherent. "Yes, he is a ruthless man. He'll try to stop me the only way I can be stopped. But I'll defend myself, I've got to defend the Constitution. I'm the only one who can do that—Bea, think of it—I'm the only person in the United States to defend—to *save* the law of the land. I'm the only one." There was another pause, filled only with heavy breathing. The now hoarse and jerky voice of the judge came out again. "He's been my friend. But my oath of office long ago—I've always tried to see that the law is upheld—it's very hard. But I'll do it. I'm an old man, I'm a sick old man. They try to hide it from me, but I'm past my useful years. But not now! *I'll be useful!* I'll kill him if I have to— Bea, don't write down all this." His voice seemed to take on a more normal tone for an instant. "No, no, I don't mean to kill him." But then his voice rose again in a grasping kind of scream. "But I'll do it! My forefathers fought for the Constitution. I can fight for it too. How can a man die better than facing fearful odds, for the ashes of his fathers and the temples of his gods?" Another pause; then he went on rather sadly. "I was so proud of him. But now I have to kill him or he'll kill me. I could see it in his eyes when I accused him or forging the certificate. Seth will try to talk me around. He's a smooth politician. But I have given my life for the law— I'll give my life for the law, Seth." The judge's voice became low. There was another short return to the normal. "Bea, I'll put this record in that big black purse of yours, on the hall table. I'll tell Seth that you have it and— Now, Bea, if there is any trouble with Seth— now, Bea, you have this tape so take care of it. If Seth gives up his plan I'll tell you and you're to forget that you know this at all. Never mention it to a soul."

The tape clicked. After a moment Rufe turned off the machine. "Too bad he didn't go on. Did you come here the night he was killed, Seth?"

Seth eyed him. "No. I knew the judge. I decided to give him time to settle down. He did come to see me at my office here. He did accuse me. I couldn't make him understand that I had no intention of becoming a candidate. Then I never saw him alive again. He was one of the best friends I had in my life. He was right. I couldn't have taken on candidacy for President even if—" Seth smiled. "Even if it was eventually offered to me."

Bea said, "Seth saved me tonight. There was someone in my room."

"Seth, you said that you didn't know the medical examiner," Rufe said slowly.

Seth lifted his arched eyebrows. "I don't. Except as a name. I've been away from Valley Ridge so much in recent years."

Rufe looked down at the desk. "And you didn't know that he spent four years as a Navy surgeon in the South Pacific."

"But what does that have to do with anything?"

"Whoever dug that bullet out of the judge couldn't have known that the medical examiner had had all that experience with bullet wounds. Of course, any good doctor could have found evidence of cutting out the bullet. But ordinarily a doctor wouldn't have looked for it. Seth couldn't have known that the medical examiner would instantly tell the difference between a normal exit wound of a bullet and an extraction with a knife. Most people would have assumed that it was only the wound a bullet would make. But the medical examiner knew at once that a knife had been used."

Clara rose, still holding the judge's gold cigar case; she walked slowly and with dignity to the judge's desk. Seth moved aside; she sat down at the desk and looked as grave and judicial as the judge himself. "This is a very serious accusation, Rufe," she said. "What it comes down to, however, is Seth's word against the judge's word. The judge told the truth. Seth admits that. But we all know that the judge sometimes was not clear in his mind." She looked at Rufe. "How long have you believed Seth shot the judge?"

Seth half smiled. Rufe said steadily, "I wasn't really sure. But at first I wondered why the person who saw me come here the night the judge was killed didn't come forward and tell the police he had seen me in his car lights. It had to be someone from out of state who either did not read of the murder or didn't want to get involved—or the murderer. The car came from the direction of Seth's house not a mile away. Then when I went to Washington old Upson told me that there was already a strong organization building up to run Seth for the presidential nomination. I knew that the judge's term on the juvenile court had been omitted from his obituary; that portion of his memoirs was missing and later found. Seth had given the obituary to Joe to phone in and omitted the judge's term in the juvenile court. Seth could have tried to get hold of that part of the memoirs and later take a look at it."

Bea broke in. "It's true. Seth did have a chance to open the filing cabinet and take out that portion of the memoirs. He was alone here in the study the next morning, Saturday, after Rufe and Tony left. But then somebody *was* in my room. Seth did come in time to save my life."

Seth nodded at her and said quietly, "I'll reserve my defense. Go on, Rufe."

Rufe continued, "Things just added up. There had to be a really important reason for the judge's murder. Then I had an idea. I read the Constitution again to make sure of my memory. If Seth had been guilty of a felony or a misdemeanor when he was young and had been sent to Millwood, it wouldn't help his candidacy if it were known, but it wouldn't prevent it legally. However, if he were born in a foreign country he couldn't be elected. I told Joe what I was afraid of. We took a quick look through Seth's office this afternoon. But it was getting late. We weren't sure we had put everything back just right so Joe made me slug him and tie him up. Then tonight Joe went back and got into the safe and there was the birth certificate. He phoned here to tell me."

"You were a little rough on poor Joe," Seth said good-naturedly. "No need for all that nonsense. If you had asked for my birth certificate, I'd have shown it to you."

"Would you?" Rufe said. There was a curious expression in his face. "A forged certificate—that does show premeditation, you know. The judge was right. What about his coat, Seth? How did you get him to remove his coat?"

"Coat? I don't know anything about a coat. Oh, yes—I remember now. That old jacket was thrown over his desk. It was a very warm night. Of course," Seth said slowly, "if your father had come over to take his blood pressure the judge would have had to remove his coat."

"No," Rufe said. "The police found it on the desk. They had examined it and folded it over a chair before you got here, Seth. So when did you see it over the desk?"

Seth's long face was still good-natured. "I grant you, Rufe, that you have a motive which some people might consider a real motive for killing the judge. But a jury wants proof. You have made out a case against me. There is no solid proof whatever. Try to convince a jury and you'll see how theoretical it is. Surely you don't think that a jury would accept as sensible evidence that tape—obviously the ravings of a sick old man! I didn't kill the judge. You say I did. Prove it."

Obrian stepped forward. "I've known you a long time, Seth. You've made a fine record. But I'm going to have to bring all this to the inquest, and the case against you is sure then to go to the grand jury. The publicity will completely finish your career. I'm sorry, really sorry. But I think you shot the judge."

"No, no!" Bea cried. "I tell you he saved my life tonight. Someone had a pillow over my face and I fought and fought and then Seth came and whoever it was knocked him down and—and—" Her voice dwindled away as a small, domestic memory struck her. "Oh," she said. "It was the rug."

"Rug?" Obrian stared at her.

"There's a little rug by my bed. The floor is polished.

184

Sometimes the rug slips and—and I suppose it slipped and he fell and then he said— Oh—" Bea turned to Clara, who held out her hand.

Lorraine said coolly, "We tried to phone Seth tonight. The line was busy. Nothing easier than to leave it off the hook so as to give the impression that he was at home and talking if anybody happened to phone." She had turned instantly from Seth to Ben, that was clear.

Obrian said, "You see, Seth, you have too many things to explain. Even if you could convince a jury you didn't kill the judge, it would end your career. But I don't think you *can* convince a jury. The minute that birth certificate of yours gets into the hands of experts . . ."

Seth had been leaning against a chair near Ben Benson. His lanky figure seemed scarcely to move, but suddenly Ben went sprawling on the floor, screaming as he went down. Everybody yelled. Rufe shot for the door and tripped over Ben, who struck wildly at Rufe. It was a nightmarish scene for a second or two. Then Seth, Rufe and Obrian were gone, Ben Benson surging out the door after them. With shocking loudness there were several gunshots echoing through the night, shouts, the thud of a car racing and then nothing.

Lorraine sat down. Clara clasped the judge's cigar case more tightly. Rufe and Obrian and Ben came back into the house. "Never mind," Obrian said. "Can't be helped." He mopped his face. "Seth was a hunter, liked nothing better than a hunting trip. He'd have been able to extract the bullet." Obrian thought for a moment. "Seth had to get out a bullet which could be identified as coming from his own gun. He must have promised the judge to give up his plans. The judge felt safe."

Rufe said, "He also, in a friendly and agreeable way, must have induced the judge to remove his coat. It really was an unseasonably warm night. But Seth would have known that a thirty-two wouldn't penetrate the coat and that he couldn't get it out. He got hold of the judge's gun, too—easy enough I'd say, the way the judge was when he was upset. Probably the judge had put his gun on his desk or in his belt or even carried it in his hand. Perhaps he wasn't entirely sure of Seth, yet Seth must have promised him to forget all about his ambition to become a candidate. It must have been that way, for apparently the judge went out willingly with Seth for a stroll.

185

Seth shot him with his own gun, then he had to dig out the bullet. He fired the judge's gun and left it beside him to suggest suicide."

Clara nodded soberly. Rufe went on, "But in the meantime Aunt Clara had set the alarm. Seth didn't know that. He came in to find the tape the judge had told him he had dictated. When the alarm went Seth got out as fast as he could. But later—"

Bea said, "Someone had searched my room twice, not thoroughly the first time when I was shut in the garage, but very thoroughly the second time when nobody was in the house."

Lorraine said, "Cecco must have seen him close the garage doors the night Bea was shut in there. Cecco waited a while before he let Bea out. That would have amused Cecco. But Cecco would not have made an appointment with him if he'd thought Seth was a murderer. He'd have been afraid to tackle him. He only meant to embarrass Seth. It would have been hard for Seth to explain."

Rufe said, "And Cecco thought that Seth might have paid him to keep quiet. But Seth believed Cecco knew more than he knew."

"Cecco had been at Seth's house this afternoon," Lorraine said. "I saw him walking down the road. He must have told Seth then whatever it was that he could use as a threat for blackmail."

"Why shoot at Bea?" Ben said.

"Probably because the judge told him that he had dictated the whole thing to Bea. Seth must have been on pins and needles for fear Bea would run the tape and know all about his motive for killing the judge." Lorraine spoke with such sharp impatience that a twinge of alarm went over Ben's face. Lorraine put her hand quickly on Ben's arm and held on.

"What happened tonight then, Rufe?" Obrian asked.

"Miss Dotty told me yesterday. It almost proved the notion I had and didn't want to have. She said that when she went home Friday night she had seen Seth's car parked in the Carter drive. Joe phoned tonight to tell me about the birth certificate. He thought it didn't look just right. Tony was already waiting with me in the drive behind that big clump of cedars. Joe came too. Miss Dotty had taken her bike to Seth's place as soon as it was dark and watched there. When he drove out she followed him and he parked again at the Carter place. We

186

were sure that Seth would make another attempt to get the tape and he had to be caught in the act. I thought we could stop him before he got into the house. But then—" He looked at Lorraine.

"I took the tape. I wanted to know what the judge had said." Lorraine shrugged but held Ben's arm.

Rufe said, "Did you open the terrace door?"

"Oh, yes. I had turned off the alarm before I came downstairs. It seemed stuffy here and I wanted some fresh air. But I didn't see Seth."

"He heard the voice on the tape. He must have got very close to the house, in the shrubbery. But he must have thought it was Bea running the tape and listening. He had to stop her. He got into the house while Aunt Clara and Lorraine and you, Bea, were in the upper hall talking and the alarm was off. He went up the back stairs. We didn't search the house. Like a fool I didn't think of that until it was almost too late. Then we broke in."

He didn't look at Bea; he only looked very white and frightened and Bea loved him. Clara said, "The judge's cigar case—"

"Oh, that was another thing, small, but Joe found it in Seth's office, recognized it as belonging to the judge, knew that the judge must have gone to see Seth the day before the judge was murdered. Seth had sent Joe out of the office to close a real estate deal. Joe forgot about the case. He intended to return it to you, Aunt Clara. After I saw that on the desk where Joe left it, I was sure Seth had killed him—but I had no real proof."

Ben said stolidly, "I'm not sure you have real jury proof yet. There's motive, yes. There's Miss Dotty's story of seeing his car the night the judge was murdered. There's his presence in the house tonight, but nobody saw him kill the judge or Cecco or shoot at Bea or—"

Obrian gave him an exasperated glance. "People don't as a rule invite other people to watch them kill somebody."

Just then the door opened and Dr. Thorne came in. "I saw the police cars," he said. "Heard about . . . It can't be Seth."

Rufe replied. "It was. And when I began to wonder about Seth I remembered what the judge said just as he died. He asked for you, Father. He said 'doctor'—then he muttered something about 'will'—but then he said 'Seth' and died. He

187

didn't want to see Seth about his will. He was trying to tell Bea that Seth had shot him."

Bea could see the rosy light from the alarm flashing. She could hear the sudden burst of the judge's voice and then the silence. But she had given the judge's words what seemed a clear interpretation then.

Obrian said soberly, "The Juvenile Court record was—before Cecco tried to do a little blackmailing—the only danger that Seth knew about. He was the judge's friend, he was the family lawyer. Nobody would have suspected him." The telephone rang, interrupting him.

Obrian was nearest and he picked it up, listened, and his face seemed to clear. He put down the receiver almost solemnly. "Well, that ends it. We don't need jury proof. Seth tried to get a gun from one of my men and somehow in the fracas Seth was shot. There'll not be a trial." He looked at Clara. "It's better that way."

It was better. Miss Dotty marched in from the terrace, took the doctor's arm and without a word marched him sternly out again.

Obrian said vaguely, "Tomorrow—the police and—" He walked out, too.

Lorraine said flatly, "I was a great fool. I'm sorry, Bea. I almost got you killed." She came to Bea and put out her hand. Bea took it. They walked hand in hand like two little girls toward the terrace, where Ben waited for Lorraine. Bea turned back to Rufe, who sat down at the judge's desk and put his head in his hands. "I was a great fool, too, Bea. I nearly got you killed for trying to get a hard and fast case."

Clara stopped him. "I expect Ben and Lorraine will want to live here rather than with his mother. So you and Bea can get married as soon as you like. I'll not be alone."

Bea's mouth opened and shut. Clara, the realist, smiled. "Lorraine would rather have been the President's wife. That is, if Seth had made it. But it didn't take her long to change her course. I expect she'll be very good for Ben really. Now let's get the date set for you two."

Bea said slowly, "Rufe, it wasn't the Foreign Office. It wasn't Lorraine. It was when you began to suspect Seth that you—oh, it seemed to me you had changed. About me, I mean."

Rufe looked up. "About you! Why, I didn't change! It was

a hard thing for me to accept, hard to try either to prove or disprove it. I didn't want to tell even you but——"

"Oh, never mind." Bea went to him and stood close, so he could put his arm around her. Clara said, "Make up your minds about the date," and walked out, holding the judge's cigar case against her cheek.

Great Mysteries by
MIGNON G. EBERHART

___**ANOTHER MAN'S MURDER**   *(B31-180, $2.50, U.S.A.)*
(B31-182, $3.25, Canada)

Dead man's bluff—the Judge had been the town's leading citizen. Now he
was dead, and it was all too clear he had been murdered. The shadow of
his death—and of his twisted life—fell heavily upon lovely Dodie Howard.
She alone kept the secret which could erupt into scandal, destroying the
man she loved. Then one night she woke to see the murderer's hands
poised over her throat . . .

___**POSTMARK MURDER**   *(B31-181, $2.50, U.S.A.)*
(B31-183, $3.25, Canada)

A strange curse . . . some might have called her lucky. Unexpected and
fabulous wealth had descended upon her. But that was only part of her
inheritance. For now her life was haunted by the terrifying specter of
murder, ready to strike and strike again.

___**UNIDENTIFIED WOMAN**   *(B31-195, $2.50, U.S.A.)*
(B31-198, $3.25, Canada)

Crazy quilt of terror . . . To a young and lovely Victoria Steane there
seemed no pattern to the murders. Yet one by one they took place—a
man found drowned, a girl floating in the river, a woman strangled in the
undergrowth. And these were just the beginning. Just one thing was all
too terrifyingly clear to Victoria. Step by step the savage murderer was
moving closer and closer to her . . .

___**HUNT WITH THE HOUNDS**   *(B31-199, $2.50, U.S.A.)*
(B31-200, $3.25, Canada)

At dusk, murder rode with the bright-jacketed huntsmen through woods
and fields. Among them was young and pretty Sue Poore, involved with
an attractive man, whose wife had been mysteriously murdered. Already
under suspicion, Sue was ripe for murder—either as victim or killer.
Death, the grim hunter, closed in for the kill . . .

___**WITNESS AT LARGE**   *(B31-205, $2.50, U.S.A.)*
(B31-206, $3.25, Canada)

Terror walks the fog-shrouded island. The pretty young girl called Sister
knows that violent murder has been done and will be done again. Who is
the unseen killer? Can it possibly be Tom, the man she has loved in secret
for so long? As she wonders, the long shadow of the murderer moves
forward to strike once more . . .

Don't Miss These Other Great Books By P.D. JAMES!